Also by Vincent Zandri:

Permanence
The Innocent
Godchild
The Remains
Moonlight Falls
Moonlight Falls (UNCUT EDITION)
Moonlight Rises
Blue Moonlight
Murder by Moonlight

THE CONCRETE PEARL

Text copyright ©2012 by Vincent Zandri
All rights reserved.

Printed in the United States of America.

Published by Thomas & Mercer
P.O. Box 400818
Las Vegas, NV 89140

ISBN-13: 9781612183527
ISBN-10: 1612183522

THE CONCRETE PEARL

by Vincent Zandri

THOMAS & MERCER

For Laura

"In case you build a tower, you must also make a parapet for your roof, that you may not place bloodguilt upon your soul because someone might fall from it."

–Deuteronomy, Chapter 22; Verse 8

"Hell has three gates: lust, anger, and greed."

–Gita

The naked man lies on his side along the edge of a steep trench. The newly excavated trench reeks of exposed clay, the rich stench wafting up from the moist floor. To the naked man, the red clay smells like the worms that seep out of a storm sewer after a heavy downpour. Naked man's got worms on the brain when he feels a boot heel press down against his rib cage, when he hears the words, "You're gonna love hell, Farrell."

He tries hard to pick his head up off the ground, but he's lost too much blood from the 9mm round that's entered and exited his left shoulder. Once upon a time he was the most gifted athlete on his high school football team. But now, twenty-odd years later, he no longer has the strength to lift his head up off the dirt. He's got no choice but to lie on his side and accept the steel-toed Red Wing work boot that digs down against skin and bone, no choice but to gaze into the empty trench, the beautiful summer sunlight spilling down onto the wormy, moist clay.

When the boot heel pushes him forward, the naked man feels himself going over the edge. But the fall is not immediate. It happens in a kind of slow motion—his wiry, six-foot-plus frame going over the side, dropping into space, spinning one complete revolution before finally hitting the clay. The impact knocks the breath from him. He feels the pain in his chest, the pain in his wounded shoulder, the constriction of his diaphragm.

But once he's able to breathe again, he's not afraid.

Maybe his fearlessness has something to do with blood loss. Or maybe it has something to do with simple resignation...knowing there's no possible way he's going to make it out of this trench alive. Maybe it has something to do with the clarity of mind that accompanies a sure death sentence.

The left side of his face lies on the cold clay floor. The clay is moist from the groundwater that seeps out of it. Like the clay, the water smells rank. As the noise from a cement truck pulling into position begins to fill his exposed ear, a small bird flies down into the trench. It perches itself on a chunk of clay only inches from his face. Just a small tweety bird—or finch, as the bird-watchers call them—with rust-colored feathers, a small black beak and opaque eyes. The bird flutters its wings, stares at the man with curiosity.

The cement truck revs its engine. Then comes the clang and bang of the aluminum chute extensions being constructed. The *naked man knows what's coming, yet he finds himself smiling. He doesn't quite know why, but he knows it's happening because he can feel his facial muscles contracting. He's weak, nearly paralyzed from blood loss. But still he tries to reach his hand out to the little bird.*

The cement truck above him roars and bucks. He knows its cylindrical holding tank must be spinning now, counterclockwise in order to pour its warm, mudlike load. A sense of urgency grips the naked man. He feels an overwhelming desire for the bird to perch itself on his outstretched finger. If he can manage it, it will be his last act on God's earth. As dumb as it seems, it would be a good, final, dying act for a man who admittedly has lost his way in life.

When the raw ready mix begins pouring down on his bare feet in a warm, white flow of gravel clumps and wet sandy lumps, the now frightened bird flies away to safety. The naked man, however, has nowhere to go. He's about to become a permanent fixture of this new construction.

It's only then that that realization sinks in—and along with it, the fear.

The concrete buries long legs. Lime burns pale skin. The naked man opens his mouth wide, lets out a scream. He screams for someone to save him. Anyone.

"Please! Help me!"

But this isn't like the good old days. Now when he cries out, there's no one around to hear him, no one to attend to his dire need—no one who cares to save his life, that is.

There is quite simply nothing left for him—the former silver spoon–fed, who-cares-about-schoolbooks golden boy who had the world gripped by the short hairs.

Nothing left at all. Not even regret.

Only the smell of worms, a deep trench, and the soft concrete that entombs his living body, fills his gaping mouth.

CHAPTER 1

How does a headstrong girl like me learn to survive in a man's construction racket? She learns to survive by taking her old man's advice, even if it does come to her from six feet under.

After all these years, I can still hear the proud baritone pouring out of the mouth of the late great John Harrison. He used to say that a building erected by Harrison Construction Company wasn't meant to last for two or even three hundred years. Like the great Egyptian pyramids, it was meant to last forever.

I can see the short but sturdy man standing on the edge of a high-rise job site, concrete foundations already poured and cured, structural steel newly erected, a big American flag perched high above us off the topmost section of a rust-colored I-beam.

"You want a tower to last, A.J.?" he'd say to me, taking my small hand in his, callused fingers squeezing me tight. "You don't skimp for nobody. You build it right the first time. No matter the cost."

But I guess even he had to admit that there were those times when a perfectly executed construct might begin to fall apart for no apparent reason. Nothing apparent to the naked eye, anyway. Maybe a tack-welded roof joist works itself loose. Or maybe a crack forms in a concrete foundation and over time expands its way up the length of a twenty-story bearing wall. In both cases, the destruction is so slow and subtle you might not take notice until it's too late.

Life is like that too.

Destruction isn't always something that hits you over the head like a claw hammer. Instead, it's something that's been building up for a long time, more like the rain that seeps into a brick wall and freezes during the winter months. The ice expands, cracks, and eventually destroys the mortar.

Case in point, my own personal Jericho came crashing down on me on Monday, June 15, barely a half hour into a hot and humid workday. Call it women's intuition or a sharply honed, built-in crap detector, but I knew something wasn't right from the moment my BlackBerry started vibrating against my hip.

I'd been trying to expedite the demolition of Albany Public School 20's basement utility room, using my equalizer (an old twenty-two-ounce, grizzly bear–clawed framing hammer) to rip down the old plywood utility panel backerboard. But even with those four-inch claws wedged in between the old, dry plywood and the brick wall, the bitch just wouldn't budge, which might explain why I barked into my BlackBerry instead of answering it with good old ladylike professionalism.

"*What?*"

"Yeah, and good morning to you too, Chief," said my assistant and former Harrison mason laborer, Tommy Moleski. "Sorry to interrupt, but we've got a bit of an emergency up here. One which requires your…ah…utmost undivided attention."

I pictured the sixty-something, blond-haired, blue-eyed Vietnam vet with the trailer phone pressed to his ear, a lit Marlboro Red balanced precariously between his lips.

"A drop-everything kind of emergency, Tommy?" I said. "Or an it-can-wait-until-coffee-break emergency?"

"Need-you-front-and-freaking-center-*now* emergency, Chief."

"Meet you in the trailer…and don't call me *Chief.*"

"How's about I call you *Sexy*?"

I caught my reflection in one of the old bathroom mirrors the school maintenance department had stored here up against the wall in the basement utility room. I still filled out my size-seven button-fly Levi's the same way I had since high school. My black T-shirt was tight in all the right places. And not a single hint of gray in my dark-brown, shoulder-length hair. So, yeah, still at least reasonably sexy.

"Be right up, Tommy," I said.

Pocketing the BlackBerry, I grumbled something about how much Monday mornings sucked, even when you got to be your own boss. Then I grabbed hold of the equalizer's rubber grip and pulled like nobody's business. The old board tore away from the wall and crashed down at my Durango-cowboy-booted feet. But then, so did half the plaster ceiling. Guess I didn't know my own strength.

Leaving the mess for later, I hightailed it out of the room and up the concrete stairs. As usual, I had a fire to put out.

CHAPTER 2

At the top of the stairs, I exited the utility room's metal access door and the hot summer sun slapped me in the face. With the equalizer gripped in one hand, I used the other to slap plaster dust out of my dark hair. Tommy called this an emergency situation, a front-and-freaking-center emergency. And by all appearances, he wasn't screwing around.

Under normal conditions, a commercial construction site is a three-ring circus filled with burly laborers and tradesman shouting out orders or carrying them out. Paint-and-taping-compound-spattered boom boxes blare classic Zepplin or Ozzy. Maybe a hungover mason mouthing off about the hostile summer heat or lying his ass off about getting laid in the bed of his pickup over the weekend. The construction site that I'd known my entire life was a rough but hyperactive place where the concrete vibrator was a "horse cock," the Port-O-Potty was the "shithouse," and an aluminum casement window that didn't quite fit a specified masonry opening was a "curly hair off."

So you might not think of a construction site as the ideal setting for a thirty-eight-year-old, liberal-arts-college-educated widow. But you'd be wrong. It's a world I happen to love.

However, there was nothing normal about the world that greeted me when I made my way out that utility door. The site was deathly quiet, and there were a dozen subcontracted workers standing in front of a scaffolding-caged school with large coffees in their hands, eyes fixed on an OSHA Emergency Response van.

I knew that the ready mix wasn't just about to hit the fan.

The ready mix had already hit and spattered.

I jogged my way across the site to the construction trailer. Inside, I found Tommy peering out the window at the van.

"We got OSHA," he said, master of the awful obvious. "Goddamned surprise inspection." Tommy was dressed in his usual uniform of a clean Hanes all-cotton T-shirt, husky Levi's, and a pair of worn Chippewa work boots he bought back when I was still in pigtails and braces. His straight blond hair was styled like someone put a bowl over his head and trimmed around the rim.

"I hate Mondays," I spat. "How long they been here?"

"Ten minutes, give or take. Pulled up right behind me when I came in."

"They show ID or badges?"

He tossed me one of those over-the-shoulder glares he does so well. "Listen, Spike, OSHA don't need no stinkin' badges."

I slapped the equalizer onto the desk, pulled a hanky from my back pocket, and soaked it with spring water from the cooler. Wiping off my face and arms, I joined Tommy at the window.

Here's the deal: OSHA, or Occupational Safety and Health Administration, had become a real thorn in my thong ever since the beginning of last year, when my professional life started caving in. In less than six months' time we had a mason who lost his left eye when a defective hammerhead shattered in his face. Then there was the carpenter who lost his index and middle fingers to a table saw. To add major insult to serious injuries, one of our laborers managed to break his back when he fell ass backward off a baker's scaffolding after drinking a quart of beer for lunch.

But that wasn't the worst of it.

I was also being harassed by a former Harrison Construction pro now turned chief upstate OSHA agent. Like me, the fiery-haired, take-no-prisoners Diana Stewart had been one of Albany's first female project managers—like me, personally trained by my father. You'd think a little sentimental leniency for "old time's sake" might be in order here. But the not-so-distant memory of the good old days wasn't enough to stop the "Tiger Lady" from picking on Harrison Construction like we were OSHA's public enemy number one, hitting us with a separate major fine for each of the three job site accidents.

Taking into account the civil lawsuits on behalf of the injured workers, plus the six-figure OSHA fines, I now found myself staring down a sum total payout just short of two million large.

I had two options: I could either file Chapter Eleven, or I could streamline the Harrison operation to just a fraction of the support staff it once employed and subcontract out any other required work like electrical, heating, plumbing, and asbestos removal.

In the interest of preserving the house that Dad built, I chose the second of the two evils. About ten months ago, I started digging out of my financial cave-in by letting the entire office staff go, laying off the full-time project managers, field supers, masons, carpenters, and laborers we kept on staff 24-7, 52 weeks a year.

Everyone but Tommy, that is.

I even rented out the North Albany office building that had been in the family for decades.

What the company de-evolution came down to was this: me, A. J. "Spike" Harrison, acting as owner, project manager, field supervisor, plus the all-important health-and-safety officer. As for my new Harrison headquarters? It consisted of the single-wide Williams Scotsman construction trailer I was now hiding out inside of, a hundred feet from the PS 20 downtown Pearl Street construction entrance. It wasn't much, but at least the firm started by the late great John Harrison some fifty years ago was still alive, if barely.

"Lock the door," I said.

Tommy did it.

Peering out the trailer window, I made out two men, both dressed in jeans so pressed you could see the creases in the seams. Anal-retentive types. OSHA-standard-issue polo shirts, hard hats, and safety goggles. No doubt the toes of their polished work boots were protected in construction-site-mandated high-strength steel.

The tall one on the left held a clipboard, while the shorter one on the right gripped a Geiger counter–like testing apparatus.

"Am I the health-and-safety officer for Harrison Construction, Tommy? Are we not in total safety compliance for a change?"

"Total compliance ain't necessarily good enough, Spike. You of all people gotta know that."

Tommy's comment smacked me right upside my hard head...

The summer I turn sweet sixteen, I beg my dad to let me work in the field on a real construction job. "Nice girls don't work on job sites," he argues. "Nice girls answer the phones, type up the bills, make the coffee." But I stubbornly twist his arm until it nearly snaps off. "I'm a tough girl," I tell him. "I can take it." Against his better judgment, he gives in, if only to get me to shut up about it. But I'm not on my first job site for more than an hour when I step on a sixpenny nail that's sticking up vertical from out of a torn-away floorboard. The steel spike impales itself through my right foot. An overnight hospital stay and numerous tetanus shots later, I become the proud owner of a new nickname: A. J. "Spike" Harrison, pigheaded female heir apparent to the Harrison Construction fortune.

The now oxygen-masked OSHA team slipped inside the school. As if on cue, the fax machine and office phone exploded to life. I sat down at my desk and picked up the phone.

"Harrison!"

"Ava Harrison, please," said the woman caller.

Ava...

Up went the red flag. Not many people referred to me by my formal name. Only bill collectors or one of several lawyers trying to sue my heart-shaped ass.

"Ms. Harrison is not available at the moment. Can I take a message?"

Eyes locked on Tommy. He gripped a hot-off-the-fax printout in his thick hands. He held up the new pages to my face. The letterhead on the top page said OSHA in the same big black letters as the van outside the school entrance.

"I'm calling on behalf of Diana Stewart at Albany OSHA," the woman said. "Please make certain Ava Harrison returns Ms. Stewart's call as soon as she receives this message. It's of the utmost urgency."

I hung up without a good-bye.

"Let's start from the start," I said. "We've got two OSHA agents crawling inside our shorts. And as far as I can tell, nobody seems to be hurt—no limbs severed, no heads rolling. Can you please tell me what the hell is going on?"

Before Tommy could open his mouth, a bullhorn-amplified voice shook the trailer. I shot up out of the swivel chair and went to the window. The student body of PS 20 was being led in an orderly but rapid fashion out the main entrance and side doors of the old school.

Tommy brushed up against my shoulder.

"This is what I know so far," he stated. "According to this fax, indie test reports for the third asbestos removal are in and they are no damned good. Tests show the school's inside air all filled up with asbestos fibers. Way off the charts." Cocking a thumb over his shoulder, "Christ, Spike, what if all those kids been exposed all year long?"

Maybe I should have seen this coming a long time ago. Back when I subcontracted a local asbestos-removal outfit for a district-funded rehab that just *had* to remain occupied by students and faculty during construction. Dumb need-for-speed architecture and engineering move if ever there was one.

Making the "occupied job site" situation even more tenuous, the subcontracting firm in charge of the removals, A-1 Environmental Solutions, was run by a man I'd known for most of my life. A tall, country club–bred rocket scientist by the name of James "Jimmy" Atkins Farrell. Jimmy had nearly flunked out of high school, yet had somehow managed to make a fortune as a "hazardous waste removal" subcontractor. Asbestos removal was his bread and butter. It wasn't anything to mess around with. If even tiny traces of the microscopic fibers contaminated the air, lives could be at risk. In the case of a school, very *young* lives.

"Total exposure," I exhaled. "That's what the Tiger Lady is thinking. Total exposure, another huge fine, the death of Harrison Construction, my dad rolling around in his coffin."

In my head, I pictured the sealed-off "No Entry" areas of the school that had already undergone asbestos removal and the one remaining area that was currently undergoing removal procedures. Since anyone who enters in and out of the removal zone has to be a licensed removal expert and all dressed up in a HEPA space suit, I had no real shot at actually observing the removal. I had no choice but to trust in Farrell's equipment, his technicians, and their abilities. Trust that they were removing the deadly stuff according to plans and specs. If they were cheating on anything, surely it would come out in the testing reports. But thus far, the testing reports had been OK.

I sat back down at my desk, shot a glance at the subcontractor/materials supplier telephone listing tacked up on the wall over the phone. I found the office number for Analytical Labs, the independent testing company hired by the school at Farrell's own suggestion to oversee his removal operation. Since the school's interior air quality was their business, it was possible they'd have an explanation for the surprise OSHA inquest.

I punched the number into the phone and waited for the connection.

When a machine clicked on, a voice said, "You've reached Analytical Labs of the Capital District. We're either away from our desks or conducting field tests. Please leave your name, number—"

I hung up.

I'd go directly to the source.

I looked up the number for Farrell's A-1 Environmental Solutions, dialed the number, and waited for an answer. But all I got was an automated operator telling me the number was out of order or temporarily disconnected. I tried the number again, connecting with the same computerized operator. Looking back up at the listing, I found Farrell's cell phone and dialed that. I was immediately transferred to his answering service.

Sitting back, I whispered, "Where in God's name are you, Jimmy?"

A bull-horned voice outside got me back to my feet and taking another look out the window. The taller of the two OSHA agents had the horn pressed to his mouth. He was shouting, his tinny voice piercing the paper-thin trailer walls. He was trying to speed up the student evacuation. The short guy pulled off his oxygen mask and started approaching the construction trailer.

I turned back to Tommy. "I need you to hold OSHA's hand for a little while...babysit them."

He shot me a quick look. "Where you goin'?"

"Something's not right," I said. "We've got an asbestos contamination and now Farrell's phone's off the hook."

"He ain't here, either, and neither is anybody from his crew."

"Which is why I'm going to take a drive over to his office, grab him by his towhead, and drag him back here. I won't be gone for more than forty-five minutes, an hour at most."

There was a hard knock on the trailer door. "This is an OSHA inspection. Please open up." The voice was deep, insistent.

Tommy grabbed his belt and hiked his loose blue jeans up over his beer belly. "It's your call, Spike," he said. "Do I let them in?"

I heard sirens.

Tommy and I both turned to face the window. A cop cruiser pulled up with an ambulance right on its tail. Holy Christ, were the schoolkids already being laid waste by the asbestos leak? A third van pulled up, this one bearing the call letters *US Environmental Protection Agency Air & Hazardous Material Division.*

"Ava Harrison," the OSHA agent persisted, "we have orders to shut down this project due to unsafe conditions!"

"They're red-flagging us," Tommy said. "Shutting us down. You still think it's a good idea to go after Farrell?"

I pulled out my beat-up BlackBerry and dialed A-1 Environmental one last time. The same automated message system told me the phone was out of service. I tried Farrell's cell again. Straight to Verizon voice mail.

I took a quick look around the trailer.

On the drafting table beside my desk sat Tommy's hard hat and safety goggles. His Carhartt overalls hung by a nail hammered into the trailer wall. I made my way to the overalls, started slipping into them.

"Whaddaya doing?" Tommy barked.

Through the window, I saw a uniformed cop approaching the door. Now dressed in the too-big overalls, I slipped on the hard hat and pulled the plastic goggles down over my eyes. The locked doorknob trembled.

Tommy bit down on his bottom lip. I knew what he was thinking. He was thinking about my hard head.

"Wait a second," he insisted, crossing the narrow space and reaching down into the wastebasket. Pulling out a spent toner cartridge, he ran his hand over the powdery ink end. He slapped some of the powder onto my face.

"There…Spike is a guy."

"Like Dad always wanted."

"What if you get through? What do I say?"

"Tell them I'm getting my hair colored."

"They ain't gonna believe me."

"OK, then tell them the truth—that I snuck out of here in disguise to track down the asbestos-removal contractor who may have contaminated a school filled with three hundred little kids."

Tommy wiped his sweat-beaded brow with a beefy forearm. I knew he needed a drink. Make that two of us. "You're playin' private dick again," he said. "Goin' after Farrell like you used to go after laborers who split town on payday."

I nodded.

Another rap on the door.

Tommy rolled his eyes. "Go now, if you're going," he said. "Out the roll-up door in storage. Nobody will see you if you go now."

Grabbing my equalizer from off the desk, I hiked it through an interior door that led into the storage portion of the construction trailer. I stepped over a collection of coiled hoses, over a Black & Decker generator, over a couple of taping compound buckets. Reaching down, I pulled open the roll-up trapdoor, lowered myself the three feet to the packed-gravel floor, then double-timed it out from under the back of the trailer and across the site to the construction lot where I'd parked my Jeep, the words *Harrison Construction* proudly emblazoned on the side panels.

Somebody had left their business card on the windshield.

It was held in place under the wiper blade. I pulled it free, got behind the wheel, and dropped the card into the empty console cup holder, unread. After stuffing the equalizer under the bucket seat, I fired up the Jeep.

Pulling out of the lot onto Pearl Street, or what was better known around town as the "Concrete Pearl," I put the pedal to the metal.

I did not look back.

Nor did I remove the goggles or hard hat until the Jeep was way out of range of OSHA's sneaky, probing eyes.

CHAPTER 3

I pulled into a convenience store parking lot, drove behind the brick building, and parked the Jeep between the free-air hose and a smelly blue Dumpster to my right. I sucked in a deep breath and peeled my fingers off the steering column.

White knuckles.

I needed a fucking minute to breathe.

I caught my reflection in the rearview. Bright brown eyes accentuated by brows that might have been stunning if I ever considered having them waxed. But who cares about shaped eyebrows on a construction site? I ran my hand through my thick hair still sprinkled with plaster dust, puckered my lips, and wet the pads of my fingers with some saliva to clean the toner off my cheeks.

Fucking Jimmy. Fucking golden boy.

How do I best describe the James Atkins Farrell I had the pleasure of knowing back in high school?

The name Einstein isn't the first thing that comes to mind. But then, he wasn't a total disaster. In terms of athletics and all-American good looks, he had the real shit going on. He was a tall, wiry, sandy-blond, blue-eyed stud. He quarterbacked the football team in the fall, played basketball in the winter, lacrosse in the spring, and in the summer months, he lifeguarded at the Schuyler Meadows Country Club—the most exclusive WASPs' nest in Albany.

By the time September came around he'd have become a golden-skinned god. In short, every female from hopeless pimple-faced nerd to hot-bodied cheerleader swooned over him. Even I fell under his spell once, shared a one-on-one heavy-petting tryst in the backseat of his secondhand Volvo station wagon.

I remember that night like it happened five minutes ago. I can still see Jimmy pulling a condom from his jeans pocket. Trojan "ultra-thin bare skin for the"—get this—"sensitive guy." Apparently the sensitive golden boy thought he was going to get a whole lot luckier that night than he'd already gotten. But in the end, I said no. And when I said no, it meant, "No way…not a chance in the world." That pretty much put an end to the heavy petting—or for that matter, any more dates with Jimmy Farrell.

So maybe the golden boy was also a lover boy, but when it came to brains, Farrell came up a couple of bricks short of a full pallet. Word is that when it came time to graduate, the high school administration required him to make up a couple of courses over the summer in order to legitimize his diploma.

That's when I lost track of him.

Then one beautiful spring day back in the late 1990s, the golden boy called on me at the Harrison Construction offices. In he walked in his finely tailored navy-blue Brooks Brothers double-breasted suit, brand-new BMW convertible parked in Dad's designated spot right outside the glass doors.

Leaning down, he gave me a peck on the cheek. In his low, warm George Clooney voice, he proceeded to spread it thick. "Sexy…hot…luscious," he whispered into my ear. "You still got it, A.J."

It was, of course, brownnosing bullshit. But bullshit or not, that's the kind of compliment you tend never to forget. Especially when rendered so eloquently by a multimillion-dollar baby like Farrell.

Reaching into his pocket, he pulled out a business card and handed it to me. He'd started a new environmental solutions business. Hazardous waste removal for contaminates like lead and oil. But his main focus would be on asbestos removal.

By the end of the 1980s, asbestos removal had become a hot business thanks to new government restrictions that banned the hazardous substance from public buildings. In order to work with existing asbestos you had to undergo rigorous training and testing. The licensed removal subcontractor had to dress up in a HEPA-authorized, environmentally independent space suit before handling the material. He was also required to isolate and seal off the "work area" entirely.

Conspicuous signage had to be posted everywhere:

DANGER
ASBESTOS

CANCER AND LUNG DISEASE HAZARD

AUTHORIZED PERSONNEL ONLY

RESPIRATORS AND PROTECTIVE
CLOTHING ARE REQUIRED IN THIS AREA

…And you got the picture super-scary clear. Listen, anybody taking on the responsibility of removing asbestos from any given building had better not be into it just for the pretty green. Taking an eye off the ball even the tiniest bit might result in somebody losing their life to a horrible and agonizingly protracted lung cancer.

Somebody like any one of those little kids pouring out of PS 20.

I remember staring down at Farrell's business card and thinking, *Is this the same guy I knew in high school? The dumb jock who couldn't pass basic algebra even when assigned special tutors? The silver spoon–fed lover boy with the ultra-sensitive condoms I denied in the backseat of his car?*

Sure, people change. Who was I to come down on him just because he'd entered into a lucrative, but risky, business? Perhaps he had very good people working for him. Knowledgeable people. Honest people.

I didn't hold my breath. But then, I didn't exclude him from my prospective subcontractor's list, either. And as the 1990s made way for the brave new century, A-1 Environmental Solutions took off like a high-speed Otis elevator, never mind my misgivings. The once academic train wreck had become a thirty-something self-made millionaire. His services were inexpensive and in demand.

What was there not to like about the handsome Jimmy Farrell and A-1 Environmental Solutions?

So while the dumb-as-a-box-of-pea-stone golden boy had figured out a way to tap into the American Dream of wealth, prosperity, and social graces, a whole lot of brainiacs who'd gone on to earn advanced degrees still struggled to pay the rent.

Hey, but ain't that America…?

Go fucking figure.

I slipped out of the Jeep, stood in the empty back lot of the convenience store, feeling more than a little out of balance. I pulled off Tommy's Carhartts, tossed them into the back of the Jeep. Breathing in and out, I tried hard to regain my equilibrium. Enough to get my thought process spinning again.

Back behind the wheel of the Jeep, I found the business card inside the cup holder.

Damien Spain, Licensed Private Detective.

A phone number was printed below the name. Nothing else. I turned the card over. Something had been written on the back. *I…CAN…HELP.*

"Who said I need any help, asshole?" I said out loud.

Felt good to say it.

I shoved the card back into the cup holder and backed out of the lot.

CHAPTER 4

Cruising Old Wolf Road in the open-topped Jeep, sunglasses wrapped around my head, with the summer wind blowing through my hair, I downshifted to make the hard right turn into the Aviation Industrial Park. I drove past the identical single-story brick and glass buildings that lined both sides of the industrial park. When I came to building No. 12, I pulled in.

The lot was empty.

It was Monday morning. A workday. Yet the place was deserted.

By contrast, the building next door at lot No. 11 was buzzing with activity. The offices of Marino Construction were surrounded by cars, SUVs, and pickup trucks.

I couldn't help but notice that a new pole barn was being erected in back. Pole barns are a must-have for construction outfits that want storage and easy access to heavy equipment. Part of the barn had already been erected. Its privacy-fenced perimeter barely hid an operating backhoe that was chewing up the earth, probably to make way for more pole barn piers.

Marino Construction had been in business as long as Harrison. Maybe even longer. About the only difference between the two competing firms now was that Marino hadn't fallen apart after the death of the founding Marino. His paunchy, slick-haired, sixty-something son Peter still presided over the general contractor's business like a street-hardened boss over a third-generation mafia family. He also held the distinction of being the father-in-law to our golden boy Jimmy. If anyone knew the word on Farrell's present whereabouts, it would be his Godfather-in-law Peter Marino.

On the other hand, maybe the temperamental Godfather would be the *last* to know.

I got out of the Jeep and made my way to the front vestibule of A-1.

A handwritten notice penned on your everyday white copy machine stock had been Scotch-taped to the glass door.

Closed Untill Further Notice

Whoever wrote the note had put two L's on the end of *Until*. The brilliant Farrell must have written it himself.

I grabbed hold of the opener and tried the door.

It was locked.

I felt the fine hairs on the back of my neck stand up on end. Maybe Jimmy wasn't answering his phones, but I never expected him to be full-on MIA. I had OSHA, the EPA, and the cops parked outside my red-flagged job site. The one person I needed to clear the situation up—immediately, if not sooner—had suddenly closed the doors of his business.

I pulled the paper off the door, stared down at it. The words didn't change. I was about to crumple it up and toss it onto the concrete walk, when I noticed something had been written on the back of the paper. A sketch. Two parallel lines that connected to a square on the far left side but that were left open at the far right. The lines had been drawn in black pencil. Below the lines were scrawled two letters: an "S" and a "C." Directly beside those, a question mark.

I couldn't imagine what S and C meant or why a question mark had been placed beside them or why I was wasting my energy on it.

Details...details.

Folding the paper into squares, I buried it in the right-hand pocket of my Levi's.

I decided to walk around the perimeter of the square building, yanking on locked doors as I passed them by, peering through dirty smoked glass. By the looks of it, the place had been cleaned out. Not a single piece of furniture or contaminate removal equipment, or even so much as a stapler, had been left behind. So it appeared from the outside, anyway. No scaffolding, no storage bags, no fifty-gallon chemical penetrate drums, no vacuum equipment, no portable respirators, no HEPA space suits, nothing.

I tried to recall the last time I'd personally spoken to Farrell on the phone. It had to be last week sometime since it was my job to personally expedite the project, which meant scheduling Jimmy for the school's third and final asbestos-removal procedure.

I tried to recall our conversation.

Did its focus shift from the final contracted phase to anything else? Had I noticed if Farrell sounded strange? Were there signs of stress in his voice? Nothing that caught my attention. But then, I hadn't been looking for anything, either.

He did, however, ask me for more money on top of the Albany School District's two hundred grand—plus I'd already paid him for two completed phases. I told him we were up to date, that he would receive his final payment upon completion of the third phase and indoor air quality sample approvals on behalf of Analytical Labs.

But he'd come up short on payroll that week, he confessed.

Ten grand would tide him over nicely until the final monies were due. Not wanting him to give me a no-show excuse, I advanced him the cash out of a Harrison cash checking account.

Not that I could afford it. But forwarding personal funds now and again was by no means an unusual practice in my business. As a matter of SOP, the GC often bankrolled at least a portion of the project. If you did it effectively enough, you racked up future favors with the subs and materials suppliers.

I brushed back my hair, felt the heat of the late-morning sun on my face, felt my temples pulsing. If Farrell's operation had shut down, if he was nowhere to be found, then I would have to face the Tiger Lady all alone. Maybe that's how Farrell envisioned it when incorrectly spelling out *Untill* on standard white copy stock.

I shot another glance over at Marino Construction, took another look at the new pole barn going up at the back of their lot. I had no choice but to go over to their office, see if anyone knew anything at all about the A-1 Environmental Solutions' sudden bugout. Farrell was married to Peter Marino's daughter. Farrell's unexpected departure from planet Earth was no longer my problem alone. Whether Marino knew it or not, this was about to become a family affair.

CHAPTER 5

Maybe making an inquiry at the Marino Construction offices seemed like the logical thing to do. But it wasn't going to look good. Not by a long shot. I not only considered Marino my direct competition, but lately, we hadn't been getting along as well as the United General Contractors Association might have hoped.

I blamed the Concrete Pearl.

The depressed, five-mile downtown boulevard had become the site of a major business improvement district called, appropriately enough, the Pearl Street Convention Center. Proposed improvements to the Hudson Riverfront roadway included a new twenty-story Hyatt hotel, a gambling casino, a convention center, an aquarium, an indoor/outdoor shopping mall, and a parking garage. With all that excitement and proposed cash about to be floating around the city, every contractor and subcontractor from Dumpster services to steel erection wanted in on the action.

Who could blame them?

The convention center was the capital city's future, its price tag estimated to be anywhere from three hundred to four hundred mil. A huge chunk of change for Albany. With my lonely school project located on the northern fringes of what would be the "redevelopment" action, you might think I'd secure Harrison a huge slice of the convention center pie.

But the bastards were shutting me out.

The convention center underwriter, Albany Development Limited, and its contracted construction manager, Marino Construction Incorporated (go figure!), had removed me from the bidder's list due to Harrison having demonstrated itself a "significant health-and-safety risk" based upon the recent rash of job site accidents. Which meant that if I ever hoped to pick up some of that redevelopment work, I would have to complete the PS 20 project without a single fuckup.

But even that was no guarantee I'd suddenly be invited to the party.

My participation in the Pearl Street Convention Center would ultimately have to be approved by Peter Marino personally (again, go figure!). So to let him in on my present crisis could very well mean pounding the final nail in the Harrison Construction coffin.

Listen, could be the final nail had already been pounded.

If Marino had a TV in his office, he might already know about the asbestos situation at PS 20—that is, if a Johnny-on-the-spot reporter had gotten word of the disaster over the police scanner. He might know all about OSHA's surprise inspection, about the entire adolescent-filled school being contaminated with the very asbestos fibers his son-in-law had been contracted to remove— and about general contractor Ava "Spike" Harrison being held ultimately responsible for it all.

I entered Marino Construction through the front smoked-glass doors.

The empty vestibule was small, narrow. A couch was pushed up against the far wall. In front of it was a coffee table covered with old issues of *National Geographic*, *Modern Builder*, *Concrete Contractor*, *Business Weekly*. Some of the same rags I used to subscribe to back when I still had a real office. Above the couch hung a framed portrait of a far younger, thinner, and apparently happier Marino than I was used to seeing on occasion now. He was standing beside his late gray-haired father—my old man's direct general contracting competition for many decades.

To my right, a forty-something woman sat behind a window that had a small hole carved out of its center. The hole was for talking through.

"Can we help you?" the woman said in a singsong voice. She was a red-haired, white-faced woman. Maybe fifty pounds overweight. When she smiled, her double chin trembled like flesh-colored Jell-O.

"My name is Spike Harrison," I said.

She just smiled at me, chins trembling, unnaturally happy for a Monday morning.

"Spike Harrison of Harrison Construction," I added.

"Of course," she said.

Behind her reception desk I could make out the large interior office space. Two or three support staff occupied identical gray cubicles, all of them women, as far as I could tell. Accounts payable and receivable, for certain. Beyond the cubicles were the project managers' offices. I knew that, in all likelihood, Marino occupied the largest of them.

I overheard a man talking...barking.

The more I listened, the clearer it became that he was arguing with somebody. Standing behind the glass, I distinctly heard, "Goddammit, Tina, when I tell you I'm going to do something, I damn well mean it, and I don't need an argument from you or anyone else. You hearing me?"

I knew the whole office could hear him. The fact that they kept their heads down, noses to their computer screens, told me they were more than a little used to Peter's tantrums.

Red, the receptionist, was still smiling like a chubby joker despite her boss's outburst. She held her wet-eyed gaze on me expectantly.

I said, "Can I speak with Peter?"

"Do we have an appointment?"

"I don't know about you," I said, "but I definitely do not."

The death-defying smile turned into a pout. "Mr. Marino is terribly occupied at the moment."

"It concerns his son-in-law Jimmy Farrell," I said. Cocking my thumb over my shoulder, "The Jimmy from next door?"

She held that stare.

"Jimmy's doing a removal for me at Public School Twenty and he appears to have disappeared. His whole office has been emptied out."

She pursed her lips. "Jimmy is married to Peter's daughter Tina," she chirped. "What a wonderful wedding they had at the country club."

I wanted to ball my fist through the glass and grab her by the chins. But then a head turtled itself out from the far corner office. The head had thick black hair and a puffy, clean-shaven face. When the eyes on the head saw that a woman was standing at the window above the reception desk, it quickly retracted back into its shell.

"Hold all my calls!" Marino barked.

A door slammed.

Red jumped a mile. How she managed to work that smile back up was a mystery to me. "Mr. Marino is unavailable at the moment," she said. "Perhaps we'd like to make an appointment?"

I knew I would get nowhere trying to get some face time with the highly touted convention center construction manager. I also knew that something had shaken him up—and wondered if that something might have had something to do with Farrell's disappearance, given that he'd been reaming out the man's wife.

"Can you leave Peter a message for me?"

Red picked a pen up off the desk. "We'd be happy to," she lied.

"Tell him that Farrell not only reneged on his contract to perform the asbestos abatement removals at PS 20 according to contract specifications, but that he split town with the school's two hundred grand, plus another ten from a Harrison checking account. And I want it back—today. Got that?"

I looked down at her hand. She hadn't written anything. "Perhaps we should have Mr. Marino call you when he gets the opportunity," she said. "What number can we be reached at?"

I dug for a business card in my jeans pocket, handed it to her through a narrow opening at the bottom of the window. She took the card, set it onto her desk. She kept smiling.

"Sorry we couldn't be more help," she said.

"Ain't no *I* in *We*," I said.

"Excuse me?" she said.

I left.

CHAPTER 6

Back behind the wheel of the Jeep, I checked my BlackBerry.

Four missed calls.

I scrolled down them all.

As expected, two more calls from Diane Stewart and two from Tommy. I deleted the messages without listening to them, then speed-dialed Tommy's cell. When I heard the country music in the background, I knew he was in his truck.

"Why aren't you on-site?" I said.

"Could say the same thing 'bout you, Chief—that is, if you weren't busy playing Agatha Christsakes…"

"It's Christie, Tommy. And I'm trying to locate Farrell but failing miserably."

"Agatha Who-Gives-a-Shit. To answer your question, I got out while I still could. They red-taped the whole place. Even the freakin' trailer. Jesus, they got me so nervous I was shittin' yellow. The newspeople pulled up in their camera trucks. Stewart's out for blood."

I told him about A-1 Environmental Solutions being no more and about Farrell's sudden departure from planet Earth. I told him about making an inquiry at the Marino Construction offices but getting nowhere.

He said he was on his way to Lanie's Bar, his home away from home in north Albany. He could better monitor the crisis from the television in the comfort of Lanie's AC. But I knew he intended to get started on an early happy hour. I couldn't blame him one bit.

I sat stewing.

By the looks of things, Farrell had exposed hundreds of kids to deadly asbestos fibers. That was one issue. The school's two hundred G's was another. The third, more personal issue was my ten G's. I stared at his empty building, at the empty parking lot. I wondered what tantalizing clues might lie inside the place, if only I could find a way in without getting busted for a B&E.

Maybe the risk was worth it.

I set the mobile down inside the cup holder and got back out of the Jeep. I reached under the seat, grabbed my equalizer. Shutting the door, I faced the abandoned offices of A-1 Environmental Solutions. With my right hand squeezing the rubber grip of the claw hammer, I walked.

I skirted around to the back of the building to the overhead garage door and the locked solid metal door beside it. I raised the equalizer, took aim, and brought it down hard onto the opener. The collision of metal against metal sent shockwaves up and down my right arm. Motherfucker wouldn't budge. When it came to Yale lock sets, they still made them like they used to.

I made my way back to the side of the building, away from Marino Construction. I came to the first window. I felt the weight of the equalizer in my hand. Cocked it back, let it fly. The head didn't go through the safety glass. It only chipped it and bounced off.

An alarm erupted. I never expected an alarm. Who was the dumbass now? The repeating siren blared. Lights flashed inside and outside the building. I peered behind me at a thick patch of second-growth woods. If anything alive had borne witness to my action, it would be of the furry, four-legged or feathery-winged variety.

I ran for the Jeep, equalizer in hand. Stuffing it back down under the seat, I got back behind the wheel. What the hell had I been thinking? Turning the engine over, I peeled out of the lot and hooked a right onto Aviation Park Drive.

I didn't give Marino Construction a second look as I flew by.

CHAPTER 7

I called Tommy back.

He was still in his truck, driving.

I asked, "You recall an address for Analytical Labs?"

If Farrell was nowhere to be found, maybe the testing professionals in charge of overseeing his work would be.

"Port of Albany," Tommy said. "You want me to turn around, head on over there, see what I can see?"

"Negative. I need you to keep on fielding the calls as they come in from Stewart and anyone else who wants their pound of flesh."

"Not much flesh left to go around," Tommy said.

"You look in the goddamned mirror lately?"

"You kissing anybody with that mouth of yours?"

I puckered up and blew him a big one. Then I hung up.

At the end of Aviation Drive, I hooked a right in the direction of downtown Albany and, beyond that, the Concrete Pearl and the Port of Albany. In my rearview, I caught sight of an APD patrol car making the hard turn into Aviation Industrial Park.

Its flashers were lit up.

So was my pulse.

At the entrance to the port I found a plywood billboard that listed all the businesses that operated inside the port facility. The list included Analytical Labs Environmental Testing Services. B32 was the indicated location.

I drove into the port, hooked a right turn immediately after crossing over the first set of railroad tracks. The port was a busy place, even if most of it was scheduled for the wrecking ball to make way for the convention center. Long and narrow, it spanned the length of the river where it ran deep and dark after decades of dredging. Dump trucks and semis occupied the veinlike network of roadways that crisscrossed one another in no discernable pattern.

I made a right turn on just such a road, eyed the old warehouses until I came to the one marked B. I pulled up to the long, tin-paneled, two-story structure where I parked the Jeep outside a metal roll-up door that had the number 32 painted on it directly above the words *Analytical Labs*.

I got out and approached the roll-up door, turned the latch counterclockwise. It was locked. The latch was old, rusty, and corroded from years of damp riverside exposure.

I took a step back.

This wasn't an office for Analytical Labs. This was a storage space.

My heart beat inside my temples.

I turned and faced the Jeep.

I could either get back in, drive back into the city, call off my search for Farrell, and face Stewart and the police on my own… Or I could keep on looking for the golden boy and my money.

So far all I'd discovered was an emptied-out Environmental Solutions and a Peter Marino who would not talk with me. Now I'd also discovered an Analytical Labs base of operations that wasn't a base of operations at all. It was a storage bin masquerading as a base of operations. What was that saying about something rotten going on in Albany?

I went to the Jeep, once again retrieved my equalizer.

I glanced over both shoulders. There was not a soul to be seen for hundreds of yards in either direction—only warehouses, fixed cranes, and heavy trucking equipment. I raised the framing hammer and brought it down hard onto the latch.

This was more like it; the lock snapped as if it were made of balsa wood. I twisted the latch, heard the metal locking bars retract. Then I pulled the door open.

The place was empty.

No…Scratch that.

It wasn't entirely empty.

It was a cavernous square space with a concrete floor and plywood partitions for walls that stored three small boxes and nothing else. In the sunlight that leaked in from the open overhead door, I pulled apart the cardboard top on the first box. It was filled with blank business checks. All of them bore the name *Analytical Labs* along with the phony business address. I opened a second box. This one contained blank accounts receivable spreadsheets. Finally, I opened the third box. It contained new letters of transmittal.

I stood up, felt the hammer head brushing against my knee as it swung at my side. Other than the boxes, there was nothing else to be found inside the place except for cobwebs and dust. I glanced down at my watch. It was going on nine o'clock. I'd been looking for Farrell for an hour and a half and gotten nowhere.

I plucked the mobile from my hip and dialed Tommy.

"Yeah, Chief."

I asked him for Analytical Labs' phone number.

He checked his materials supplier telephone list, recited it for me. I committed it to memory. I asked him if it seemed strange that the address to what was supposed to be a legitimate business operation was really a storage bin that stored a whole lot of nothing except blank business forms.

He laughed, told me he'd known more than one drinking buddy over the years who used one of those places as a permanent residence.

"You recall Analytical Labs performing services on any previous Harrison projects?"

"Not that I recall," Tommy said. "But I don't pay much attention to the testing outfits. Ain't up to us to hire them. Usually the removal contractor hires somebody on behalf of the owner."

"Despite the fact that the owner should never trust the removal firm to hire its own tester. But they all do it out of convenience anyway."

"Convenience," Tommy said. "Stupidity."

"Ignorance and laziness," I said.

I hung up on Tommy and dialed the number I memorized for Analytical Labs. I waited for a human voice, but I got the same answering service that I'd connected with via the landline back inside the construction trailer.

Tommy was balls-on correct. I never paid much attention to the testing services that came and went from any given construction project, simply because I didn't have to. Had I ever talked with an AL technician since starting PS 20? Never. That had been Farrell's responsibility.

Protocol.

When the answering service beeped, I left my name and number, told the dead air that I needed to speak with someone regarding PS 20 ASAP, that the situation was urgent.

I hung up, knowing in my bones I'd never hear from them.

I reached up, grabbed the roll-up door, pulled it back down. It shut with a resounding hollow metal bang. I returned the now broken latch to the horizontal "locked" position, just for appearance's sake.

Back at the Jeep, I slid the equalizer under the driver's seat, got in, fired up the six cylinder. I pulled away from warehouse B and beat a direct path for the port exit. When I came to Pearl Street, I didn't cross it in the direction of the city. Instead, I hooked a right, driving north toward the suburbs.

The day had started out strange. The more I found out about the missing Farrell and his missing operations, the stranger it got. That in mind, I decided the moment had come to break the golden rule of construction professionalism.

It was time to pay an unannounced visit to the golden boy's private residence.

CHAPTER 8

No need to consult a phone book for the Farrell home address. I already had a pretty good idea of its location. He lived about three miles up the road from me in a newly constructed McMansion that had recently sprung up alongside a thousand identical McMansions inside a posh pastel-colored development called East Hills.

I couldn't be certain which place belonged to him. But it wouldn't be all that difficult to locate, knowing his penchant for expensive cars and motorcycles. I simply drove until I located a cookie-cutter mansion that sported a larger-than-usual custom garage. It didn't take me long to find just such a garage, the name *Farrell* printed on the plastic Lowes mailbox out front. *Bingo!*

I pulled up the sloped, circular drive and parked at the crest, where a set of pretty marble-topped steps rose up to greet a massive Center-Hall Colonial. I got out, climbed the stairs up to the landing, fingered the doorbell to the sound of an ominous gong.

My heart raced a little while I waited.

When I made out the sound of footsteps, I perked up, stood at attention. I stored my sunglasses inside my leather jacket. Then I spit on the pads of my fingertips, brought them to my face, and rubbed the damp fingertips into my skin, trying to bring out some of the blood in my cheeks. I could only hope that none of the black toner still stained my fingers.

When the door opened, she stood before me like an angelic apparition. Tall, fake blonde, blue-eyed, and Gold's Gym slim, this woman could have fit the bill as Farrell's female alter ego. But I recognized her as his wife.

Tina Marino, Peter Marino's daughter.

"Can I help you?" Tina asked politely, long lashes blinking.

She was dressed in white tennis shorts, a tank top fashioned to stop just short of her flat belly, exposing the silver hoop that pierced her navel.

She didn't recognize me. Which made sense. She had to be at least ten or eleven years my junior. I vividly recalled the old days, when she ran around the country club in Pampers.

I smiled and said, "I'm looking for your husband."

She looked at me—rather, looked into me with deep-blue lasers. "I know you," she said.

"We met many years ago," I said, holding out my hand. "Spike."

"Excuse me?" she said with scrunched brow.

"You would remember me as A.J. or Ava Harrison," I clarified. "Our dads were business associates. Well, competitors."

Her heart-shaped mouth went from pout to corner-of-the-mouth smile. Or was it a smirk? She took my hand in hers. It felt like a soft, cold, wet fish against my calluses. We both might have been born of similar construction stock, but I knew then that, unlike me, Tina had never shown any interest in entering the family biz. Standing there, surrounded by all that marble, I had to wonder who'd made the right decision. Who chose wrong?

I couldn't pull my hand away fast enough.

"Please come in."

The interior was IKEA heaven, with a little Stickley tossed in to make things interesting. To my left was a large parlor filled with a big brown leather sectional couch, a teakwood coffee table, and a wall-mounted plasma. The screen on the plasma was almost as wide as the picture window that made up the exterior wall directly across from it.

To my right was a dining room with its long table and chairs, the walls covered in an eclectic assortment of prints and original artwork. Directly ahead of me was a large marble-floored foyer and a wraparound staircase that led upstairs. Nailed to the wall beside me was a framed black-and-white photo. It showed Jimmy and Tina on their wedding day, posing for the lens in front of a large old oak tree on the country club lawn, he in black tux, she in pearl-white taffeta. The photo came straight out of a *Town*

& Country magazine back issue, which, by all appearances, had published news of their marriage. While a smiling, wide-eyed Tina looked ravishing in the photo, Farrell looked proud and, dare I say it, smart.

"Now, what's this all about?" Tina asked.

"We've run into a problem with the asbestos removal down at PS 20," I said. "It requires your husband's attention."

Her eyes blinked rapidly, her sexy bottom lip assuming a pout position. The invisible cat had got her tongue.

"So, is your husband home?" I pressed.

Blue eyes continued boring holes into me. "I remember you now," she said. "From the country club when I was little. You went to school with James. You're a contractor like Daddy."

"Yes," I said. "Like Daddy." Then impatiently, "Tina, I really need to speak with Jimmy about the crisis situation at PS 20."

She crossed long, ripped arms over an ample chest, cleared her throat, peered down at the tops of her tennis shoes. "He's gone," she said.

"Excuse me?"

"Ms. Harrison—"

"Spike."

She seemed taken aback.

"When I was a kid," I explained, "I stepped on a big nail the size of a spike. It impaled me through my foot." I raised my hands like *Get it?* What I didn't tell her was that my grandfather's long-dead beagle had also been named Spike. Why confuse the poor kid?

"Spike," she said, eyes filling, "my husband went fishing on Saturday morning and has not returned since."

The floor shifted under my boots. "He hasn't called in?"

She shook her head, wiped her eyes with the backs of her hands. I couldn't help but notice her manicure. I made loose fists with my hands, felt my jagged cuticles. Sometimes I felt like a man with boobs.

"You tried calling him?"

She sniffled, tried to compose herself. "All I get is the answering service."

"What about the police?"

"Daddy…," she began, then stopped to clear a frog from her throat. "My father wanted to wait another day…to see if James would show up."

A million and one questions ran through my brain, the major one being, *Does Farrell have a squeeze on the side? Is that what this is all about?*

"I imagine you must be quite upset," I said. "But by the looks of things, your husband…*James*…has chinsed out on the asbestos-removal phases of the PS 20 contract, placing a lot of people in considerable danger."

Her eyes were wide, unblinking. Big tears began to fall.

"I just left his office, and guess what, Tina? No more office. Meaning our James has chewed and screwed. Flown the coop. Bolted the scene."

Nothing but open, tear-filled eyes.

I said, "And he did it with most of a two-hundred-fifty-thousand-dollar contract in his pocket, plus another ten that I personally advanced him."

More tears.

"Now, Tina, think hard. Do you know *where* he might have gone fishing on Saturday?"

She stared at me through a haze of salt water. Her whole body was trembling.

"You sure he went fishing at all?"

"Fly…fishing," she said, nodding. "That's what he told me… and I…believed him."

"Did you see him leave the house with all his stuff—waders, fishing poles?"

"He left at dawn," she said. "He used to go with Daddy almost every weekend. Then they stopped for a while." Taking on an ironic smile, "Lately, they've been going out again quite often."

"You'd still be sleeping at dawn," I said.

She pursed her lips, squinted her eyes. "I had doubles scheduled for ten a.m. at the club…plus Pilates."

"Of course you did," I said. "But if Jimmy did actually go fishing, do you at least know *where* he went fishing?"

"He doesn't tell me those things," she said, wiping both sides of her face with the backs of her hands. "He doesn't tell me where he goes, what he does, when he goes there."

"I'm not surprised."

"Well, that's not exactly right."

"Which is it, Tina? Did he tell you where he was going or not?"

She wiped her eyes again. "He didn't tell me, exactly. But I know that he and Daddy used to do a lot of fishing on the Desolation Kill near Lake Desolation. Do you know the place?"

I nodded. "I used to fish there myself as a child. With my grandfather. We used to camp on the lake sometimes. Do you know exactly where on the Kill they used to fish?"

She exhaled and breathed in, like all this thinking was hurting her brain. "A bridge or something…out of Greenfield?"

I knew the place. So did the entire upstate fishing community. I reached into my pocket, pulled out one of my Harrison Construction business cards, and handed it to her. "My advice is to call the police department right away. No matter what your father recommends."

"I was just about to do that very thing. It's been forty-eight hours."

She had a point. Like Tommy had alluded to earlier, about our occasional "runaway" laborers, I'd gone through my fair share of construction workers who got paid on Thursday, then suddenly and inexplicably flew the coop on Friday, no forwarding address to be found. Many times I'd gone in search of them. The last thing the missing person or I needed was for the cops to get involved. Anyway, I knew it took forty-eight hours before the police considered someone missing.

"If you should suddenly hear from him," I added, heading back to the front door, "please be so kind as to call me. Or better yet, please have Jimmy…*James*…call me."

She stopped me in the vestibule with a question. "What could be so wrong at Public School 20 that you must see my husband in person?"

The question gave me pause. Hadn't she heard me? It was as if asbestos contamination didn't qualify as an emergency that could explain my sudden presence at her East Hills mansion. She suspected an ulterior motive, probably something to do with a crush I might be harboring for the old golden boy. Was she aware of my high school backseat romp with her husband?

I said, "I need answers from Jimmy. It's a matter of life and death for a whole lot of kids who've been exposed to asbestos fibers for months."

She set an open hand atop her flat belly, hiding the silver hoop. A gesture I instinctively translated as *baby aboard*. Was Tina carrying the missing Farrell's offspring?

I put my hand on the polished brass knob, twisted it, opened the door. Whether it was out of politeness or anxiousness need to get rid of me, she went to hold it open. But I told her I could let myself out.

"Spike," she said, "can I ask a question?"

I nodded.

"Does James have…another woman in his life? Someone I'm not aware of?"

I looked at her from outside on the landing.

Her expression had gone from teary-eyed emotional to stone cold in two-point-five seconds flat. All the cash that surrounded her, all the suburban lavishness, the country club tan, the personal trainer bod, the plasma TV, the waxed bikini line, the Nike tennis clothes, the *Town & Country* wedding write-up…None of it seemed to be making her the least bit happy. I was beginning to think the same thing about the incredible disappearing Mr. Farrell—Mr. Happy-Go-Lucky-Go-Suddenly-Missing.

"I have no way of knowing," I told her. Not because I didn't want to make her suicidal, but because it was the truth. I just didn't know or care about what women he might be poking in his spare time. All I wanted was for him to make right the asbestos problem at PS 20, if there was indeed a problem, then give me my ten grand back.

"Please make certain he calls me," I said, starting down the front steps. But half under my breath, I added, "I'm not going to jail on behalf of Jimmy's fuckups."

Tina might have heard me had she not already closed the door on her broke-down East Hills palace.

What's a headstrong girl to do?

I got back in the Jeep, feeling a bead of sweat drip down the center of my chest. The realization began to sink in. I wondered what had to finally give way for a man to suddenly abandon his life. Just split the scene, Jean, slip out the back, Jack…

What the fuck? Farrell hadn't gone fishing.

He was gone baby gone.

He wasn't coming back.

Farrell was…

Gone from PS 20.

Gone from his Aviation Industrial Park offices.

Gone from his home and his trophy wife.

Gone from father-in-law Peter Marino.

Gone from A-1 Environmental Solutions.

Gone with the school's two hundred large, plus my ten.

I looked down at my hands gripping the steering column. My knuckles were white and my hands cramped. Heart pounded against sternum. If you could've seen through my clothes and skin, you wouldn't have seen the blood running through my veins. You'd have seen it shooting.

I had nowhere else to go other than back to the job site. There was no other place to go looking for Farrell. Maybe it was time to do what I should have done earlier that morning when I found out Jimmy had split the scene. I pulled out the BlackBerry and punched in 911.

I held my thumb on the SEND button. My thumb trembled. The early summer sun beat down on me. The BlackBerry began to vibrate against the palm of my hand due to an incoming call. The sudden vibration startled me.

Two choices appeared on the screen. ANSWER or IGNORE.

I recognized the incoming number. It was Marino Construction. I hit ANSWER, placed the phone to my ear.

"Harrison."

"Ms. Harrison?" It was a woman's voice. Bobbie, the redheaded receptionist. "Please, I have to make this quick. But I was here when Mr. Farrell emptied out his offices on Saturday."

"How would you know?"

"I was in the office catching up on some paperwork. Jimmy was packing up his office next door. Rather, he was overseeing a moving company doing all the work. He brought some boxes here to Marino Construction. He met with Peter inside Peter's office. They argued."

"About what?"

"I couldn't tell, really, they were flinging so many names and accusations. But I do recall something that stuck out."

"I'm listening, Bobbie."

"They were doing a lot of screaming. About money, cuts, fair shares, and Tina. They argued about another girl too. I think her name was Natalie. It was like they both had an interest in her, whoever this Natalie was."

"What else can you tell me?"

"They fought over a baby."

My stomach did a flip at the sound of the B-word. "What baby?"

"I don't know."

"Is Tina pregnant?"

"I don't know. Peter hasn't said anything."

"Why are you volunteering this information? Why place yourself and your job at risk?"

"Because I thought you should know. And like you said, 'Ain't no *I* in *We*.'"

She hung up before I could thank her.

"A baby," I whispered to myself, picturing Tina pressing the palm of her hand against her exposed, flat belly. Or maybe it was the mysterious Natalie who was pregnant? Pregnant with Jimmy's or even Peter's baby.

I gave up on redialing 911. What the hell was the nature of my emergency, anyway? The nature was that something else was going on besides Farrell simply splitting town.

I backed out of Farrell's driveway, contemplated doing something that seemed entirely stupid but, at the same time, made perfect sense: heading north to Lake Desolation. Maybe Farrell hadn't really gone fishing in the pure-sportsman-outdoorsy-one-with-Mother-Nature sort of way. But what's a skull-strong construction babe to do?

She goes fishing with the one lead she's got left.

CHAPTER 9

Driving.

Highway 87 north until I came to Exit 12, just below Saratoga Springs.

From there I drove west into farm country, following rural Route 84 all the way out until I spotted the lake though the trees on the left and eventually the stream that fed it—the Desolation Kill. I drove the Jeep fast over winding, hilly country roads, not worrying about speed, only about trying to find Farrell before my absence from the PS 20 job site became more conspicuous than it already had to be.

Motoring around the pine-treed perimeter of the lake, I came to the bridge.

I recognized the short metal-span bridge as the same one my grandfather took me to back when I was a little girl. I took it slow over the bridge until I cut the wheel to the left, cruising onto a wide section of gravel-soft shoulder that had been cut out of the thick second-growth woods. I put the Jeep in park and killed the ignition.

I took immediate notice of a sign that had been nailed to the trunk of an old oak tree, the words *Public Fishing Access Area* engraved on it. It also displayed the hours of regulation fishing: 7 a.m. to 7 p.m. Below that, in smaller script, were the words *No Parking After Hours. Vehicles Towed at Owner's Expense: $75.00.* Obviously, Greenfield was concerned about not providing its teenage lovers with a secluded place to suck face.

Also displayed on the sign were the name and phone number of the towing company, Dott's Garage.

I opened my briefcase, pulled out a yellow estimating pad, jotted down the number in one of the slots normally reserved for a construction item. Naturally, I had my doubts that Farrell had come here at all. But if he had come here, was it possible his car had been towed from this very spot? And if it had been towed, why had he abandoned it in the first place?

I set the estimating pad back down on top of the briefcase, opened the door, and slipped out of the Jeep. Immediately, I was struck by the smell of pine trees. The sweet scent transported me back to my childhood. So did the stream rushing over the rocks under the bridge, the iron structure forming a kind of echo chamber that amplified the sound.

I pictured Farrell standing in the gravel lot, no doubt dressed in overpriced Orvis waders and vest, fly rod in hand. I saw him trekking the short path down to the stream.

But then, that was stupid. If he had come here, his pockets bulging with my and the school's money, it hadn't been to fish. It just didn't make sense.

I followed the path. Its dusty gravel floor was stamped with footprints from the dozens of fishermen and women who'd come and gone since the fishing season began back in the early spring. I came upon the stream and its strong-flowing, metallic-smelling water.

I took a look around the place. A half dozen spent cigarette butts littered the bank. The kind of cigarettes you rolled yourself. Each of them looked like the little roach end of a joint after it was smoked to death, but I sensed these cigarettes had been filled with tobacco. No stoner in his or her right mind would leave a half dozen roaches hanging around. But just to make sure, I picked one of the little butts up and smelled it. Just as I suspected. Cigarette tobacco.

I tossed the butt back down and noticed an empty beer can. Budweiser. Tossed onto the bank not far from that, a used condom. Just looking at it made my stomach turn. The empty wrapper had been flung onto the ground as well.

Trojan ultra-thin bare skin.

Well, what do you know? Jimmy Farrell's personal choice of lovemaking protection. Not far away from that, a can of Skoal chewing tobacco. Wintergreen flavor. Coincidence of coincidences, Jimmy chewed Skoal tobacco—wintergreen Skoal, to be precise. Farrell might have been one hell of a gifted dumb jock back in high school. But I knew from experience that he did harbor that one very bad habit that I found particularly repulsive, especially when I kissed him. He still chewed the stuff, even when making the rare visit to the PS 20 job site.

What a trail of pretty disgusting bread crumbs our Jimmy had left behind.

My pulse picking up, I reached down for the can. I'll be damned. It was still full. Who the hell would leave a full can of this stuff behind? Even if the owner had suddenly decided to quit, he'd at least have carried it out with him and gifted it to a friend who still chewed the rancid stuff. I wasn't entirely sure what good it would do me, or if this stuff really did belong to Farrell or not, but my gut was telling me to hold on to the can of chewing tobacco. Starting back up the embankment toward my Jeep, I greedily gripped the can of Skoal like it was not only the key to uncovering my ten thousand dollars, but also to uncovering the location of the missing Farrell himself.

I straightened up and, the can of chewing tobacco still in hand, walked back up the embankment to the parking area and my rig.

Opening the door, I set the Skoal tin inside my briefcase along with the estimating pad. The mobile was lit up like a Christmas tree. Four missed calls, three new messages to go with them. The first was from Tommy, the next two from the Tiger Lady. The fourth and last was a number I matched up with the business card stored inside the cup holder: Damien Spain, Licensed Private Detective. Ignoring the messages, I speed-dialed Tommy's cell. When he answered it, my ear filled with background noise coming from Lanie's.

"Where the hell you been, Spike?"

I told him.

He assured me that he'd been fielding calls as they came in since our project trailer answering service had been programmed to automatically forward them to his cell. He, too, had been hounded by Diana Stewart, had assured the OSHA chief that we were doing everything in our power to rectify the asbestos contamination.

He'd also received a call from a field reporter at the local Channel 13 news. A woman named Chris Collins, who was looking for comments regarding the asbestos leak at the public school. I asked Tommy for her number, jotting it down on the estimating pad.

"What's your directive, Chief?" he asked.

I didn't have one. Yet. "Turns out I can't locate Farrell by the end of the workday, so we figure out another plan of action."

"What kind of plan?"

"Fuck if I know," I said.

"Confidence is a good attribute in a situation like this," Tommy said. "So is being pigheaded."

I hung up, sat back, thought the communications situation over.

On my behalf, Tommy had already fielded OSHA's calls. He'd taken care of calming the big guns down. Short of calling my lawyer, giving him the green light to burn through what was left of my cash reserve to oversee the communications issue, Tommy was the best I could do. I sensed that, at this point, if I personally spoke with the Tiger Lady without a solid explanation as to how Farrell's asbestos-removal screw-ups had gotten past me—the general contractor—I would not only begin implicating myself, but I might say something for the record I might regret later on. That is, I might end up the target of a few more major fines. Which, at this point, looked inevitable.

I did, however, have a plan, no matter how fragile.

What if I took the initiative, contacted the media directly? What if I put on my best public relations hat and contacted Collins at Channel 13 news, offered her an exclusive on the PS 20 asbestos affair? Maybe by cooperating with her I could get my message out to Farrell, wherever the hell he was. Maybe he would be tuning into the news, tuning into the blame that I was about to toss onto his skinny-ass lap.

CHAPTER 10

I dialed the number Tommy relayed to me for Collins's cell phone, waited for a connection. When she answered, I politely identified myself, kindly offered her an insider's exclusive to the asbestos-leak story, and then told her most of what I knew. Just the facts—no opinion or conjecture. I told her everything from OSHA's job site invasion first thing this morning to the school's hasty evacuation, to the asbestos test results proving inside air contaminated with asbestos fibers, to my failed attempts to contact the man responsible for the crisis.

What I did not tell her about was the money he took off with. Mine or the school's. Nor did I tell her he hadn't shown up to his East Hills home in two days.

Why did I choose to hold back?

I'm not a detective. But I did know this: If Farrell couldn't be located, then the authorities would no doubt focus every bit of their attention and blame on me. No point in giving them a head start by advertising the fact that Farrell had flown the coop.

"All I'm really aware of," I told Collins as I peered out the Jeep onto the pine-tree-lined road, "is that I've acted according to the contract documents for the safe and effective removal of existing asbestos material inside Public School 20."

"But as the general contractor, aren't you ultimately responsible for the health and safety of the school's inhabitants?" she asked. "Even in the event of death?"

I didn't want to lie. She'd obviously done some homework on the subject, and for all I knew, she might have had a copy of the asbestos specification laid out on her desk.

Scratch that...

I didn't want to get *caught* in a lie.

I told her I was responsible insofar as my subcontractor, A-1 Environmental Solutions, was responsible. Was I was passing the buck here? Yes and no. Yes, in that, as the general contractor on the job, I'm ultimately responsible for what goes on, from the beginning moment when a shovel breaks down to the last moment when the owner takes over final occupancy. But no, in that I am only one person, and I can't possibly monitor every square inch of space inside a big school renovation any more than the President of the United States can monitor every bit of America or even the world at once. You have to rely on your support staff. You have to rely on trust. Trust that the subs you hire will do their jobs according to plans and specs and according to an unwritten moral and ethical code. I'd always known Jimmy as a good-looking guy who could care less about academics, but I'd never known him to be a crook. I sensed in him a genuine willingness to make good at the environmental solutions business, and thus far, he'd been a great success. So in the end, yes, I was responsible, but also, no, I wasn't responsible, and I believe that Collins understood my precarious, if not downright dangerously exposed, position in all this. Because her next question nearly took my breath away.

"Ms. Harrison," she said, "hypothetically speaking, what if it happens that one of the school's students or faculty members should develop an asbestos-related cancer like mesothelioma or asbestosis? How would you react to an accusation of negligence? Would you assume full responsibility?"

How was I supposed to answer that one without a lawyer present?

This wasn't me trying to explain myself with honesty to the media. This was me on trial for something that was essentially out of my control no matter how much I monitored the situation. I can stare all day at asbestos-removal workers coming and going from the dangerous abatement area, but asbestos fibers are invisible. How am I supposed to know how good a job they're doing until the test reports are in or something like OSHA shows up and performs a surprise inspection?

Outside, on the sleepy road, a rare car was passing. It was an old, restored Dodge Charger. The Charger was going by slowly, the driver no doubt taking an interest in who had parked in the public fishing lot. A fisherman, probably, looking for a secluded place to drop a line. Having passed, he suddenly sped up, the Charger engine roaring as the car crossed over the bridge.

Collins asked me for an immediate face-to-face interview at the school job site. "Take just fifteen minutes of your time," she said, like it was some kind of enticement.

"Not convenient," I said. "I have a crisis to diffuse first."

"This is important news."

I pulled the BlackBerry from my face. "Chris, you're breaking up on me," I lied.

"Can you hear me now?" she barked.

I thumbed END.

I speed-dialed Tommy.

"I need for you to look into something."

He told me to wait while he grabbed a pencil.

"Shoot, Chief," he said.

"I want to know how much asbestos needs to be in the air in order to cause lung problems for people ingesting it. Also, how long do those same people have to be exposed to the fibers before they're affected?"

I could tell by the silence that Tommy was writing it all down.

"Thought you'd maybe know the answer to this stuff by this point in your stellar career, Spike," he said.

"I'm no expert, Tommy," I said. "That's what engineers and certified removal experts are for. Get it?"

"Got it, Chief," he said. Thinking out loud, he mumbled, "Number of asbestos fibers per cubic centimeter of air." Then, in a louder voice, "What else?"

"Keep a low profile until I tell you different. Take a spin back to the job site; make sure it's secured. I don't care if the joint is red-flagged. Padlock the trailer door. I don't want the cops or OSHA or EPA nosing around any more than they already have."

"Maybe you should have hung around the site more than you did today."

"Maybe I should wrap a coaxial cable around my neck, hang myself from the scaffolding."

"What would your old man say to that?"

"He'd tell me to take a long fucking deep breath and count to ten."

"'Cept he wouldn't use the F-word."

"Sometimes the apple doesn't fall far, but it can roll a long way away."

"You got a call from some guy, calls himself Spain, like the country. Says he's a private detective."

"And my mobile's a private number."

"Says he can help, Spike. Says he's been looking into Farrell's screw-ups for a while now and that he can help you."

"I'll take it into consideration," I said.

"Will I hear from you later?"

"You gotta ask?"

I slapped the phone down. If I had my choice, I would have tossed the mofo into the lake. I decided to exit the Jeep one final time, make one last sweep of the place before I pulled out. Might as well try to be thorough while I was all the way up here. I looked at the trees, at the bridge, at the stream and lake. I turned and looked at the country road and the farm field across from it. I looked high; I looked low.

I might not have noticed it had I not peered down at the tops of my boots. Something glinting in the midday sun. At first I did a double take but then took a couple of steps toward the shiny object. Bending at the knees, I felt my heart skip a couple of beats. I reached into my back pocket, pulled out a white cotton handkerchief, wrapped it around the fingers on my right hand, dug out the object from the sand and gravel.

It was a spent shell casing. A 9mm, the jacket new and chrome shiny.

My heart sped up. My dad had owned guns. He acquired his pistol permit when his first cousin had been elected an Albany County judge and could push the application through the thick wall of bureaucratic red tape and background checks. He wanted the option of being able to carry a concealable pistol for safety reasons. It wasn't all that long ago contractors found themselves carrying around cash payrolls in their pickups.

At his insistence, he wanted me to do the same. An order to which I reluctantly acquiesced as I approached my mid-twenties despite my stubborn streak. Although I shot a pistol for target practice on many occasions, I never could get used to the volatility of a handgun, preferring the relative safety of my equalizer. But I recognized a 9mm shell casing when I saw it. I also knew when one had been recently fired. I brought the open side of the shell to my face, inhaling fresh powder.

The smell was strong, acrid, but not unpleasant. How long would it have retained that scent? Not much more than twenty-four, maybe forty-eight hours at most. And I should know. When I was a kid, I used to save the spent shell casings from my dad's guns whenever he'd go shoot with his friends. I tried to make jewelry out of them. I still own a pair of brass-bullet earrings that went great with a ripped T-shirt and a pair of ratty combat boots during my punk rock days.

Wrapping the casing up in the handkerchief, I looked down at the gravel for any bloodstains. I didn't see any. At least not with the naked eye. The June days had been bright, hot, cloudless, and dry. But the past two nights had been different. The hot, humid weather produced stormy weather and scattered cloudbursts. I was no expert, but it was possible that the blood residue could have washed away.

Farrell's blood?

I had to wonder if the weather and I were combining to contaminate a possible crime scene. "Too late now," I whispered to myself.

I took the wrapped-up casing with me to my Jeep. Back behind the wheel, I slipped the shell into the briefcase along with the Skoal canister and the estimating pad.

Closing the briefcase back up, my eyes caught the sign nailed to the oak tree.

VEHICLES TOWED AT OWNER'S EXPENSE

I added up the particulars: a missing Jimmy "gone fishing"…a Wintergreen Skoal chewing tobacco tin…a spent 9mm shell casing…a spent condom that I knew to be Jimmy's preferred brand…no sign of the golden boy's ride…

Chalk one up for the headstrong girl. Maybe it had been a good idea to make the scenic drive up to Lake Desolation, after all.

I fired up the Jeep.

Next stop, Dott's Garage.

CHAPTER 11

I hadn't pulled away from the public access fishing parking area when my BlackBerry vibrated against my hip bone.

"Whaddaya got, Tommy?"

"FYI," he said, "all types of asbestos fibers are dangerous if you inhale them. I think we both knew that already. But check this shit out: No amount of fibers in the air is considered safe. And I mean no amounts. Zero. Zilch. Which means even a tiny amount can contaminate PS 20."

"You're right, Tommy," I said, my stomach feeling like a common brick was lodging itself inside it. "I'd always assumed there was an acceptable level, no matter how miniscule."

"Thanks for making me look that shit up, Spike, because now you got me all paranoid. Jesus, you and me right now could be suffering from the beginnings of some killer asbestos disease like asbestosis or meso...mesothel..."

"Meso-thel-ioma," I pronounced for him.

"You could be dying, Spike. I could be dying. You know how much of that fibrous crap I've torn out and tossed away without a mask in my day?"

Tommy had a point. In my early days laboring for Harrison, I, too, had handled old asbestos insulation without wearing protective gear. I'd spent two days my senior high school summer tearing it from the basement of an old bowling alley that was being renovated into a computer tech center. For a brief second, I pictured the insides of my lungs as though staring at an MRI. I wanted to imagine healthy pink lungs. Instead, I saw something that resembled burnt toast. All drama aside, maybe Tommy was right. Maybe we were dying a slow death and didn't know it yet.

"Did anything say how long you have to be exposed to the stuff for it to affect your lungs?"

"One hour, one month, one year. It doesn't matter. Problem is, you can't tell when the shit is in the air or when it's hurting your lungs. It's got no odor, no taste, no feel, nothing to let you know that the air you're breathing is tainted with death."

"Mother of God, Tommy, could you possibly paint a grimmer picture?"

"Hey, you fucking asked, Chief."

"Yeah," I whispered, thinking of all those little kids in PS 20. "I did have to ask, didn't I?"

I heard the sound of Tommy shuffling through some notes, the Lanie's jukebox going in the background. "It gets better," he went on. "There's something called a latency period. All asbestos diseases have this latency period—that's more or less a gap between the time you suck in asbestos fibers and the time you start feeling sick. The latency period can be as short as a few months or as long as, like, thirty years."

My stomach dropped down around my boot heels. "So it's true, then. There could be any number of sick PS 20 kids or faculty as we speak."

"And here's where it gets way worse," Tommy added. "All asbestos cancers and diseases are not just real hard to treat; they're near *impossible* to treat. They're also impossible to cure."

"That much I already knew," I said. "I just wasn't sure I believed it until hearing it come from your mouth."

"You remember that song back in the seventies—'Werewolves of London?'"

"*His hair was perfect,*" I quoted.

"The guy who sang that song, Warren Zevon…he died of meso…"

"Mesothelioma," I pronounced for him again.

"Meso-whatever-the-fuck…Anyway, Zevon dies decades after spending too much time writing songs in his grandparents' asbestos-insulation-filled attic. Steve McQueen bought the farm over it, too, after only a three-month exposure in his old LA town house. Three freakin' months, Spike!"

I took a moment to breathe but had a little trouble doing so, like my lungs were full of asbestos insulation.

I wasn't sure if what I felt was more rage at Farrell or outright fear for those kids who attended an asbestos-contaminated school all year long, never mind three months. All on my watch.

My watch.

My fucking watch...I should have been screaming at myself.

"What's next, Chief?"

The coax cable and the scaffolding, Tommy, I wanted to say. *Aren't you listening? Bring enough cable for the both our necks...*

But enough of that thinking. I had to keep my head together. Keep my world from falling apart any more than it already was. I inhaled a breath and pressed the phone against my ear with a trembling hand.

"I'm heading to Dott's Garage in Saratoga," I told him. "I have a hunch Farrell's Beemer was towed there over the weekend."

"Whad' you expect to find inside it?"

"Maybe a detailed itinerary describing the golden boy's destination, including phone and fax numbers."

"Very funny."

"Can you tell I'm pretty much just making this up as I go?"

"Beats the alternative."

"What's that?"

"Suckin' up the entire blame for something that ain't all your fault."

CHAPTER 12

Driving east on my way out of the open farm country toward Saratoga Springs and Dott's Garage. Maybe it had something to do with the rise in anxiety level, but as the surrounding green fields faded and the suburbs took over, I couldn't stop myself from picturing Jordan, my husband of five short years. Saratoga had been one of Jordan's favorite places, especially in August during the thoroughbred racing season.

We'd first met at Harrison Construction ten years ago...

As the senior project manager, I'm responsible for overseeing the entire team of project managers, which at the time includes Diana Stewart. Jordan is new to the Harrison team. He's been hired by my father as a senior supervisor. It's his responsibility to visit every job site, making sure that everything from excavation to framing to roofing is progressing steadily and according to schedule.

It's not long before I learn that Jordan is not the kind of man to sit idly at a desk inside the Harrison Construction offices. When he isn't working, he's running cross-country. When he isn't running, he's lifting weights. When he isn't lifting weights, he's hiking or fly-fishing or playing guitar.

He stands five feet eight, maybe one hundred seventy-five pounds. Who is taller depends upon whether or not I wear flats or heels.

But Jordan still exudes confidence.

He is covered in muscle. And I do not hesitate to refer to him as "muscle head" from time to time. It's a term of affection that always makes him stick his tongue out at me from between thick lips accented with a trimmed mustache and a goatee. But it's not the muscle or the energy or the Marlboro Man image that attracts me most to Jordan.

The little things make me love him.

The way he bites his bottom lip when in deep thought, the way he subtly rubs the back of his left hand with his right when he's nervous, his stuttered laugh, and his ear-to-ear smile. It's the way he constantly opens his mouth when he chews his food so that I have to tell him to keep his mouth closed. Or the way he will, on occasion, show up at my office door after everyone else has gone home for the day; the way he'll close the door behind him, come to me, and without a word, undress me, lift me up in his arms, set me down gently on the drafting table...

Dad loves Jordan too.

Dad's old-school—a single parent who always wanted a son. He molds Jordan into the "super" supervisor every Harrison worker can come to respect. It's not at all unlike Jordan to jump out of his truck, grab a shovel, jump into a trench, help out with pouring a footing. Or maybe he'll temper the mud for a mason, working the line like a common laborer. Or maybe he'll just sit down with a carpenter, share a smoke, a hard roll, and coffee...shoot the shit.

Dad and I, we're not the only ones who love Jordan, though.

That's where the real trouble starts.

You could see the love cooking in Diana's eyes whenever Jordan blew into the office, the pockets on his work shirt and Carhartt vest filled with packing slips and receipts that required processing by our accounts payable. Diana, with her fiery red hair and killer bod, would always request her standard five minutes of the chief super's time—time for the University of Virginia grad and Albany, New York, native to discuss, in her faux Southern accent, the material deliveries on any given job she might be managing. Or maybe she'd want to go over a blueprint detail that just didn't quite jibe right in the field. Maybe a corner where the copper flashing butts up against a concrete block with no possible means for moisture to escape.

But we all knew the truth.

What Diana wanted was a little face time with my boyfriend, who sooner than later became my husband. But that was all right by me. Seriously. I was secure in my relationship with Jordan. Diana wasn't a threat to either one of us. Like her phony Southern belle voice, we'd laugh about her little crush. Besides, she was a good ten years older than the both of us. We interpreted her little infatuation as a compliment. Nothing more.

It's while the two of us are visiting the Tiger Lady–managed Pearl Street Key Bank rehab project when Jordan makes the mistake of his life. Instead of taking the interior stairs, he decides to climb a dozen-plus scaffolding levels to confer with Diana and to check on a newly replaced cornice.

As always, it makes me nervous when he insists on climbing hand and boot to the top of a building. But you just can't shake the boy from the man when it comes to Jordan. You just can't shake his need to be moving, doing anything but sitting. On that particular morning when he makes the climb, I can't help but think that a big part of him is showing off for my benefit, for my entertainment!

But that doesn't make it any easier when only moments later he's laid out on his back in the hospital, his body a train wreck of shattered bones and lacerated flesh, his brain now swelled against the insides of his skull, bleeding out the ears and nostrils. Still, he tries to move, tries to get up. Having somehow survived a sixty-foot fall, he's peering up at me from the bed in the ICU trauma unit, bruised eyes pleading. I think it's not like he wants to tell me something. It's like he wants me to rescue him from that hospital, as if I can simply strap a shattered man on my back, carry him out of ICU, out the front door of the Albany Medical Center forever...

Looking back on it all these years later, stealing Jordan from that hospital is exactly what I would have done, knowing then what I would come to know shortly thereafter: that he would never step out of that hospital alive.

CHAPTER 13

Dott's Garage and Used Auto Parts was located at the far north end of the village, along the rural hinterland between downtown Saratoga Springs and the suburban enclave of Wilton. It had been converted from an old full-service gas station into a fenced-in ghost town for towed or repo'd cars, vans, and trucks.

I pulled up to the first of the two parallel concrete islands that had once upon a time supported gas pumps. What had been the gas station now served as Dott's office.

I knew about Dott through Jordan, who used to come here to buy used parts for his vintage 1968 Chevy three-on-the-tree pickup. The guy was a local legend of sorts, a grease monkey who cherished Elvis, lived in a fenced-in time warp, always complaining about a sex-stingy wife no one had ever met.

I got out of the Jeep and ran both hands through my hair. Just for the hell of it, I unbuttoned the third button down on my work shirt. A little skin and a black push-up bra never hurt. I stepped inside through the glass-and-wood door and was hit with the smell of motor oil. The toxic odor combined with a cloud of cigarette smoke. It made me wonder which site boasted the worse interior air quality: the air inside Dott's office or the asbestos-contaminated air inside PS 20.

To my immediate left hung a wall-mounted bulletin board, its surface mostly covered with key rings that hung from little hooks and nails stabbed into the corkboard. I made a cursory search for the sterling silver skull-and-bones key ring that belonged to Jimmy's beloved black four-door Beemer, the ride he always drove to the job site during his less-than-occasional visits. The board was filled with keys, but as I'd hoped it would, the silver metal skull stuck out from the crowd.

Beside the bulletin board was an open door that led into a two-bay service garage. Both bays were occupied, the first with an old tow truck, the hoist-and-boom kind you don't see much anymore, and the second with an old black Cadillac convertible, something a president might sit in back in the '60s to wave at his adoring public—that is, before assassins started using open tops as an excuse for playing Kill the Commander in Chief.

To my right was a vending machine that must have come with the place back when Dott purchased it from the gas company. Judging by the sunbaked wrappers, the candy bars it stocked had come with the machine too.

Directly ahead of me was an old metal desk like the kind my dad used to keep in the basement back when I was a little kid, when he ran Harrison Construction from out of our West Albany home. There was a man sitting behind the desk in a swivel chair. His jet-black dye job was slicked back in an Elvis ducktail. He was dressed in grease-pit overalls that looked as if they hadn't been washed since "Jailhouse Rock" topped the charts. Elvis was sitting way back in the chair, eyes glued not to a desktop buried in paperwork but to an old black-and-white TV set on a metal stand. On the screen, the Yankees were playing the Boston Red Sox. There was no score.

He'd heard me come in, but Dott took his time turning to me. "Help you?"

"Please don't get up."

He smiled, sense of humor beaming through nicotine-painted teeth.

"I've come to collect my boyfriend's Beemer," I said.

"You have ID?"

On the television, Johnny Damon was up at bat against his old team. This was back near the end of Damon's stint with New York, but I guess I never could get used to him being a Yankee. The first pitch was too high, too inside. Damon had to pull his head back at the last millisecond or risk losing it completely.

Dott let out a groan. "Sox are still out to kill that boy for desertion."

"Don't you think he's adorable?" I said.

He just grunted while we watched Damon pop it up on the next pitch. Dott stood up then. All six feet six of him. He squinted down at me, eyes locked on the narrow exposed space between my size Bs. On the television, the game switched over to a promo for the upcoming Channel 13 news at noon. Field reporter Chris Collins stood in front of a PS 20 project trailer wrapped in red tape. "A local school under rehabilitative construction is evacuated after it's discovered that deadly asbestos fibers have been contaminating the air for more than nine months," she said into a handheld mike. "Just who's to blame for the contamination? Tune in at noon to find out."

I cleared my tight throat.

"I brought in a black four-door BMW from Greenfield last Saturday night," Dott said. He pulled a ticket from the stack on the counter, looking from it to me. "What's your boyfriend's name?"

"Jimmy. Jimmy Farrell."

Nodding, "Registered to a Mr. James Atkins Farrell of A-1 Environmental Solutions." Eyes back on me.

"Yes, that's the one."

He said, "I called the number for that Environmental Solutions joint, but all I got was a Ma Bell voice recording."

Jimmy must purchase his vehicles through his company. Which explained why Tina would not have fielded a call about her husband's towed Beemer.

To Dott, I said, "I had the same problem last week when I tried him at the office. A-1's been knocking heads with the phone company."

"You got ID?"

I took out my wallet, showed him my driver's license.

He pulled a pair of reading glasses from the pocket on his overalls, slid them on. He studied the license. For a beat, I thought he might recognize me from the local news reports—that is, if my name had been mentioned, my image broadcast. He pulled the glasses back off, cleared the frog in his throat.

"You got something that tells me you're James Atkins Farrell's significant other?"

"No."

"Can't let you have the car."

He studied me like he had studied the license. I'd been living in a man's world for a long time now. I knew all about pigheadedness. I knew Dott wasn't about to change his mind.

"Can you tell me where the car is, at least?"

"Why d'you wanna know that?"

"James is very particular about his cars. Maybe it would be OK if I just took a little walk to check it out, make sure it wasn't damaged during transport. I won't be needing the keys for that."

He came around the desk. "State troopers issued the call for the tow. I'm not entirely sure they'd want you snooping around without the proper authorization."

The room went silent other than for the baseball game.

"Let me see your pockets," Dott said.

"Pardon me?"

"Let me see your pockets, make sure you aren't carrying a second set of keys."

I pulled out the pockets on my pants and jacket. Aside from a small stack of Harrison business cards, they were empty.

"Now let me have your wallet."

"Say what?" I said, eyes wide.

"Let me have your wallet…please. I'll keep it right here, out in plain sight, on the counter."

Why Dott felt the need to give me such a hard time I had no idea. Maybe he suspected something fishy was going on. Maybe he was having fun with me. I decided to play along anyway. I pulled the wallet from my back pocket, set it on the counter.

He looked at the thin leather wallet, then at me. "Pretty little thing," he said.

"How sweet of you to notice, Mr. Dott," I smiled. And then, "Oh, you meant the wallet?"

He laughed, winked.

"Location of Jimmy's car?"

"Over around the back side of the garage, about a hundred feet yonder. Brand spankin' new black Beemer. But you probably already know that, seein' as you're lucky James Atkins Farrell's personal squeeze."

I walked out, the door slamming closed behind me.

I didn't go directly to Farrell's ride. I had to find a way to get at the keys and get inside it. The lot was buried in all sizes and makes of automobiles, some of them pricey new models: Cadillac, BMW, Mercedes-Benz, Lexus. There was a snow-white Hummer parked a couple of cars ahead of where I'd parked the Jeep. One of those sporty, half-sized Hummers that's supposed to be more fuel efficient than the tank-sized job Arnold Schwarzenegger used to drive around LA.

I got in the Jeep, backed out through the fenced-in perimeter of Dott's Garage, parked it on the street. Reaching under the driver's seat, I pulled out my equalizer. I gripped the hammer tightly, rubber against palm. Then I made my way on foot back in through the open gate.

I took a glance inside the office to make sure Dott was back to sitting at his desk, his back to the door, Yankees/Redsox baseball game monopolizing his undivided attention.

I then made my way over to the snow-white Hummer and stood beside it. I raised the equalizer and swung it hard into the right rear tail light, shattering it.

The Hummer's alarm system exploded to life.

I about-faced, ran like hell for the open gate and the Jeep, where I tossed the hammer onto the driver's seat. Then I sprinted back through the gate for the far side wall of Dott's offices. When the big man came barreling out the front door toward the Hummer, I snuck my way back inside his now empty offices. Reaching up to the tackboard to my immediate left, I grabbed hold of Farrell's keys. Then I grabbed my wallet off the desk, shoved it in my back pocket.

I kept an eye out for Dott. I found him reaching inside the open window on the driver's side door of the SUV, searching desperately for a way to kill the alarm. He was cursing like an overworked truck driver wired out on NoDoz.

That was my cue to exit the office and make an all-out sprint for Farrell's Beemer.

CHAPTER 14

I aimed the electronic key-lock device at the black BMW.

It sprung to life.

I opened the driver's side door first, took a quick look around. I wasn't looking for anything specific. I was searching for anything that might help tell me where Farrell had fled to—a receipt, a ticket stub, anything. But in typical Farrell fashion, the vehicle interior was clean. Not like it was driven off the lot yesterday, but close to it. It even still had that new-car smell.

But when I looked down at the pedals, I could see that the rubber mat had some gravel and dirt on it. The same gravel and dirt from the public fishing access parking lot? I could only assume that it was. I looked at the electronic gas gauge lit up on the dash. The tank was mostly full, like Farrell had filled it up in Albany just before making the drive up here.

While the Hummer alarm kept on blaring, I closed the driver's side door, made my way around to the trunk, sprung it open with the key-lock. For a split second, I expected to see Farrell's lanky body stuffed inside it, a small hole in his forehead where a single 9mm cap had penetrated it. But the trunk was filled with something else. Set beside a spare tire and the tools required to change a flat was a shovel and two five-gallon taping compound buckets. I reached in, felt the buckets. They were filled with liquid and heavy. I could only assume that what I was looking at were cleaning materials for asbestos removal.

I grabbed hold of a bucket handle, pulled it closer to me, felt the liquid sloshing around inside the plastic container. Using my fingers like pliers, I pried the lid open. The smell was enough to knock me over. The liquid was brown, and floating inside it were little clam-like organisms. I couldn't imagine what they were or how they helped clean up asbestos. All I knew was that the brown liquid smelled a whole lot like something it very much resembled.

I placed the lid back on the bucket, closed the trunk, went around to the passenger side, and opened the door.

I leaned in farther, took a good look into the backseat. Backing out of the open door, I stood up straight, resting my forearms atop the BMW's roof. I gazed out upon the fenced-in automotive ghost yard. The Hummer alarm had finally stopped.

I thought about the empty shell casing that now resided inside my briefcase, along with an empty Skoal chewing tobacco container. I pictured the used condom and cigarette butts that littered the bank of the Desolation Kill. Then I thought about the bigger picture, about the OSHA investigative team arriving at PS 20. In my head, I saw the school being evacuated. I saw the APD cruiser pull up, a cop get out. I saw the faxes that indicated asbestos-contaminated air. I pictured having handed over an additional ten G's to Farrell just last week. A sign of good faith gone bad.

Maybe it all added up to Farrell's disappearance.

Maybe it didn't.

Maybe I was making the mistake of my life trying to play private detective instead of playing the role of responsible general contractor.

One thing was for sure: I knew in my bones that he had met someone at Lake Desolation on Saturday morning. Someone he could not possibly meet up with in public. Someone he had to meet all the way out in Nowheresville, where no one would see them together. Maybe the no one in question was why Tina didn't seem all that quick to recover her husband's car—or her husband, for that matter. She hadn't called the police, after all.

No doubt about it, Farrell was meeting someone on the sly.

Question was, had he survived the meeting?

I decided to duck back inside the car, take one last look around. For what it was worth.

I opened the center console storage compartment. Like the trunk and the backseat, it was pretty much empty. I did, however, find a couple of CDs. *Jimmy Buffett's Greatest Hit(s)* and an audiobook of *The Secret*. Farrell always did have his finger on the global cultural pulse. *Not!*

For the sheer hell of it, I pulled out both disks, opened the plastic cases. I knew that's what they would do on *CSI: Miami*. Look inside the cases for some hidden photograph or ticket to some foreign destination or a suicide note. But the only thing I found inside was CDs and their respective liner notes. Slapping them back into their storage compartment, I shut the lid.

Then I opened the glove box.

At first glance, it, too, appeared to be empty. I rummaged around a bit with my left hand. There was the leather-bound BMW owner's manual. Pulling it out, I set it onto the empty passenger seat, opened it. In the little document storage fold, I found an insurance card, a New York State driver's registration card made out in Farrell's name and A-1 Environmental Solutions, and of course, the full-color owner's manual.

I knew that, with the Hummer alarm stopped, it was only a matter of time before Dott put two and two together.

"Come on, Jimmy," I whispered. "Give me something else to go on."

That *something* appeared for me in the form of a business card.

I snatched it up, read it.

THE THATCHER STREET PUB
HOME OF FREE PIZZA THURSDAYS

I turned the card over.

It had a phone number written on it in blue ballpoint, along with a red lipstick impression of kissy lips. The name *Natalie* had been written in the middle of the lips in the same blue ballpoint, just above the phone number. I recalled my conversation with Marino's receptionist, Bobbie, a little while before. She told me that Farrell and Marino had argued over someone named Natalie.

I brought the card up to my face, smelled it.

There was the waxy, sweet smell of the lipstick, along with a hint of perfume. Maybe Chanel No. 5 or some cheaper imitation. Maybe I was a woman living in a man's world. But I was still a woman. And I knew that the red lipstick impression, the perfume, the phone number…They were meant for Farrell so that he would not forget Natalie.

Now, neither would I.

Natalie, whoever the hell she was, could very well be the reason behind Tina's tears: *"Does James have another woman in his life?"* Natalie might have been the one to meet up with Farrell on Saturday. She might know precisely where Jimmy fled to and why. Natalie, unlike Tina, might know precisely where my asbestos-removal subcontractor was hiding and for what reason. Finally, I had in my possession some real clues. From a used condom I felt sure was Jimmy's to spent shell casings to buckets filled with smelly liquid to the calling card of a woman named Natalie.

Things were looking up for the hardheaded girl.

I buried the card inside the interior pocket of my leather jacket.

I was about to back myself out of the Beemer when a hand touched my shoulder.

CHAPTER 15

"Please back away from the vehicle," the man said.

I pictured the business card hidden inside my jacket pocket, the name *Natalie* scrawled over a lipstick red kiss imprint. I reversed myself out of the car, stood up.

He was a man of medium height, slim, with a tan complexion. He wore dark jeans, black boots, and a light-blue button-down over a black T-shirt. Over that he wore a black lightweight leather jacket. His face was clean shaven and Ray Ban aviator sunglasses masked his eyes.

He reached into his jacket pocket, produced his wallet. He flashed a laminated photo ID. Damien Spain, Licensed Private Detective for the State of New York. I didn't have the chance to read the small print before he flipped the wallet closed, returning it to his inside jacket pocket. For the couple of seconds that his jacket remained open, I took notice of the hand cannon tucked securely away in a black nylon holster attached to his black leather belt.

"Why you going through Farrell's impounded BMW?"

I told him.

He crossed his arms, black-booted feet set squarely on the packed-gravel lot. "Ms. Harrison," he said.

"Call me Spike."

"I understand the spot you're in with Farrell, Spike," he said. "I think I can help."

My pulse picked up. In the back and front of my mind, I pictured Dott. I knew he'd be coming after me once he figured out that'd I'd taken Jimmy's keys and my wallet back. As soon as he killed that alarm. "Who are you working for, Mr. Spain?"

"That's confidential," he said.

"But you know all about my problems at Public School 20."

"Word travels fast in *Smalbany*…especially when you own a police scanner."

"How very clever."

"Habit of yours to go 'round stirring up wasps' nests?"

"I need to find Farrell."

He nodded, said, "It's imperative that you no longer attempt to investigate Mr. Farrell's whereabouts on your own. That includes snooping around his residence and inside his vehicle."

"And what is it you suggest I do, Spain?" I said. "I've got a potential lethal asbestos exposure to over three hundred kids, plus thirty faculty and support staff. And it's all on my head."

Spain lowered his head, looking down at the tops of his black leather boots. "My no-shit-Sherlock opinion?"

"No-shit-Sherlock."

"Work with me. Assist me in finding him. We do that, we'll expose him for what he really is—a cheat."

"Any idea where he might have run off to?"

"I've been tailing him for weeks. Now that he's gone, I haven't the slightest clue."

"Who's your client?" I asked again.

He stared at me for a bit. Until he shook his head. "Tina Farrell is my client," he said. "Or *was* my client, I should say. Now it's the Albany County District Attorney's office."

I sensed Spain was being straight. Or else he wouldn't have divulged the names of the clients paying for his bread and butter.

Spain slipped his hand in his black pants pocket and pulled out a card, handed it to me. "Call me," he said. "We both want the same thing—Farrell on a silver platter."

I shoved the second of the two Spain business cards into my jeans pocket. "I'll give it serious thought," I said.

He smiled. "You're a hard nut to crack," he said.

"So I've been told."

I knew I was pushing my luck with Dott. That, eventually, he'd discover the BMW's keys missing from the tackboard. Maybe he already had. Maybe he'd already called the police. The Hummer alarm wasn't going off anymore. Time to make a quick escape.

"Nice meeting you, Spain," I said, handing him the key ring, taking slow steps away from the car.

"Whaddaya want me to do with these?" he said, holding up the keys.

"Do some investigating," I said. "But beware of old man Dott."

He sighed.

I turned, made my way back across the automotive graveyard under the cover of all those abandoned and repo'd cars and trucks. Moments later, I snuck my way out the open gate.

CHAPTER 16

What's a headstrong (and slightly panicked) girl like yours truly to do when she starts running out of options?

She decides to eat something—something sweet and fattening with a who-gives-a-crap number of calories. The more fattening, the better. Maybe some caffeine to wash it all down.

Heading south on Route 87 back toward Albany, I spotted my salvation out the corner of my right eye. I pulled off the highway and pulled into a Dunkin' Donuts for a big coffee and a plain donut. Sustenance, construction style. I stood outside the Jeep, coffee and donut set on the still-warm hood, pulled out my mobile, and dialed Tommy.

I pictured his stocky body planted on the corner stool at Lanie's Bar. I asked him the obvious question: Had he heard anything from Farrell? I wasn't the least bit surprised when he said that he hadn't heard diddly.

"You speak to Diana?" he asked me.

"Still avoiding that one," I said, picturing the fiery red-haired OSHA Tiger Lady. "At least until I get back into town."

I took a bite of donut, washed it down with a small sip of hot coffee. I waited for the initial signs of the sugar-and-caffeine rush. Then I told Tommy about the abandoned BMW and about PI Damien Spain, who had somehow tailed me to Dott's garage.

"You know what I think?" Tommy said. "I think our preppy boy took the money and went bye-bye forever and ever, amen."

My insides dropped.

Tommy spoke to my silence. "If you were the cheating, extorting Farrell, would you want to be seen again?"

"Case closed?"

"Fuckin' A," he said.

I fingered END, took another bite out of the donut, and pondered my situation while I chewed.

What's a stubborn girl supposed to do?

She faces the inevitable.

I speed-dialed the number for the Harrison Construction Company's longtime lawyer, Joel Clark, left a message on his voice mail to call me back as soon as possible regarding the red-flag situation at PS 20. In my head, I pictured my Harrison Construction cash account balance turning bright red.

Cutting the connection, I already knew what he was going to suggest—that OSHA, the EPA, and the principal members of the project be brought together for an emergency summit to clear the air, get the school cleaned up, get the rehab back on track. It would be the right thing to do, maybe the only thing that could potentially save my ass.

But there was one overriding problem with that rather simple solution.

Diana Stewart.

In the time she'd been away from Harrison Construction, she had not only developed a hatred of me, she'd begun enacting her vengeance. It wasn't enough that she'd fallen hopelessly in love with my husband. It was as though I had purposely stolen him from her.

Based on the three severe fines she'd nailed me with over the past twelve months alone, I'd developed the distinct feeling that the Tiger Lady would stop at nothing to see my life go permanently south. It was even possible that Stewart was more hardheaded than I was. Which meant I wasn't about to throw myself at the mercy of her court. I knew that if she had her way, Farrell's negligence would result in the last wilted straw for Harrison Construction.

No way I could allow that.

A voice inside my head whispered to me. The voice belonged to my dad. The voice told me to go back to the job site. I knew enough not to ignore the old man, even if he was dead and buried.

I ate the rest of the donut, got back in the Jeep with my coffee. A little spilled onto the console when I pulled back out onto the road.

Oh well, one of those fucking days.

CHAPTER 17

In the dusk, the PS 20 job site was deserted. It was also as quiet as a church. The kind of quiet that surrounds you, buries you with anxiety. You couldn't miss the red plastic tape attached crime-scene style to both the construction trailer door and the school's main entrance. A large banner had been posted directly to the four-foot-by-eight-foot Harrison Construction site sign. In big black letters it read,

DANGER: Health Hazard. Do Not Enter. OSHA

Per OSHA mandate, there were two black skull-and-crossbones warnings conspicuously painted on both the top and the bottom of the banner. It was the kind of warning you might see posted outside a minefield in Afghanistan.

Sitting inside the Jeep on an abandoned lower Pearl Street, I thought for a split second about heading into the trailer to retrieve my files. But the door to the trailer had been secured with a lockbox.

I opened the glove box, grabbed hold of the Black & Decker flashlight stored inside it. Killing the Jeep, I got out and made my way toward the school. I passed by the red-ribboned job trailer, a neat stack of dry-concrete-encrusted scaffolding planks, and a brand-new pallet of common brick. I approached the school but stopped just short of the padlocked doors.

The brick school was covered with scaffolding. The third asbestos abatement and removal was to take place up on the fourth floor of the school. Shining the flashlight up at the fourth floor, I could see where workers had removed a window casement to facilitate the portable, flexible ductwork ventilation equipment.

I knew that if I couldn't get in through the school's doors, I could climb the scaffolding and literally rip my way through the flex duct.

Chances were I wouldn't find anything up there that would shed light on Farrell's location. But then, maybe I would get an idea of how he'd been cheating both the school system and me.

I turned off the flashlight, stuck the handle end into the waist of my jeans, and started to climb.

I climbed hand over foot, quickly scaled two separate sections, and started on my third. Looking down, I could see that I had approached fifteen feet off the solid ground. I was the health-and-safety officer for Harrison Construction. I knew that all it took to kill a person was a fall from ten feet. Jordan had fallen from a height of nearly sixty feet onto hard-packed gravel. He'd survived, but only for a few hours.

I climbed up past the third section, then onto the fourth, my palms now coated with a slippery layer of sweat, making each attempted grip of the crossbars a dangerous proposition. But I managed to make it to the top of the fourth level, where I hung my torso over the planking and swung my legs around. Standing, I looked out onto the PS 20 site and the downtown Albany city skyline. With the warm wind buffeting my face, I felt like I was on top of the world.

There was little time to lose. If there was a cop lurking in the vicinity, I would be as good as caught.

I turned to face the white flex duct that ran like a headless snake from the interior of the school out onto the scaffolding. I was familiar enough with the material to know I didn't need a knife to rip into it. All I needed was strong fingers.

The material might as well have been papier-mâché it tore apart so easily. It took only seconds before I was able to climb right into the school through the window opening.

I pulled the flashlight from my waist and flicked it on.

I faced a four-sided empty space. It was not a space separated by plaster and masonry walls, but by supposedly "airtight" plastic-covered temporary partitions. In the center of the room sat a machine that looked like it had been lifted off the set of a sci-fi flick. It was the air-filtration device that would suck in the bad asbestos-tainted air, filter it, and then blow it out through the window opening via three sections of flexible ductwork.

I carried the flashlight to the machine, opened up the lid, and peered inside. I looked for the thick round filter that was utilized for the cleaning process.

The filter was gone.

I wondered if Jimmy had been stupid or flat-out evil enough to do without it, or if OSHA had confiscated it during their surprise inspection. I had no way of knowing. This was the first and only time I'd been inside the area since the asbestos removal began.

I took another look around.

The asbestos floor tiles and ceiling panels were gone. So was all the old crumbly insulation that had been wrapped around the old ceiling-mounted radiant heating pipes. There was no doubt in my mind that much of the obvious asbestos insulation had been removed. But the question remained: How safely and responsibly had it been removed? If test filter samples were any indication, A1-Environmental had been performing the removal minus the ventilation process. And by doing so, Farrell must have been saving a bundle while at the same time placing an awful lot of people at risk, most of whom were between the ages of five and thirteen. The question loomed large: Was cheating so profitable that he was willing to place the lives of all those children at risk?

No freakin' way.

I couldn't help but think that something else was going on here besides a simple cheat-for-extra-ching kind of Mickey Mouse operation. That something had split town along with Farrell.

There was a noise. A dull bang, followed by what I thought might have been a footstep.

I killed the light.

I couldn't be sure where the noise had come from. The fourth floor or down on one of the other levels. I shoved the flashlight back into my pants and made for the window opening.

I climbed back out onto the scaffolding platform, took a good look around at the construction site and the designated contractor parking area. No cop cars visible. But that didn't mean I wasn't being watched.

I dropped down to my knees, then eased my left leg over the edge of the platform. Exhaling a breath, I eased myself down over the side. I was gripping the topmost steel bar while searching for some solid footing when I first heard the siren. The siren was coming from the direction of the lower Concrete Pearl. The siren was getting louder with each hand over foot motion I made on the slow climb down the scaffolding.

My heart shot into my throat. The siren got louder, more intense. I descended as fast as I could without losing my footing or my handhold.

The siren blared.

I had no choice but to ignore it while I inched my way down, the moist palms on my exposed hands slapping the metal scaffolding bars, my booted feet cramping in the narrow "V" sections where the vertical crossbar supports joined together.

Out the corner of my left eye, I saw the cruiser pull into the designated contractor parking lot and stop.

Oh, fuck me.

A second later, I made it to the bottom of the scaffolding tower, sweat beading my brow and the back of my neck. The cruiser lights were still flashing, but the cop had turned off the siren. The parking area was maybe one hundred fifty feet away. I could see the cop as he stood up outside the car and flashed the business end of a flashlight in my direction. I fell flat onto my stomach and hid myself behind a stack of empty pallets, my breathing fast and labored, my heart jammed into my throat. I waited until the light shifted away from me, then I lifted myself up and, as light-footed as humanly possible, sprinted across the job site under the cover of darkness. I didn't stop until I reached the open road, praying all the time the police offer hadn't heard me scampering away from a very unhealthy PS 20 building.

CHAPTER 18

By now, my back was covered in sweat, mouth dry, heart beating a mile per second. I drove in silence. On the bypass I passed a backlit billboard that read, *Hurt on the Job Site? Call 1-800-LAW-1010! Get the Money You Deserve*, and another with a massive black-and-white photograph of a sickly bare-chested man, *Exposed to Asbestos! Mesothelioma is Lethal. Call 1-800-GET-HELP.*

The world was full of things that killed you, especially on construction sites.

In the end, only the lawyers survived.

Eventually, I pulled into a convenience store parking lot. I needed something cool and wet to calm me down. I'd managed to slip that cop, but I knew that if I'd been caught breaking into my own red-flagged job site, I would have faced immediate arrest. My little PS 20 B&E hadn't been worth the risk. But then, when I decided to do something, there was no talking me out of it. My stubborn streak was notorious. So my dad reminded me on a daily basis (apparently I took after my mother).

Inside the brightly lit store, I patted my left pocket for some petty cash. The pocket was empty. There was an ATM located in the far corner of the store. I went to it.

I pulled out my wallet, slid out the MasterCard debit card, slid it down the designated vertical slot. When the machine asked me for my four-digit PIN, I punched it in. It asked how much cash I wanted: $20, $40, Quick $60…

I punched in $40.

The machine told me I would have to pay three dollars for the privilege of getting at my own money. It asked me if I wanted to continue despite the extortion.

Yes or no?

I fingered YES.

The machine asked me to be patient while it contacted my bank and processed my request.

Stacked on the linoleum floor beside me was the evening edition of the *Times Union Newspaper*. The headline read, "Albany Elementary School Contaminated." Below that headline was a small teaser: "Pearl Street's PS 20 tainted with asbestos fibers; students exposed to deadly carcinogen."

There was a second Concrete Pearl–related story printed farther down on the front page:

"Common Council Ponders Albany Development Proposal for June Convention Center Groundbreaking."

The ATM issued an electronic beep. I refocused my attention on the machine. When the main screen reappeared, it said, *Request Denied. Insufficient Funds.*

Ice water shot up and down my spine. I shot a glance over my right shoulder at the cashier standing behind the counter up at the front of the store. She was a tall African American woman. Thin and attractive and college young. She wore a brown acrylic vest over a white tank top. The vest said *Stewarts* on it in white block letters. She was painting long fingernails while listening to hip-hop on a portable boom box. The hip-hop drowned out the complimentary piped-in Muzak.

She returned my glance with a glare.

I cancelled the transaction, got my card back out, went through the whole procedure again.

Same result.

Insufficient funds.

I knew I had more than fifteen G's in the Harrison Construction "petty cash" checking account. That's after taking into account the ten I'd advanced Farrell for his payroll. There had to be a glitch in the automated teller machine system.

I turned, walked across the store floor to the coolers in the rear. I picked out a tall Diet Pepsi, brought it back with me over to the counter. I set it down.

I handed the young woman my debit card. She set the nail polish brush back into the bottle of red nail polish. She looked at the Diet Pepsi, condensate bleeding down its sides. She looked at the debit card beside it.

"The card…just for a fuckin' Pepsi?" she said, blowing on her wet nails.

"Just run it please," I said. I was in no mood.

She glared some more, did a mock head bob, and shoveled up the card with the nails on her dry hand, ran it through the computer register.

She waited.

I waited.

The card didn't take.

An old man had walked into the store. Now he stood behind me, clearing his throat. I turned to look at him. He was gripping a stack of blaze-orange lotto quick-draw tickets in his hand. I knew he was anxious to cash them in, anxious to play again and again and again.

"Card…don't…work," the cashier said slowly, like maybe my head was full of gravel. "Insufficient…funds."

"There's plenty of money in there," I said.

"Computer says you tight, yo."

The old man behind me cleared his throat. Again. "Finished?" he said.

I took back my debit card, leaving the Diet Pepsi sitting on the counter in a small pool of its own condensate.

Outside the store, I called the number printed on the back side of the debit card. The automated operator said to press "2" for balance information. Then the operator said, "Account placed on indefinite hold." The computer voice was both pleasant and to-the-point direct. She said to contact a bank customer representative at the 800 number listed on the back of the card.

Ending the call, I redialed the 800 number.

I pressed "0" for a human animal.

The automated operator told me I'd have to wait forty-five minutes for the next available customer representative. Muzak followed. A tinny version of Michael Jackson's "Thriller."

Yeah, this was a thriller, all right.

I wanted to fucking punch somebody or something, starting with the convenience store ATM. Instead, I made the decision to drive straight home. Better to drown my sorrows in Budweiser beer than to commit aggravated assault.

CHAPTER 19

Ten minutes later, I was walking across the parking lot outside my apartment building. My BlackBerry vibrated. *Joel Clark, Esq.*, said the ID.

"Joel," I said, pressing the phone to my ear.

"What prompted you to hire Farrell?"

"You gotta ask? His asbestos-removal bid was low. He got the job fair and super square."

I pictured the graying lawyer seated behind his mahogany desk inside a tenth-floor high-rise office, desk drowning in piles of paperwork. He apologized about being in depositions the entire day and therefore so out of touch. Then he told me he'd already seen the papers and the television news. But he wanted my take. He wanted me to tell him everything from the time I arrived on the PS 20 job site that morning up until now.

I told him everything, standing right out there in the open lot. From the moment I split the job site all the way up to being denied cash from the convenience store ATM. By the time I was done, it was dark out. The parking lot lamps were illuminating the lot in a hazy orange afterglow.

"Jesus, you're one headstrong wrecking crew of a woman," he barked. "You're lucky you're not already standing in county lockup for tampering with state evidence. You'd gotten yourself snagged up on that PS 20 scaffolding, that's exactly where you'd be."

But now that the scolding was over, he told me to keep out of touch.

"Damage control," he called it.

He counseled me not to speak with Stewart or with anyone from the press (meaning Chris Collins) or any one of the project principals directly (the project principals being the architect and the school board president). He would take care of the communications issue first thing in the morning. If at all possible, he wanted to arrange an emergency project meeting at his downtown office tomorrow afternoon with the intent to resolve the safety situation at the school. Only when it was possible to re-enter the main building legally and without risk would we address the issue of performing removal procedures all over again. This time according to plans and specs.

"You're gonna have to take a serious hit on this, Spike," he said. "You're gonna have to hire another asbestos-removal company, get them on-site ASAP, if only to show good faith."

The muscles in my stomach tightened. "How do I pay for that?" I said. "It could run a hundred grand."

"By back-charging what you can to Farrell's A-1 Environmental Solutions."

"FYI," I exhaled, "Farrell is paid up to date, plus."

"You advanced Farrell funds—"

"For the sake of expediting the project."

"That's the school's money, Spike."

"Not exactly. I advanced him ten large from a Harrison cash account so he could make payroll. Why do you think I'm personally on his trail?"

"Well, you're going to have no choice but to put up what cash you can, then go after Farrell's bid bond. I'll take care of the bond issue from here in my office tomorrow."

He didn't say anything for a second or two. But I got the feeling there was something else on his mind.

"It's too late now, Spike," he said, "but you should not have left the job site for any reason."

Joel was right. Dad taught me better than that. By being absent, I'd only made it look like I had something to hide. I tried to put myself in the shoes of all the PS 20 mothers. I wasn't a mother myself. But I knew they'd be worried sick about their children.

"One more thing," he said. "Keep in mind if one of those kids or faculty members should start screaming cancer, you're going to find yourself in more trouble than you ever thought possible."

My sternum went tight at the thought of a sick child. I decided to put it out of my mind the best I could.

"What do you want me to do with the shell casing? And what about the other stuff—the chewing tobacco tin and the Thatcher Street business card?"

"Don't touch any of it more than you have. Pack it up and drop it off at my office. We got a real missing persons case—or, God forbid, a homicide—the cops will want to confiscate it all."

"So what do you suggest I do now?" I said, voice betraying me by cracking mid-sentence.

"Like I've been trying to tell you," Joel said, "lay low and do the right thing."

"Listen, what about the hold on my petty cash account?"

Joel sighed. He was a big man who was good at big sighs. "My guess is the school has placed a lien on your accounts pending rectification of the asbestos contamination."

"They want their money back is what they want, Joel."

"They're simply trying to protect themselves. I'll see about bonding the liens tomorrow morning once I go after Farrell's bid bond."

"What do I do for money in the meantime?"

"Use your personal checking account."

"All thirty-five cents of it?"

What I didn't have the guts to tell Joel was that, lately, I'd been using the Harrison cash accounts as my own personal accounts.

"You must have credit cards."

"Harrison Construction AMEX," I said, knowing I had maybe a grand left on it before it was maxed out.

"Just use that," Joel said. "Pay it off later."

With what? I wanted to say.

I hung up, retrieved my briefcase from the Jeep, and headed for my apartment, which was located, appropriately enough, in the basement.

CHAPTER 20

I made my way into my bedroom. From out of my pocket I pulled out the misspelled "Closed Untill Further Notice" note with the odd sketch on the back. I set it, along with my briefcase, on the desktop. I turned on the laptop. While I waited for it to boot up, I touched my lips with the tips of two fingers, pressed them to Jordan's mouth—the Jordan who appeared for me in the framed black-and-white studio headshot I kept of him beside my computer.

I went into the kitchen, grabbed a cold bottle of beer, brought it back into the bedroom with me. I sat down at the desk, logged onto the Harrison Construction website, and typed in the password that accessed my e-mail. The new e-mails fell one by one into a vertical column, like rapidly stacked bricks. There had to be thirty or more new messages, most of them from the Tiger Lady.

It had been one hell of a long Monday. I couldn't help but wonder if I'd accomplished anything. Maybe I wasn't any closer to finding Farrell, but I was a little closer to finding out what had happened to him.

I opened the briefcase, pulled out all the items I'd collected at the public fishing access site. I picked up the spent shell casing, took a good look at the back rim where the pin had left its indentation mark.

Winchester 9mm rounds, 362 grains. Chrome plated.

Had Farrell been shot, his body ditched somewhere, his car towed to Dott's? Obviously, homicide was a possibility. According to Joel, anyway.

I picked up the Skoal chewing tobacco can.

I had no way of proving it, but I did know that Farrell enjoyed his Skoal and I knew the discarded tin might have belonged to him and no way in hell he would have left a full tin behind. If it did belong to him, it was proof that he'd made the drive to Lake Desolation on Saturday. What I could not prove was what had happened there or why he went there in the first place. Who or what had been shot? And where had Farrell disappeared to as a result of it?

I had no idea.

I fingered the "Closed Untill Further Notice" note, turned it over, glanced once more at the sketch. Two wavy but parallel lines connected at one end to a kind of square. Under the sketch, the letters "S" and "C" and a question mark. I couldn't imagine what they stood for. I couldn't even begin to come up with possibilities.

"Santa Claus," I whispered to myself. But it was quite possible that a whole bunch of innocent kids had been exposed to a deadly carcinogen for nearly a year and this was no joke.

I set the paper back down, sat back, locked eyes on my husband's still-alive brown eyes. "I'm in a real fix this time, Jordan," I said. "You were in my boots, what would you do?"

I heard his voice inside my head: *It's a mistake to stop looking for Farrell.*

I picked up the business card, turned it over, eyeballed the impression of lipstick red lips, the name *Natalie* written over them in blue ballpoint. Turning the card back over, I took note of the bar's phone number. Without thinking about it, the BlackBerry appeared in my hand. I punched in the number.

After five rings, someone picked up. "Thatcher Street," a man's voice said. Stern, gruff.

"Natalie, please," I said.

"Hang on," said the man. I heard him slap the phone down hard onto the bar. There was an audible commotion coming from somewhere in the background. Then the phone being picked back up.

"This is Natalie." Soft, tentative. Afraid, maybe.

My pulse picked up with the sound of her voice. A voice Farrell would be familiar with.

"Hello?" she said, begging for a response. "Hello?"

"I'm sorry," I said, satisfied that Natalie truly existed and was in fact at work tonight at the Thatcher Street Pub. "Wrong number."

I killed the call.

I took another drink of beer, stared into Jordan's brown eyes. He told me to give Farrell's cell another shot.

"You never know..."

I did it.

The call was immediately transferred to the computerized answering service. This time, instead of allowing me to leave a message, the recorded voice told me the mailbox was full. The connection cut.

That was it, then.

It didn't take a No-Shit-Sherlock to know there'd be no chance of contacting Farrell now. At least by phone.

Another glance at my husband.

"Why not try Tina again?"

I fingered in the number for the Farrell residence.

Tina answered after only one ring, as if she'd been waiting by the phone. "This is Tina," she said, formal and polite.

I wondered if she'd picked up my name and number via the caller ID.

"Tina, this is Spike Harrison," I said. "I was wondering if by chance you've heard from your husband."

"I'm sorry," she said. "No."

Her voice had gone from deadpan to hurt. I pictured the spent shell casing. Was a missing persons case in fact about to turn into a murder?

"Tina," I said, "does Jimmy own a handgun?"

She hesitated for a beat. Then she said, "I don't think so."

"You sure?"

"Sure as I can be," she said, a double hint of doubt in her voice.

"What about your dad?"

"What the hell is this?" she snapped. "What are you trying to get at?"

"What kind of tobacco Jimmy chewing these days?"

She thought about it for a moment. Then, "Skoal," she said. "Packaged in a cute little green container."

"He been known to grab a beer or two at the Thatcher Street Pub down in Albany?"

"Sure."

"Christ, Tina, call the fucking cops right now."

Suddenly, commotion. Another voice coming to me from over the connection. A man's voice. "Who is this?" the voice demanded.

I told him.

"This is Tina's father, Peter," he said. "Can I ask the purpose of your call?"

"Peter, this is Spike Harrison. I've been looking for Jimmy—"

"Ms. Harrison," he interrupted, "at present we are dealing with a family crisis. Your intrusion is not appreciated."

I wanted to tell him to stop pretending he didn't know me. But he hung up before I had the chance to get it all out. When the CALL ENDED signal revealed itself, I dialed the Farrell residence once again. But this time all I got was a busy signal.

Phone off the hook.

Setting the cell back down, I took one more good look at Jordan. "Well," I said, "what now?"

As if directed to do so, my eyes found their way to the Thatcher Street business card. Drinking the rest of my beer, I got up from the desk. I took a quick look around the bedroom, at the queen bed, the simple dresser, the framed shot of Jordan and me on our wedding day that hung on the wall above it, the body-length IKEA dressing mirror set in the far corner, my bathrobe hanging from it, blocking out most of my reflection.

"Been a while since I went out for a drink," I said.

I stored all the evidence, minus Natalie's card, inside my desk drawer. Then I got up and went to my dresser. Inside my underwear drawer, I grabbed a ten and two fives from out of a coffee can where I hid some emergency cash and quarters for the laundry machine. I shoved the cash into my jeans pocket along with my BlackBerry and Natalie's calling card. Grabbing up my keys, I exited the apartment by way of the back terrace door.

CHAPTER 21

I backed out of my parking space, pulled out onto the apartment complex road that led me to the main drag. I couldn't help but notice another set of headlights in my rearview. Another car pulling out of a spot in the building lot next door to my own.

I didn't think much of it at first. People were always coming and going from the apartments at all hours of the night. But these headlights followed me all the way up the complex access road. When I made a left onto the main road in the direction of downtown, the lights followed me.

I pressed my foot on the gas, tried to create a little distance between me and those headlights. Then I killed my lights altogether, hooked a quick left down a neighborhood street perpendicular to the main road, and gunned the Jeep. I also prayed that no cops were patrolling the area.

Having made it to the end of the street, I once more looked into the rearview.

The headlights hadn't made the turn.

Maybe I was growing paranoid. But better safe than stupid and sorry.

I put my lights back on, turned right, and followed Broadway all the way to where it intersected with the lower Concrete Pearl, not far from the Thatcher Street Pub.

CHAPTER 22

Thatcher Street was a throwback to the days when lower Pearl Street thrived as a Barbary Coast of smoke-billowing factories and mills that lined the banks of the Hudson River. There were lumberyards, steel mills, paper factories, shipbuilding plants, and ports of call that made the riverfront a longshoreman's paradise. Everywhere you looked you would find strongbacks dressed in dungarees or overalls, lifting and hauling everything from one-hundred-pound bags of iron ore to sandbags to newly cut wood planks.

All these years later, the mills and factories had been relocated to Mexico and China, leaving only the unemployed and the rusted and rotted-out building shells lining the Concrete Pearl. But the Thatcher Street Pub had somehow survived. Maybe one of the reasons behind its survival was its topless bartenders. The bar still attracted tough guys who worked with their backs and rough necks. But nowadays, you could also find the occasional stockbroker, lawyer, or doctor bellying up to the bar alongside them.

I walked in through the front screen door.

Every set of male eyes turned to me. I felt the eyes burn holes into my skin. I made my way to an open spot at the near end of the long bar, not ten feet away from the unoccupied pool table.

As the faces of a dozen men scattered about the bar returned to their beers, shots, and mixed drinks, I took a good look around. In a word, the place was a dump. Not at all what I expected of a topless place where maybe a half dozen mostly naked women traipsed around behind the bar or waiting tables. Or so I'd been told.

But not this place.

Located at the far end of the bar was the kitchen. The door to the kitchen was open. I saw a big man with a dirty butcher's apron wrapped around his belly and chest. There was a spatula gripped in his hand. He seemed to be arguing with someone who stood just beyond my line of sight. When that unknown person revealed herself a couple of seconds later, I wondered if I'd found Jimmy's Natalie. She was the only woman on duty. Or so it seemed.

Wiping her eyes with the back of her hand, she composed herself, took her place back behind the bar. Eyeballing me—her newest customer—she made her way over.

I pegged her for between twenty-five and thirty. She wore only a sheer black satin thong that fit snug around her narrow hips. She was a brunette like me, her eyes brown and a little puffy from tears, her skin sunlamp tan. She wasn't what I would call tall, but she wasn't short. Her long hair was as striking as her narrow waist.

As for her breasts, they were a little bit smaller than my own. What Jordan would call "pert and spunky." She was attractive. Certainly attractive enough to find work in a nicer joint than this one. She forced a smile, never once giving me any indication about how odd it was that a lone female would just happen to walk into a man's bar and order a drink.

"What can I get you?" she asked in that same soft, gentle voice she'd used on the phone.

"Corona," I said.

When she slid down to the steel cooler, pushed back the lid, I could see that she was wearing a pair of baby-blue Nike Air running shoes on her feet. The sneakers looked kind of silly up against all that exposed skin.

She uncapped the beer, brought it to me, set it down on the bar. "Need a lime wedge?"

"Naked is good," I said.

She smiled like I was making a joke.

I laid out a five spot on the bar, told her to keep the change.

She was about to turn away when I said, "Natalie?"

She turned back quick, smooth hair moving in a wave as she did it. "How'd you know my name?"

Before I could answer, one of the male patrons down the bar held up an empty beer bottle. "Nat," barked the gray-bearded man.

Nat ignored him.

"I'm an associate of Jimmy Farrell's," I said.

She just stared at me. Into me. I sensed that if she'd possessed an Adam's apple, it would have bobbed nervously up and down.

"I need to find him," I said.

"You the police?" she said.

"Natalie," Gray Beard called out. Louder this time. Booze-soaked baritone bouncing off the plaster walls.

She turned, slow. "Hold your water, Roger," she said. It was a scold. Big old Roger began to pout, his bottom lip protruding out from underneath a thick gray mustache.

I leaned over the bar, close to her face, tried to talk under my breath. "I'm not the police," I said. "I run a construction company. Farrell was subcontracting for me on a job at PS 20 just up the road. He seems to have run off without finishing the job and with quite a large portion of both the school's and my money in pocket."

Natalie shook her head, crossed her forearms over her chest, as if suddenly embarrassed about her seminakedness. "What do you want from me?" she asked. Her pretty face suddenly became a tight canvas of exposed nerves.

"I'm aware that Jimmy and you were friends," I said. "I thought you might help me figure out where he took off to."

She inhaled, exhaled. "I haven't seen or heard from Jimmy in weeks," she said. "He used to come in sometimes after work. We get a lot of construction workers in here."

She was holding back on me.

"But you were friends."

"He was a client," she stressed. "Good customer. Good tipper."

"Natalie, my patience wears thin," shouted Gray Beard.

"Did you see each other outside the pub?"

Natalie's eyes went wide. "We're not allowed to fraternize with the clientele," she said.

"But you were friends," I pressed.

"Like I told you," she said, "he was a good customer. That's all I have to say about it."

Interesting how she kept speaking in the past tense. For a split second, I thought about pulling all the cash from my pants pocket, handing it to her. Maybe some pretty green would jog her memory. But I had the feeling all the cash in the world wouldn't make an ounce of difference to Natalie, much less a mere extra fifteen bucks.

I slipped off the barstool, dug a Harrison Construction business card out of my pocket. Before I handed it to her, I grabbed a stubby pencil from the lotto quick-draw container, jotted down my personal e-mail address on the back.

"Please, Natalie," I said. "More than three hundred kids have been exposed to asbestos fibers every day for more than nine months. If I don't locate Farrell, their life or death will fall squarely onto my shoulders. If you'd rather not speak about him here, at least e-mail me with something."

She took a minute to absorb what I'd said. Then she took the card from off the bar, slipped it behind the string on her thong, where it remained pressed up against her right hip.

I made for the door. But before I opened it, I turned to see her standing before Gray Beard. He was leaning his bull-like torso over the bar, a bill of large denomination lodged between his teeth. He was attempting to stuff the bill between Natalie's pert-and-spunkies. As his belly laughter filled the narrow barroom, Natalie peered at me over her left shoulder.

For just a second, our eyes locked.

A feeling of dread washed over me.

I sensed that Natalie had lied to me, that she knew exactly what had happened to Farrell. And that it was not good.

CHAPTER 23

I couldn't have been driving the Concrete Pearl for more than ten seconds when another set of headlamps appeared in my rearview mirror. Halogen headlamps that looked like a pair of bright-white glowing eyes. The eyes stayed with me, the unidentified vehicle on my tail while I motored the open-topped Jeep the full two miles to my apartment complex.

This time I wasn't going to try to duck my stalker.

By the time I pulled into the lot, my pulse was pounding in my temples, my palms moist against the rubber-coated steering wheel. I wished I had Tommy with me.

Pulling into my designated space, I killed the engine. The vehicle pulled up directly behind me, the now too-close rearview headlamp reflection blinding me.

A sea change occurred then.

Fear turned into anger.

I pulled the equalizer out from under the bucket seat. I squeezed the rubber grip, threw open the Jeep door, got out.

I faced the stalker head-on.

CHAPTER 24

At first, I saw only a silhouette standing beside the car. A dark shadow against the dim streetlamp light. I recognized the car as a compact but pricey Lexus two-door. The dark figure I did not recognize. Until she spoke.

"Take it easy," she said in her false state-of-Virginia voice. An accent she'd adopted while attending UVA.

I felt the weight of the top-heavy claw hammer drop to my side, the sharp claws brushing up against my knee. "Aren't you breaking the rules of engagement, Diana? Following me around like that?"

I remembered Joel's order not to make direct communication with the Tiger Lady. Too late now.

My former Harrison coworker took a step forward, smooth red hair and trim body glowing in the inverted arc of sodium lamplight. "I come as an old friend," she said. "Off the record. My Lord, I've been trying to reach you all day." When she said "Lord," it sounded like "*Laward*."

I knew by now not to trust her friendly air. I also knew something else: to deny her the face time she wanted, off the record or not, would be to bury myself even deeper.

"Old friend?" I asked, squeezing the rubber hammer grip.

"I've never stopped liking you, Spike," she said. "It's just that I have to do my job to the best of my ability. Innocent lives depend upon it."

Turning, I opened the Jeep door, slid the equalizer back beneath the driver's seat, headfirst. Shutting the door, I shoved the keys into the right-hand pocket of my leather jacket.

"Still carrying around your trusty equalizer, I see?" Diana asked.

I didn't give her the benefit of an answer. Besides, she already knew it. Instead, I told her she'd better park in the visitors' lot across the green. "I'm apartment One-R, bottom floor," I said.

"I know," she said, turning back for the Lexus.

Isn't that just like the Tiger Lady? Always one step ahead of me.

CHAPTER 25

The first job Diana did for Harrison, we were the low bidder on a General Electric Company project to build their brand-new, state-mandated wastewater treatment facility. It was a big job requiring the construction of footings and foundations for eight 50,000-gallon tanks—the identical make and style of the steel tanks you might find inside an oil refinery.

My father was worried.

His bid had come in more than two hundred thousand lower than the next-lowest bid. A discrepancy of more than 10 percent. No matter how many times he checked and rechecked his bid sheet, he could find no errors. The problem, he thought, had to lie in working with the tanks themselves. There must have been something about those tanks the competition knew and he didn't. Something complicated and time consuming about their installation.

Dad looked like a lost soul, standing in the middle of the office floor, scratching his receding, gray hairline, eyeglasses sliding off his nose. He just could not put a finger on his estimating mistake, other than the fact that he had never worked with big-ass tanks before.

Neither had Diana.

But that didn't stop the headstrong woman from tapping into her sharp mind. She brought up the fact that the challenge wouldn't arise in the handling and construction of the tanks themselves (the steel erection subcontractor would handle that), it was coming up with the required radius for the circular concrete foundations that had to be poured to precise specifications. The margin of error would be measured in millimeters, not centimeters or inches.

"That's why the other bids are too high," she pointed out, eyes glassy with excitement. "The other GCs lack confidence. They're worried about getting the foundations wrong. They all loaded their bids up with a shitload of contingency money."

My father shook his head, unable to hide his blushing face. For a lifer construction pro, he would never get comfortable with the gutter language the rest of us loved so fucking dearly.

"You're sure about this?" he said.

"I know all about padding a bid," Diana said, smiling, that faux Southern drawl affording her words a touch of the devil.

She then pulled a piece of blank paper from the copier. She had an idea. Taking pencil to paper, she drew out a series of circles. First a half circle, then another half circle butting up against it to make a completed 360-degree circle. The idea would be to create circular templates out of plywood. Build them in half-circle segments, off-site, under controlled conditions, according to the precise steel tank specifications, then ship them into the construction area. When the riverside site was properly cleared, we would hire a couple of union millwrights to set the plywood templates on level, compacted earth and then set the concrete forms into position according to them. The concrete would be poured in a perfect circular shape while the anchor bolts would be set with zero margin of error.

Diana's idea not only worked, Harrison construction crews completed the wastewater treatment facility in record time, netting my father a low six-figure profit. It was a feather in Diana's cap, but an even larger feather for the Harrison Construction reputation. The General Electric Company wrote a letter of testimonial on our behalf, stating that the wastewater treatment facility was one of the most flawless projects ever undertaken at the Hudson River plant.

Diana not only received a major raise, my father bought her a new car. She was also the recipient of a new nickname. From that point on, she was looked up to as the gutsy, hardheaded "Tiger Lady" of Harrison Construction.

That was then.

Now we sat across from one another at a round metal café table that barely fit inside my galley kitchen. I nursed a beer while Diana sipped a cup of hot tea. She was wearing a knee-length skirt and a navy cotton button-down for a top. No jewelry—OSHA rules. Befitting a woman of about fifty, her thick hair was cut to shoulder length but was still lush and somehow elegant. On occasion, she brushed it back with the fingers of her right hand.

We locked eyes from across the tiny table. "Mind if I smoke?" she said, pulling a pack of Marlboro Lights from her small black shoulder bag.

"Violation of OSHA rules," I said. "How curious."

"Perhaps even ironical," she said, holding up the cig as if waiting for my permission.

I shot a quick glance over my right shoulder. The window above the kitchen sink was wide open. "Can't argue with ironical," I said.

She smiled and set the cig between her lips.

"Let's have it," I said. "How'd you know I'd be at Thatcher Street?"

She lit up with a Bic lighter, exhaled a cloud of blue smoke. "My office is housed in the old EnCon building on upper Pearl. I was heading home when I spotted your Jeep."

In my mind, I saw the Harrison Construction logo printed on the side panel—the R's formed by a graphic representation of inverted ninety-degree civil engineer's rulers.

You can run, Spike. But you cannot hide.

Wish I could say the same for you, Jimmy.

"You were following me earlier too," I said.

She shook her head. "Not me."

"OK, whatever. But why'd you decide to follow me from Thatcher Street instead of just coming inside?"

"Not my kind of place." She smiled.

A jab.

"I like it," I lied. "No one bothers me there."

She squinted trimmed brows like I was messing with her.

"Why'd you come here?" I asked.

She worked up a false smile. "I'm worried about you. PS 20 is a disaster. A major health hazard and major safety risk."

I laughed. "You're worried," I said. "Three major OSHA penalties in the past nine months alone, and now you red-flag the school."

"I have no choice but to enforce the safety of all the job sites that fall under my jurisdiction," she said, the smile now wiped off her face. "We both share in that responsibility."

"I've done nothing but comply with OSHA regs," I said out the corner of my mouth. "If I didn't know any better, I'd say you and your agency have been harassing me."

She shook her head, stamped out her cig. "You don't believe a word of what you just said, do you?"

I stared into my beer bottle. I wasn't sure what to believe. "Back to my original question," I said. "Why are you here?"

Lifting her mug off the table, she drew a small sip of tea, ran an open hand through her hair, once more painting that smile on her mouth. "I've come to offer my help," she said.

"You want to help, call off the dogs. Or at the very least, call the situation what it is—Farrell's personal screwup."

Another shake of her head, hair moving around her narrow face like a red wave. "I can't do that and you know it." Making a pistol with her right hand, aiming the barrel at me, "You hired him."

"We talking off the record?"

"Sure."

"What if I'm able to locate Farrell, somehow convince him to come back with me to face the charges of negligence directly? Would that take the heat off me?"

She cocked her head, eyes glowing in the dim light spilling down from the old ceiling-mounted fixture. "I don't see how it couldn't. But he'd have to be willing to own up to everything, from cheating on the asbestos removals to rigging IAQ test samples, to deceiving you, to running away from it all."

I might have mentioned the issue of running away with the Albany School Board's two hundred grand, plus my ten. But theft was out of OSHA's jurisdiction.

Diana smiled, wry, inquisitive. "You're not serious about going after him," she said in the form of a question. "You'd never find him. And even if you did, he'd never take responsibility, short of putting a gun to his head."

The Tiger Lady was right on the money.

"So why are you here?"

"The team of project principals meets with your lawyer tomorrow. I'll be there. So will the Albany County DA."

My stomach tightened up.

"I suspect the press will be there too," Diana continued. "TV and print press have already been hounding me. Especially Ms. Collins at Channel Thirteen." She pronounced "Ms." like *Meeaazz*.

In my head, I had a sharp vision of the shapely, miniskirted reporter.

"Do yourself a favor. Show up to the meeting. Tell the truth. Plead your case, but apologize for unknowingly hiring a bad sub. Admit that the school is entirely contaminated, uninhabitable, perhaps beyond help. Your contrition will be taken very seriously."

"In other words," I said, "you want me to plead guilty to negligence and you want me to do it in front of the county prosecutor. I'm not so sure my lawyer would go for it."

She stood up from the table. "It's your only hope and Joel Clark knows it. Your only way out of this while retaining some dignity for you and Harrison Construction."

"What exactly can you promise me if I were to show up and make this…ah…little public act of contrition?"

"I can't promise anything. But what I can do is push for the most minimal fine possible."

My heart pounded. So loud even she had to hear it through flesh and bone. "I'll take your advice into consideration."

Biting her bottom lip, Diana picked up her mug off the table, carried it to the sink, set it down. "Thank you for the tea," she said in her polite, counterfeit Virginia twang. Suddenly, she seemed eager to leave. "Sorry I couldn't come up with better news."

She walked out of the kitchen, into the living area, taking the keys to the Lexus off the table, holding them in her hand.

I said, "One more heavy fine and Harrison will be dead and buried."

She nodded sadly and headed for the back terrace door. But before she stepped out, she took notice of a framed picture of Jordan I kept on the upper eye-level shelf of the floor-to-ceiling bookcase.

She paused silently, reflectively. Until she said, "You must really miss him." This time when she spoke, there was no hint of Virginia drawl.

In the photograph, Jordan was dressed in his blue-jeaned work shirt, worn Levi's, brown suede cowboy boots. He wore a red-and-black Harrison hard hat on his head. He was standing atop the tracks of a large yellow CAT dozer that had just moved a couple tons of earth into a massive pile. We had only been engaged for a few days when I'd snapped the shot of him with my digital.

"Every minute of every day," I said, eyes locked on his.

She bit her lip, nodded. As she gazed at Jordan's image, she seemed to be a million miles away, alone with her own thoughts of my deceased husband.

Until she turned back to me.

"Please peel away your stubborn skin. Show up alongside your lawyer tomorrow. I promise I'll do everything in my power to see that you receive a fair and balanced hearing."

With that statement, the old Diana had returned. But I didn't trust the fake Southern belle as far as I could throw her.

She opened the door.

"Tomorrow evening this time," she added, stepping out into the night, "this will all be resolved and you can get on with the business of rebuilding Daddy's business."

"I'm holding my breath," I said, closing the door behind her.

CHAPTER 26

I slipped on the chain, turned the deadbolt.

Who the hell was she kidding? By this time tomorrow I could *get on with the business of rebuilding Daddy's business*?

By this time tomorrow I'd be lucky if I wasn't facing criminal charges.

When I was a kid of no more than ten, I went through a frightening phase. I liked to steal my dad's old framing hammer from out of his truck and smash things with it. Bottles, cans, old Barbie dolls...Made me feel good to smash them. Until my dad put a stop to it.

Now I wanted to use my equalizer to smash Diana Stewart's Lexus headlights. No, that's not right. I wanted to smack her upside her red head. Now, *that* would feel good. First her, then Jimmy Farrell. Then I would smack my own hard head for being caught so unawares at PS 20. Ignorance is not bliss when it comes to placing little kids in danger.

Diana Stewart...the Tiger Lady. She hadn't come here to help me *off the record*. More than likely she'd come here hoping to lure me into a trap that wouldn't be sprung until all the interested parties met for tomorrow's PS 20 meeting.

Heading back inside the kitchen for another beer, I saw that Diana had left her smokes behind. Marlboro Lights. My old brand. The opened pack was calling out to me with a sweet singsong voice.

Cancer Medusa.

I didn't pick up the pack off the table and embrace it like the nicotine addict I used to be. That would make me feel too much like a real smoker. Instead, I simply snatched the one butt that was already poking out of the pack, filter end first.

I found some old matches in the junk drawer, lit one up, blew the smoke through the open window. The heart-racing but soothing nicotine head rush enveloped me. Maybe I hadn't smoked in two years, but the brain never forgets an addiction. The brain never stops jonesin' for a butt.

Legal heroin.

The BlackBerry vibrated softly in the next room. I took the lit cigarette with me to my leather jacket, which was set on the antique chair back in the living room. I pulled the mobile from the interior pocket, checked out the caller ID.

My new friend Damien Spain.

I answered it.

"You've been snooping again," he said. "Thatcher Street."

My internal lightbulb flashed on. "You're the one who's been following me."

"You and me," he said, "we can help each other out. Stop being pigheaded and at least give it a chance." He sounded a little drunk and like he was trying to catch his breath. "How's about I come over and we talk about it?"

"Get over yourself, Spain. I'm not that easy."

"You need me and my investigative knowledge; I need you and your construction knowledge."

"How do I know you're not just trying to get into my pants?"

"You don't."

"I'll think about it." I ended the call, set the ringer for the highest setting, and plugged it into the charger. Then I locked up the rest of the apartment, turned off the lights.

Back inside the kitchen, I drank and smoked the rest of my cigarette in the dark.

I cried a little too.

CHAPTER 27

Before hitting the sheets, I managed to go through my nightly ritual of checking my personal e-mail. I'd received one new message, from Natalie, bearing the subject heading "Not Spam."

I opened the message. It read, "Maybe this will help you... Please don't call me or call *on* me anymore."

A file had been attached to the e-mail. I downloaded it.

It was an MPEG. The movie came up, began to play.

Immediately, I recognized Farrell in the frame. I also recognized Natalie. She was wearing a Santa hat and not much else. Mr. Golden Smile was pushing a small pile of crumpled bills into Natalie's black G-string. The setting was Thatcher Street. Colorful strands of Christmas lights had been tacked to the pine walls. In the far corner, beside the dartboard, was a fake Christmas tree with pics of nude women for ornaments. Classy touch.

Farrell looked positively plastered.

He leaned in over the bar, kissed Natalie. Not innocently on the cheek, but on the lips, so that the two of them seemed to melt in one another's arms. A woman knew how to recognize true love when she saw it. Despite the cheap video, you could almost see Natalie blush. With the sound turned up, you could hear the voice of the cameraman. He was telling the happy couple to smile. He laughed a little. Then he said, "I want me a little of that, Nat sweet-lips."

By the time the twenty-three-second video clip ended, no doubt was left in my mind. The cameraman's voice belonged to Peter Marino.

I played the clip again, and again, and yet again.

I might have been more than a little drunk, but it didn't take a sober soul to know that Natalie and Jimmy cared for each other.

More than a bartender would care for the average customer, anyway. And not only did they care for each other, but Jimmy's own father-in-law didn't seem to care in the slightest.

Or did he?

Does Jimmy have another woman in his life? Yup, you betcha, princess.

"The plot—she thickens," I mumbled to myself. My voice sounded strange. I couldn't help but laugh.

I saved the MPEG on my PC before I closed down the e-mail and the computer altogether. Peeling off my clothes, I threw myself on the bed and passed out.

That night, I wrestled with the sandman.

Buried beneath the sheets in black panties and T-shirt… under the erupting volcano…

I'm lying on my back in a deep hole. It's like a grave, only somehow I know it's not a grave. It's a trench. Voices come to me from outside the opening. But I can't see any people. I just see bright sunlight. Suddenly, a bulge forms along the left trench wall. The bulge gives way. The wall caves in on top of me. Then the other wall collapses. The sandy, wet soil buries me. I try to inhale but breathe in only dirt and sand. I'm gagging on the wormy soil that fills my mouth and nasal passages until a set of hands reaches in for me, pulls me out…

My father.

The dream shifts to a different place, a different time…

I see Jordan. He's climbing the scaffolding that surrounds the KeyBank building exterior down off the lower Concrete Pearl. I see his muscular body grabbing onto the iron crossbars, see him plant booted feet on the first section's lowest cross brace, watch him heave his body up onto the second section, then the third and fourth, until he is far above the solid ground.

Standing outside the Jeep in the construction site lot, I watch my husband and I feel my heart beat triplets in my chest.

A voice breaks me from my spell. A voice and the figure of a woman.

Shielding the sun from my eyes with my right hand, I look up to the top of the scaffolding. It's there I am able to make out Diana. The project manager stands foursquare on the topmost scaffolding tower section, her knees pressed up against the metal parapet's edge. She's tossing me a wave, not like we're Harrison Construction coworkers, but best friends.

"Jordan," I hear her shout in slight Virginia drawl, "there's a perfectly good set of stairs inside the bank building."

Although I can't hear him, I know my husband is laughing. It dawns on me that he's not only having fun, he's showing off.

He gets to the top, climbs up over the short rail, onto the planking.

Safe and sound.

I turn back to the Jeep.

Suddenly, a commotion. That's followed by a sickening thud. I feel the thud in my chest cavity as much as I hear it. Like a watermelon smashed against a concrete slab. I look over my shoulder. I don't believe what I see. Can't believe it.

Jordan.

On his back. On the ground.

CHAPTER 28

Morning came down hard with a hangover the size of a cement mixer.

The BlackBerry exploded from the opposite end of the apartment. What dumbass switched the ringer from vibrate to the loudest ringtone possible? Would that dumbass be me?

Motherfucker…This had better be good!

I rolled over. It hurt to move. Hurt to breathe.

With burning eyeballs, I glanced at the clock radio—the same clock radio I've had since college, when I didn't get hangovers even after drinking and smoking all day and night—7:30 in backlit, white-on-black letters.

I shed the covers, pulled myself up, swung my legs around, and planted my bare feet on a cold hardwood floor. A quick look in the mirror across from me revealed a hardheaded monster with a sagging face veiled by a nest of dark hair. I only smoked a single cigarette, but my throat was on fire.

What kind of idiot starts smoking again two years after quitting?

That idiot would most definitely be me…

I got up, made the trek through the bedroom to the living room, plucked the BlackBerry off the charger, and thumbed SEND. "Yeah."

"Turn on Channel Thirteen," Tommy ordered. "Then call me right back."

I hung up, grabbing the remote to turn on the TV.

Channel 13.

By the looks of it, a live report was being broadcast from a hospital room. A young African American boy was sitting on a hospital bed, bare-chested, little legs dangling down off the white-sheeted mattress. On one side of him stood a grown woman. His mother? On the other, a suited man with a face I recognized. I'd voted for him in the last election for Albany County DA.

Derrick P. Santiago.

A well-educated, handsome, coffee-with-milk-skinned, fifty-something man. A late bloomer in terms of politics, but an up-and-comer in the Albany political scene nonetheless. Maybe a future mayoral candidate.

Crime reporter Chris Collins was already in the middle of interviewing the prosecutor.

"...And you're certain, Mr. Santiago, that this eight-year-old boy's condition is directly related to the asbestos fiber contamination of Albany Public School 20."

A statement posed as a question that made my heart skip a beat.

"This little boy, Nicolas Boni, a third grade student at PS 20, has been experiencing lung pain and difficulty breathing for some weeks now. The pain and discomfort has increased in recent days. Over the past twenty-four hours, the medical staff of the Albany Medical Center has conducted extensive tests. I'm told it's quite possible that Nicolas has contracted mesothelioma, a lung disease that occurs from prolonged exposure to asbestos fibers."

"But are you attributing Nicolas's condition directly to the asbestos contamination at PS 20?"

The critical question.

"I believe the disease, which is known to be terminal, was contracted as a direct result of asbestos contamination much like the gross contamination discovered yesterday at the school."

My head spun. I felt suddenly off balance. I braced myself by setting my hand down flat on the table, arm straight and stiff.

Collins put the mike to her own heart-shaped lips. "Are you looking to bring an indictment, Mr. Santiago?"

The mic back in the politician's face, his dark, soil-colored eyes were not focused on Collins but on the TV camera. On me! "My office is aware of the fact that Mr. James Farrell, owner and operator of A-1 Environmental Solutions, was hired by Harrison

Construction for the very sensitive job of removing all the existing asbestos material at the school.

Obviously, Mr. Farrell doesn't fear conviction by the county. Because we know without a doubt that he not only neglected to properly remove and dispose of the asbestos, he purposely and maliciously falsified indoor air quality testing samples. Since, by law, Harrison Construction is required to oversee the removal process, we believe it's possible they were aware of these false samples and did nothing to stop them. We now have a sick child because of these crimes, and who knows how many more to come?"

"Why would Harrison Construction put themselves at such risk?"

"Obviously, in the interest of completing the project on time, or even improving upon the project schedule. Which, in the end, increases Harrison's profits. Ava Harrison, the owner of Harrison Construction, may very well be named as a conspirator in the indictment against Farrell. We'll be presenting what we have to a grand jury as early as tomorrow morning."

"What kind of charges will the two business owners face if more children like Nicolas come forward? Or what if the disease proves terminal? Would the county go after Harrison and Farrell to face homicide charges?"

The little boy's mother began to weep. The little boy simply looked on, deer-caught-in-headlights confused.

"I cannot comment on that possibility at this time," Santiago said.

Collins turned to the camera. "It should be further noted that Farrell has been missing since this past Saturday after leaving his mansion in Albany's posh East Hills suburb for a fishing trip just outside of Saratoga Springs. In the meantime, sources tell Channel 13 that his business, A-1 Environmental Solutions, has been shut down, the offices emptied out. Numerous attempts to contact him have proven futile.

"While we hesitate to speculate on the nature of Mr. Farrell's disappearance and the sudden, if not suspicious, nature of A-1's apparent bug out, the facts are certainly consistent with a guilty man fleeing from justice. That leaves Ava 'Spike' Harrison alone to answer to charges of negligence in what has now become the life-and-death case of Public School 20.

While it should be noted that Ms. Harrison made herself available for comment briefly by phone yesterday afternoon, her statements shed very little light on both the school's contamination or about Mr. Farrell's disappearance. Since that time, Ms. Harrison has been absent from the job site and unavailable for further comment."

The camera shifted its focus from Collins to the sad, frightened little boy. Then it panned out to show the entire hospital room, the television news reporter taking up the entire right side of the screen in her red minidress and matching jacket. To her left were Santiago, the boy, and his still quietly weeping mother.

"This is Chris Collins with a special live report for Channel Thirteen News at the Albany Medical Center."

I picked up the remote, thumbed off the TV.

Then I collapsed into the chair like a bucket-load of raw earth.

CHAPTER 29

I wasn't sure how long the BlackBerry had been ringing before it registered with my brain. I was still sitting in the wood chair, hard head buzzing with adrenaline.

I picked up the phone.

Tommy said, "We both know that Farrell ain't just hiding. He's gone for good. What they want is somebody to thunderbolt to the crossbeam now, and you're it, Spike."

"That what you think this is?" I said. "Witch hunt?"

"You know what else?" Tommy barked. "I wanna tell you to take off. If more sick kids come popping out of the woodwork or if that poor Nicolas kid buys the farm"—pausing for effect—"well, then Christ help us all."

"Especially his poor mother," I said.

Call waiting chimed in.

Joel Clark. He'd obviously made it to the office bright and early. Maybe he'd slept there.

"Tommy," I said, "I've got to go."

"Wait just a second," he said.

"Make it quick," I said.

"How you holding up through all this? You want me to come over?"

"How'm I holding up?" I said. "Let's put it this way: I used to be pretty; now I'm just pretty fucked up."

I hit SEND, putting out one fire only to start another.

"The good news is that you're innocent until proven guilty," Joel said, his steady voice coming at me over his speakerphone.

"Reassuring," I said, my voice still a whimper.

He turned off the speaker, picked up the handset. "Meet me at the Miss Albany Diner in one hour. Can you manage that?"

"I might have trouble holding down solid food."

"Long night?"

"What about your meeting with the PS 20 project principals and Diana Stewart?"

"Postponed until later this afternoon when I've better prepared myself to handle these new allegations and developments. In the meantime, don't even think of going near that job site."

Yesterday, he was yelling at me for being conspicuously absent from the school. Now he wanted me to avoid the place at all costs.

"Joel," I said, "I still have a contract to fulfill."

"Not anymore you don't," he said. "The Albany School Board is already looking into a new GC to finish it up. You—*we*—can expect a letter of dismissal to arrive via messenger to my office sometime today. From what I understand, the paperwork is already drawn up and attached as an amendment to the original contract."

"Can they do that? Fire me like that?"

"They already have." He breathed in, exhaled. I heard him rattling some papers. Then he quoted, "'The performance of work under this contract may be terminated by the Owner, in whole or in part, for cause or whenever the Owner shall determine that such termination is in the best interest of the Owner. Any such termination shall be effected by a notice in writing—'"

"I get it, Joel." My head was heavy, my balance teetering like a detached sandstone cornice. "The Tiger Lady came to see me last night—off the record."

Big Joel issued one of his big sighs. "What did you tell her?"

"I told her nothing."

"Then what the hell did she want?"

"She offered her help."

"She knows something we don't. Do. Not. Trust. Her."

"I didn't…I won't."

"One hour," he said, then hung up.

CHAPTER 30

What's a thickheaded girl to do?

Do the right thing.

Meet up with Joel. Talk the whole rotten situation through. Weigh my legal options, figure out a way to make good the asbestos foul-up without damaging my reputation—what was left of it, that is, with two million G's in OSHA penalties and civil lawsuits already pressing down on my shoulders like heavyweight blocks, and everything my dad ever worked for his entire life reduced to me, Tommy, and a dwindling cash account.

Or I could do the wrong thing.

Farrell was gone. He wasn't coming back. Nor would I ever see a penny of my ten G's. With a sick child having entered the PS 20 equation, it was only a matter of time until I took a major fall off a high scaffolding tower. With Farrell disappeared, somebody would have to bear the burden of responsibility. Like Tommy said, I was *it*. Maybe I could follow Farrell's lead, bond the liens the school put up against me, empty out what was left of the Harrison bank accounts, head for the Canadian border. From there, maybe Europe.

Like Elvis sang, *I'm caught in a trap.* A classic case of buried if I do the right thing, maybe not so buried if I take my chances, do the wrong thing, and disappear. Whoever said running away was never an option was full of crap. Just ask Jimmy Farrell—that is, if you can find him.

My head hurt.

In the kitchen, I pulled the big bottle of Advil from out of the cabinet. I swallowed four with a cold glass of tap water. The hard water tasted like rust. On the counter, I glared hatefully at Diana's cigs. I picked them up, tried to crush the pack in my hand. But the pack wouldn't crush. Something rigid was stuffed inside it. I tore the pack open. Diana's Bic cigarette lighter had been stored inside the pack. It was exactly the way I used to prevent myself from losing my own lighters back when I smoked.

I pulled the lighter out and nearly fell over.

I hadn't noticed it when she lit her single cigarette last night, but the lighter did not belong to her. Now, without her hand cupped around it, I was able to recognize the old lighter. It was an old translucent blue plastic model with a New York Giants football helmet logo printed on both sides. The red, white, and blue logo had faded over time. The paint had been nearly worn away from age and job site wear. Still, I knew this lighter the instant I saw it in open daylight. I'd purchased it, after all.

Purchased it for Jordan not two weeks before he died.

My body was trembling.

Back in the bedroom, I set the old lighter into my desk drawer, along with the rest of the evidence I'd collected the previous day.

What the hell was Diana doing with Jordan's lighter after all this time?

If she simply found it somewhere, why had she held onto it for so long? She had to have known it belonged to Jordan. She smoked with him whenever the two met on a job site. How many times had he lit a cigarette for her with this very lighter?

In my head, I saw the faces of my enemies—Diana foremost amongst a lineup that included Farrell and Santiago. I swallowed something cold and bitter. I wanted revenge. Vengeance. Even the Bible allowed for vengeance, so I'm told.

I closed the desk drawer hard.

Then I went into the bathroom, turned on the shower. It would take every ounce of my willpower—my hardheadedness—but for now, I was going to make the right choice.

I was going to keep my appointment with my lawyer.

CHAPTER 31

I met Joel at the Miss Albany Diner on Pearl Street, maybe a stone's throw from the Thatcher Street Pub to the north and PS 20 to the south. The old trailer-and-hitch-style mobile eatery had been permanently grounded decades ago beside the old RCA building, the six-story concrete monstrosity topped off with a gigantic fifty-foot-high plaster-and-mesh Nipper the Dog. The black-on-white Nipper sat obediently atop the flat roof's edge, big black eyes peering down on the Concrete Pearl like a monster guard dog. His heavy body bolted down by chains and iron bars, tail end pointing to the Hudson River like an insult.

The diner, the giant plaster dog, the RCA building…Much of it would be relegated to the wrecking ball in a matter of months to make way for the new-and-improved Concrete Pearl Convention Center.

Joel was a slick, divorced, middle-aged lawyer from the construction law firm of Couch, Clark & Levine, which was located in the center of Pearl Street where it intersected with the city's more populated downtown business district—a three-block area that was to be spared demolition. By the time I made it to the diner, the breakfast crowd had disappeared. He'd already started on a plate of eggs over easy and buttered wheat toast. The runny yellow yokes were bleeding all over the white plate.

"How can you eat that?" I said, taking a seat on an empty stool beside the tall, barrel-chested man.

"The egg is considered by many to be the perfect food," he said, wiping the egg from his face with a paper napkin. "Hey, Cliff," he barked across the counter to a short, squat, balding man with a white apron wrapped around his torso. "Coffee for my client."

Without a word, Cliff retrieved a white ceramic mug from the stainless steel shelf mounted to the wall above the grill.

"Thank Christ." I exhaled a long, drawn-out sigh.

"Looks like somebody hit the sauce a little too aggressively last night," Joel said with a roll of his gravel-colored eyes.

Cliff came over and set down my coffee. I picked up the hot mug with both hands and took a sip. The hot liquid entered my system like new blood to a dying limb. Coming up for air, I scanned the old diner—a habit you can't help but pick up in my trade. The counter was made of light oak that had been covered over during a renovation of sorts with a laminate top. Easy to clean. The walls were finished in their original material, however—stainless steel panels that, over the many years of their existence, hadn't quite lived up to the name "stainless."

"So what's your advice, Counselor?" I said, stealing another sip of coffee.

Joel sopped up the remaining egg yoke on his plate with the bit of toast and ate it. "Let's move to a booth," he said, lifting his big torso up from off his stool.

We grabbed our coffee mugs and took seats across from each other inside one of the empty booths.

"This is the way I see it," he sighed, his eyes staring down into his coffee. "The law is very clear in the matter of a general contractor's responsibility for a negligent subcontractor—"

"Meaning?"

"Meaning that you are just as responsible as Farrell for the asbestos screwup. Maybe even more so since you personally signed off on the daily worksheets presented to you by A-1 Environmental Solutions. Same worksheets that would accompany the filter testing samples passed on to the independent air-testing contractor hired by the school—Analytical Labs."

"The Analytical Labs office is a phony," I said.

"Forget about that," he said. "Doesn't mean a thing. It's the worksheets I'm worried about now."

The worksheets.

Joel's reminder of them hit me like a sledgehammer to the gut. Farrell hadn't been all that stupid. Following the contract to the letter, he had personally asked me to sign daily worksheets at the end of every workday in which his lackeys performed asbestos removal. The worksheets assured A-1 Environmental Solutions that I had not only examined their work but that I had approved it as having been performed according to plans and specifications. But that was all bullshit. Because even though I knew the workers were removing the asbestos and carting it off-site, I had no way of knowing just how good a job they were doing and if they were performing in accordance to plans and specs. The answer to that would come out in the test reports.

"Those slips act as legal disclaimers, Spike," Joel said. "They effectively shift the burden of responsibility from Farrell to you." With another sigh, a shake of his head, his eyes lifting up from the coffee cup, settling on me, he continued. "Don't believe me? Check out the Air-Monitoring Clause of your contract with the school—paragraph one-point-zero-two which states in part, and I quote, 'The general contractor shall oversee air-monitoring activities during every work shift in each work area during which abatement and removal activities occur in order to'...something, something, something...So, tell me, why didn't you check the work if you knew Farrell was going to make you sign those daily worksheets?"

"Because you know as well as I do that it's impossible to determine if the asbestos has been removed according to contract documents," I said, looking down into my coffee. It was bleak and black. Like my future. "I'm not a certified removal expert any more than you are, Joel. That's why I hired Farrell. I had to trust him to do the job the right way. When I signed those sheets, I could only hope the testing reports would come back with a clean seal of approval. And they did."

"Until OSHA showed up, that is," Joel said.

"OK, so what's all this leading up to, Joel? Give it to me straight, no mixers."

My BlackBerry vibrated against my right hip. I pulled it out of its holster. What I saw gave me pause. The caller ID read, *Marino*

Construction. A six-digit number followed, along with a new voice mail indicator.

"Somebody you need to speak with?" Joel probed.

I shook my head. "Just Tommy," I lied. "I'll call him back as soon as we're done."

Which I hoped would be soon. I might have jumped at telling Joel the truth about who had just left a message on my cell—Farrell's father-in-law. But judging by the way our conversation was going, I decided to trust in my gut, keep the call to myself. Because what if Marino was calling me to let me in on details of Farrell's whereabouts? You could be damned sure that I would act on them, Joel's order to stop looking for the negligent sub or not.

"I won't sugarcoat it for you, Spike," Joel said. "If the grand jury agrees there's a case here, Santiago is going to hit you with an indictment of asbestos-removal negligence just for starters. Thus far, I've persuaded him to hold off on anything having to do with that kid Nicolas. At least until it's proven his condition didn't come from his living situation at home."

"Living situation?"

"Poor kid lives in the South End projects. That's the real evil of asbestosis and mesothelioma. It likes to prey on poor people who can't afford a brand-new mansion in East Hills."

"Like our boy Jimmy."

"In my opinion," Joel added, "your best defense is to simply cooperate in every possible way with Santiago's investigation. Forget what I said before about staying away from the job site. Go back to your office right now, have Tommy help you gather up all the paperwork you have on PS 20, stuff it all into some banker's boxes, deliver it in person to my office by the end of the day. When I meet with the project principals this afternoon, I'll let them know you're doing all you can to make things right, not only with the school, but with the law. At the end of the day, you and I will both sit down with the prosecutor, strike up some kind of deal."

"Trailer's been lockboxed by the cops," I said. "How'm I gonna get in?"

"I'll make the necessary calls as soon as we leave here."

I felt my body go from defeated to outright angry. Joel was changing his mind like some women change clothes. First, he wanted me to make a presence at the school; then he wanted me to stay away. Now he wanted me at the school in order to empty out my files, present them to Santiago, along with a dozen long-stemmed roses. I hadn't even been offered the chance to put up a fight and my lawyer was all set to surrender.

"Shouldn't it be Farrell striking up that deal, Joel?"

He sat up. "Farrell's gone. This is the real world and someone has got to answer and that someone is the general contractor in charge of Farrell." Leaning into me, he continued. "Jesus, Spike, read your goddamned contracts. That's your Jane Hancock on those daily worksheets. Farrell might not seem like a genius, but he knew what he was doing when he got you to sign off on them." Joel sat back hard.

I exhaled, said, "What do you think will result from your closed-door meeting with Santiago?"

"He assures me that if you cooperate fully with his office and with the discovery of all documentation, it's possible you'll face only fines—at the discretion of the court, of course."

"And if it's proven the child is sick because of the PS 20 asbestos contamination?"

"That's an entirely different ball of wax. It would also be out of my jurisdiction as a construction lawyer. It would mean hiring a criminal defense attorney."

I had nothing to say. Even if I opened my mouth and tried to speak, I knew nothing would come out.

Joel leaned forward again. "Listen, Spike," he said, "don't think about that right now. Just concentrate on the negligent asbestos-removal problem. Large fines on top of the ones you've already been nailed with could mean Harrison Construction will finally go under. But at least you just might avoid a criminal prosecution."

"Jeez, now I feel warm and cozy."

"You've made some bad decisions, and now you have to pay for them. At least Santiago is willing to work with you."

I felt like crying. The tears actually built up behind my eyeballs. But somehow, I would not give Joel the satisfaction of big tears falling. I inhaled deeply, exhaled a calming breath.

"When is Santiago going to announce his indictments?" I said.

"Like I said, I meet with him and the project principals this afternoon at the job site. Grand jury will meet first thing in morning. They'll present the specific indictments to the court. They may summon you to be present at the hearing."

I nodded and took one last sip of the coffee. It was cold now, like the fluid that filled my spine.

I slid out of the booth.

Joel stayed put, his thick hands still wrapped around the coffee mug.

"I'm really sorry about all this, Spike. I really am. And I know how your dad would feel about the whole thing. But the circumstances of the matter are not in your favor."

"Just answer me one more question," I said. "Who did the Albany School Board approach to take over PS 20?"

"Marino Construction," Joel said. "Why?"

The muscles in my neck tensed up. "Farrell's father-in-law," I said. "Nice touch. Christ, Joel, Marino Construction and A-1 Environmental Solutions are located right next door to one another."

"I know how it looks, Spike. But the school board's decision is out of my hands."

Joel smiled. Why, I had no idea.

"I trust I'll see you this afternoon with the paperwork?" he posed. "And don't forget to bring me that stuff you collected up at that stream—the shell casing."

I recalled the physical evidence hidden inside my desk drawer—physical evidence that could very well be tied to Farrell's disappearance. Joel wanted to get his hands on it. Suddenly, that was the last thing I wanted.

"I'm glad you're finally making the right decisions," he went on. "I thought you might choose to fight the indictments, not cooperate…you and that hard head of yours."

He was still smiling.

The pigheaded lady wasn't.

"Who said I was giving in?" I said.

"What's that mean?" he said.

"Tough girls don't go down easy." I winked before turning my back on him and walking out of the diner.

CHAPTER 32

Outside, I punched in the number for Marino on my mobile.

He answered, "Marino Construction."

"I'd appreciate an explanation, Mr. Marino," I barked. "Farrell's disappearance, his whereabouts, your ignoring me, your involvement in all this…And since when is a workaholic contractor so interested in fly fishing?"

"Meet me at the port in ten minutes and I'll tell you what I know."

"Why should I meet with you just because now you're good and ready?"

"Because you don't have much of a choice, young lady."

"I'm not so young anymore, Marino."

"We're starting the demo on the old port warehouses, make way for the convention center."

"Thought the common council was still stalling on their approval?"

"Let's just say I'm burning with optimism's flame. Ten minutes."

"OK, I'll play it your way. But I need answers."

"There's a big tanker getting loaded up—big old rusty thing with river water streaming out the bilge pumps. Just like you see in the old Bogie movies. I'll meet you at the stern…That's her ass end."

"I'm pretty familiar with one of those."

"I'll look out for you."

CHAPTER 33

Marino was in his mid-sixties. One of those construction lifers like my dad who lived the business 24-7, who wished it was physically possible to do everything by himself (from project layout to project closeout), and who would retire only when his casket was nailed shut, the grave filled in and compacted with two yards of raw earth.

According to project specs, of course.

Dressed way too casual in alligator loafers, loose slacks, and a purple oxford, he stood a couple of inches taller than me. He was heavy in the middle and out of shape, his face clean shaven, pale, pug nose mapped with red and purple veins. In his hand, he held the chain-and-leather leash that attached itself to the meaty neck of his pride and joy—a white and black-eyed pit bull he'd christened Sonny, in honor of the character in the *Godfather*. Or so legend had it. Sonny was looking up at me, showing me his fangs, making little halfhearted lunges against the leash. The little monster was praying for a chance to wrap his jaws around my neck.

As promised, the dark-haired, unibrowed Marino stood along with his killer pooch at the stern end of a docked cargo merchant ship. Behind us, a crew of leather-skinned construction workers was busy tearing down one corner of a long metal-sided warehouse. In the air was the fishy, gamey smell of the river combined with the oil and gas vapors that escaped the ship's idling engines.

He held out his free hand while holding a tight rein on Sonny.

I wasn't sure what to do with the hand. But I knew that to refuse it would not be a good idea. Keeping one eye on Marino and the other on Sonny, I took the big callused hand in mine. He squeezed it gently and held onto it. It was like being clutched in the claw of a giant lizard.

"I want to apologize for the way I spoke with you over the phone last evening," he said in a deep staccato voice, his hand still holding, if not caressing, mine. "As you can only imagine, my daughter has been under considerable stress lately. Naturally, when she's stressed, so am I." Finally, letting my hand slide away from his and offering me some safe separation from Sonny, he continued. "I can bet your dad—God rest his soul—knew the feeling all too well."

Marino was a master at speaking part savvy businessman and part tough-guy contractor. Not a bad attribute in this business. When he smiled, he revealed a mouthful of newly bleached teeth.

"I knew your dad well," he said. "He taught me many things about our business. Many things that I shall never forget." Raising his right hand, he pressed the tip of a sausage-thick index finger to his lips, as if it helped him to think. "Despite those things, there is one rule he insisted upon above all others. Do you know what that rule might be, Spike?"

I shook my head, hoping the sermon wouldn't take long.

He said, "Trust no one, but make damn certain everybody trusts you."

"Dad's version of 'Keep your friends close, but your enemies closer.'"

"Precisely." Marino laughed.

Sonny snarled and barked.

I took a step back.

A crashing noise startled me. Over Marino's shoulder, I saw that a large piece of metal siding had come crashing down to the dock. I took a breath and told myself to stop being so jumpy.

"Farrell," I said, growing impatient. "Where is he? Where's my money? The school's money?"

The contractor raised both big palms to me, telling me to hold my horses. "This business with my son-in-law has not been easy on my family," he said. "At first, I placed my trust in James. I trusted him because my daughter was in love with him and he seemed like such a clever, successful young environmental solutions executive."

That was a first. Someone referring to Farrell as "clever."

"I even went out of my way to see that he was introduced to the right developers, architects, and engineers. I personally carted him to Albany Development when they started talking about a redevelopment for the Concrete Pearl and the waterfront—when they initiated talks about the issuance of bonds. That was nine years ago, back when the project seemed like a five-hundred-million-dollar pipe dream. But now that it's looking more like reality, James is nowhere to be found." Raising his hands, bringing them back down fast, slapping the sides of his meaty hips, "I did everything a good father-in-law can do to help his daughter's husband attain professional prosperity and still keep my head above the law."

"No payoffs or collusion, in other words," I interjected. But in my head, I replayed the video of Farrell lovingly kissing Natalie, the father-in-law recording the moment for posterity.

"Naturally," Marino said.

"But Jimmy betrayed your trust, didn't he?"

He bit down on his bottom lip. "It was worse than that, young lady. I betrayed myself. I broke my own first rule. The rule your dad went out of his way to teach me."

"Jimmy began to fuck the dog."

"Let's just say, for the sake of argument, that James cut corners to maximize profits. Because who's ever really going to know if the asbestos in any given building has been properly removed or wrapped?"

"Authorities like OSHA and the EPA test for proper interior air quality," I said. "The independents like Analytical Labs test for it too." I thought about yesterday's visit to the storage garage just a couple hundred yards from the warehouse Marino was tearing down.

"But why test again and again when initial tests prove satisfactory?"

My gut started speaking to me again. It told me Marino knew full well his son-in-law was cheating on asbestos-removal projects. Maybe cheating for years.

"Where's Jimmy's hiding?"

He shook his head.

"Where is he, Peter? I've got to know!"

"My dear Spike," he said, "calm yourself down. Don't you think that if I knew where he was I would be there myself, personally dragging him back to his wife and responsibilities?"

"I know for certain you two argued on Saturday when he moved out of his offices. What were you fighting about?"

He stared into me. "Yes, we had some words, however brief."

"Loud, too, I heard."

Sonny barked, lunged at my ankles as if he didn't like my attitude. If it weren't for Peter holding tight to the leash, holding him back, the little monster would have impaled his teeth into my leg.

"What did you talk about, Peter?"

"About his hasty decision to get out of the environmental solutions business." Marino once more tossed his free hand in the air. "It's bad business to leave clients hanging. Clients whose contracts have yet to be fulfilled."

"Yeah, it's called stealing," I said. "There're only two reasons why a business owner like Jimmy would shut down in the middle of a job. The first is he's broke. And the second is he's running away from someone or something he's scared of."

Sonny growled.

Marino said, "I tried my best to talk him out of it. Tried to impress upon him the legal ramifications of what he was about to do. But you know James and his..." He let the thought trail off while he gazed out on the river and the massive docked ship.

"His what?" I pressed.

He turned his attention back to me. "Well, let's just say that the handsome James is like a beautifully constructed mansion with all the lights on, but there's no one home—ever."

"Yeah, the golden boy is a dud...I get that. So if he willingly left by his own accord, where the hell did he go and why did he do it?"

"If only I knew."

"Who's Natalie?" I said.

He tossed me this wide-eyed look of shock and awe, followed by a grin. "A common…bar…whore," he said.

"Why'd you videotape Jimmy kissing her? I'm sure Tina wouldn't like it."

He slowly nodded, looked into me instead of at me, like he couldn't imagine how it was possible that I'd gotten my callused hands on that video. "Last year's Christmas party. We were innocently drunk—a father- and son-in-law bonding kind of thing. Better times for us and our businesses back then."

"Didn't look all that innocent to me. Looked like Jimmy was cheating on your daughter by sucking face with a half-naked barmaid. That's what got caught on tape. Who knows what was happening behind closed doors?"

"I wasn't aware of anything more than a kiss," he said.

"What about employees?" I said, deciding to drop the Natalie business. "Maybe they'd know what rock Jimmy slithered under."

Another shake of the head. "The three or four employees he required at any one time would be set up in another town by now, working on another job."

"What'd you do, Peter? Pay them off to keep quiet, leave town?"

Sonny lunged again.

"Sonny, heel!" Peter shouted, yanking back hard on the leash. Then, smiling at me, he said, "I'll let that little comment slide. Temporary help was the best policy for my son-in-law in terms of maintaining a profitable business. It was my idea to begin with."

I was getting nowhere fast. "What about the police? Anyone file a missing persons report yet?"

"Filed last evening. I wanted to wait for as long as possible before getting the authorities involved. I'm sure from where you're standing, you understand my apprehension over messy legal matters."

For a time, we both eyed the river while Sonny sniffed the pavement, searching for an insect to kill.

After a while, I said, "You're taking over the PS 20 job."

The big man nodded, contemplative eyes on the river.

I added, "Under the circumstances, Peter, you don't see your direct involvement as a conflict of interest?"

He turned back to me. "I'm a professional," he said. "When the Albany School Board asked me to take over, I dropped everything. You realize it's a direct possibility that PS 20 will pull up stakes, move uptown to make way for the convention center. It means that not only will I be able to negotiate their existing property for the Pearl Street Convention Center, but the district will also require a new school facility." He smiled. "You know how the game works, Spike. If I can make the project principals happy now, I just might have a shot at negotiating a badly needed Pearl Street parcel."

"How nice for you," I said. "Taking into account your status as the convention center construction manager, you just might have a monopoly on the entire boatload of new Concrete Pearl work."

His smile faded. "What I do in the interest of Marino Construction," he said, "I do legally."

"What about Albany Development Limited?"

"I'm a member in good standing of the board of trustees."

"I'd say you're getting your cake and devouring it too."

"That's the American way, Spike. Land of economic prosperity and opportunity."

"Funny you talking about opportunity, when Harrison Construction has been shut out of the convention center. I have you to thank for that."

Peter reached out with his claw, set it heavily on my shoulder. When he squeezed it, I felt my stomach do a flip.

"You're a health-and-safety liability," he said. "And now the DA is talking about indictments. Do yourself a favor, Spike; ignore that hard head of yours and put Harrison Construction out of its misery. Bury it and forget about it."

He slipped his claw off my shoulder. "I have a proposition for you, young lady," he said. "When this thing blows over, I want you to come work for me. Who better to finish up PS 20 than the GC who started it?" He was smiling, bushy eyebrows perked up at both ends like the devil.

"Somehow I'm not sure my presence on-site would be greatly appreciated by the Albany School Board."

He shook his head again, the wiry ends of that devil eyebrow trembling in the stiff wind. Sonny farted and went back to panting. "You'd run the job from the office," Peter clarified. "Not a soul would know the difference."

How ironic. In just a few minutes' time, I'd gone from certain state indictment to a job offer. All over the same asbestos-contaminated Pearl Street school project.

He tossed a quick glance over his shoulder at the warehouse demolition and his crew of construction workers. "I'd better be getting back to my job," he said. "Remember, I asked you out here because your dad gave me advice once and now I'm here to pass along some advice to you. I know he'd want you to do the right thing. Your best bet is to cooperate with Santiago and this will all pass you by very quickly."

He was grinning when he turned toward the demo-in-progress warehouse, dragging Sonny behind him. But before taking more than five steps, he turned back to me. "Oh," he said, "I almost forgot."

I locked eyes with him.

"As you know, my daughter spoke to me about your unscheduled meeting yesterday at her residence. She mentioned how anxious you were to locate James to hunt him down, as it were—and that you might have even gone out to the spot where he was thought to have gone fishing last Saturday morning."

He pursed his lips like a load of wet clay was weighing heavily on the mind.

"I can only assume you also located James's new BMW at Dott's Garage. You even might have searched it, perhaps in hopes of finding some sort of clue that might lead to his whereabouts."

"What are you getting at, Peter?" In my mind, I pictured the spent shell casing. I pictured all the stuff I'd collected thus far, the evidence Joel wanted me to pack up and deliver to his office—A-S-A-fucking-P.

"If you've discovered anything, Spike," he said, "anything at all that might aid official investigators in their search for my daughter's husband, it would be in your best interest to reveal them to me personally. Naturally, you understand?"

I understood loud and clear. Marino must have already put two and two together. He must have known I had found something up at the Desolation Kill and in Farrell's car, or he would have never said a word about it. He wouldn't have asked me to meet him. The job offer, the advice, the kind words about my old man—transparent frosting to lull me into his confidence.

But then I had to ask myself this: How did Marino know about the evidence in the first place? And why would he care? Was it possible Marino was with his son-in-law at the public access fishing area just prior to Jimmy's disappearance?

It was time for me to end this meeting.

I took a step back. "I'll think the job offer over," I said.

"Remember, young lady," he said, "if you found anything… anything at all…I would very much appreciate knowing about it."

I kept backing up, careful not to back up off the pier into the river.

Something occurred to me then. "Peter," I said.

He shot me a glance.

"If you're so sure PS 20 is going to be relocated uptown," I said, "why bother finishing the project up at all?"

"*Ours is but to do and die,*" he quoted with a devilish smile, yanking on Sonny's leash.

I turned and walked away, the hairs on the back of my neck still standing up on end.

CHAPTER 34

Driving. Out of the port toward the Concrete Pearl.

At a stop sign, I dialed 4-1-1 on my BlackBerry. I asked for the main number to the Albany Police Department. Information dialed the number for me. When an APD switchboard operator came on the line, I told her I needed to speak with someone who worked on missing persons. She asked me if I was a reporter.

"Just a concerned citizen," I said.

She asked me the name of the missing person. I told her. She told me to hold.

When she came back on the line, she said that a report had been filed yesterday, late afternoon.

"By whom?" I asked.

"Intra-departmental," she said.

"In other words, no one from Farrell's family filed it." A question.

"OK, what TV station you work for?"

I hung up before she ran my number.

Marino lied about filing the missing persons report on his son-in-law.

Big surprise.

What did it all mean?

It meant he either didn't care about Jimmy's well-being or the last thing he wanted was to have to speak with the cops. The real answer probably lay somewhere in between.

The phone vibrated. Spain's name came up on the caller ID.

And I was the one everybody called stubborn?

I thumbed IGNORE and drove in the direction of PS 20.

CHAPTER 35

I pulled up to PS 20—or *almost* to the site, once I saw that there was a party going on that I had not been invited to. I watched it from a distance, the Jeep hidden behind a stand of overgrown pines that bordered the northern edge of the school property.

I'd come not to collect my project files in accordance with my lawyer's carefully considered counsel but to take them home with me. Hide them until I figured out a better plan of action than simply giving up.

But I was too late.

Just outside the trailer stood the team of project principals. The gawky Albany school supervisor, the bearded architect, DA Santiago, along with two or three uniformed APD. A blue-jeans-clad Diana Stewart also occupied her little personal square foot of blacktop. She stood beside Joel Clark and one more person too—Private Detective Spain.

Maybe I should have answered his call, after all.

The bigwigs were standing in a semicircular formation around the set of aluminum steps leading up to the red-flagged project trailer door. It's not that I had forgotten about the *come-to-Jesus* between the project principals—the meeting in which Joel would represent me in my absence, where he would announce my full cooperation to surrender my files, and me, to the DA. It's just that it wasn't supposed to happen until later in the afternoon. According to Joel, I had plenty of time to get at my files.

So much for trusting my lifelong lawyer.

The trailer door opened up. The party took a collective step aside to avoid the unidentified man who was carting my metal file cabinet out on a dolly, down the steps to an awaiting GMC suburban.

Another car pulled up.

A Porsche convertible.

Marino.

He hadn't been far behind me. He got out of the car like a movie star, shook hands with several team members, including Santiago and Joel. He ignored Spain. He was wearing razor-thin sunglasses and had a bright smile planted on his face, no doubt visions of dollar signs flashing through his brain. Here the Italian-American contractor came to save the day now that the health-and-safety liability had been tossed off the job, now that his son-in-law had been officially reported missing, not by him or Tina, but by the APD themselves.

I threw the Jeep in drive. As I pulled away, I took one more look over at Santiago. I also took one last good look at the devil-browed Marino, at Joel, at Stewart…

At Spain.

Had the private detective called to warn me that my files would be confiscated by the cops? As I slid out from behind the trees, I was certain the PI caught sight of me. My eyes focused in on the rearview mirror, I watched him silently watching me as I drove away from the school, out of sight, but not out of mind.

CHAPTER 36

It was going on half past one when I pulled into Lanie's bar.

I spotted Tommy's black Ford F-150 pickup parked right outside the entrance. As soon as I walked in, I saw that he occupied his usual corner stool behind the pool table and the popcorn machine, a full bottle of Bud set before him. The stool gave him a good unobstructed view of the ceiling-mounted television.

I sat myself down on the empty stool next to his. He automatically ordered me a draft beer from the young woman tending bar.

The dark-haired college girl looked up from the magazine she was reading, retrieved my beer, set it down in front of me. "Take it out of here, Tommy?" she asked, digging manicured fingers into the pile of cash laid out on the bar.

"'Course," Tommy said. Then, turning to me, he said, "Santiago is threatening to indict you. What now?"

I took a small sip of the cold beer, then told him about the confiscated files. "Joel wants me to give up," I said. "Wants me to cooperate with Santiago, strike a deal with the county. Word is I'll be fined. No prison time."

He looked at me hard. "You haven't done shit," he said, voice bitter. "Any more than you cut that carpenter's fingers off earlier this year."

I fell silent for a moment while my heart sank and bled for all the mothers of the kids I might have had a hand in infecting. Maybe Tommy was my ally in all of this, and maybe he was trying to keep my spirits up with his version of a guilt-free pep talk. But the fact is, I did feel guilty. Dammit, if only I could have reversed time, I would have at least refused to sign those daily worksheets. Refused to sign them until I could be certain the building was clean, apart from those interior air quality reports Analytical Labs was providing. But who would ever guess that a guy I'd known nearly my entire life would cheat on the job I hired him for and then split town?

I sat stewing, my eyes veering from the bartender who was back to reading her magazine and the television that was tuned into the twenty-four-hour local news—Tommy's personal information source. The bartender's black boy-beater T-shirt fell just short of her navel. Her tight belly sported a brand-new *phat tat* of a green palm tree bending in the wind.

"Any clue where your old lover boy took off to yet?" He followed up with one of his grins.

I took a sip of beer and glared back at him like, *Don't even go there.*

Then I told him I had no new word on the subject. But I was able to tell him about the liens placed on the Harrison accounts. I told him about my little introduction to Natalie in the flesh at Thatcher Street, about how upset she'd seemed, about how she'd denied knowing a whole lot about Farrell—that is, until she forwarded a short MPEG to me proving she and the golden boy were more than just barroom acquaintances and how Marino, of all people, acted as cameraman. I let him know about my surprise meeting with Diana last night and I told him about my impromptu meeting with Marino at the port late that morning.

Tommy took it all in, especially the part about both Marino and Diana wanting me to turn myself over to Santiago, just like Joel wanted. "Marino," he said. "Bastard is taking over our job even though his son-in-law caused this entire mess."

Not exactly, Tommy, I wanted to say. I had something to do with it too. But I knew he wouldn't hear of it.

"Listen, Tommy, I have to lay you off for a while," I said, downing the rest of my beer before sliding off the stool. "I want you to put in for unemployment."

"I need a vacation, anyway," he said. "But not until I help you get out of this mess."

I reached into him, kissed him on the cheek.

"Easy," he said. "People know me here."

No one else occupied the bar. Only the bartender, her eyes still buried in her mag, that little palm tree swaying with her every breath. She was young enough to be Tommy's granddaughter.

"My apologies, Romeo," I said.

"I'm worried about you," Tommy said. "You've been doing a lot of snooping in the past twenty-four hours."

"You think Marino is scared about what I uncovered at that fishing hole—the bullet casing?"

He sat upright on his stool, crossed thick arms over barrel chest. "Could be that, by finding out about what happened to Farrell, you also stand the chance of uncovering something about Marino. Something buried deep he doesn't want you to uncover. And that's always some dangerous shit."

My mobile vibrated.

Joel. No doubt calling to inform me that the Harrison bid files had been confiscated by county authorities. He'd also want to pin me down for a time when I would voluntarily surrender myself to Santiago.

I ignored the call.

"I've got to go, Tommy," I said.

"You watch your back, Spike. Who knows what kind of worm can you pried open? Think about it. You found a shell casing and Marino knows it. Someone had to have fired a gun that produced that shell, for whatever reason. Maybe I always thought of Farrell as a stuck-up, preppy dumbass, but let's hope that the reason behind his disappearing act ain't got nothing to do with that shell casing."

"Now I think I know what I have to do," I said.

"What's that?"

"Something I should have done yesterday. Instead of handing the evidence over to Joel, I'm going to hand it over to the police."

CHAPTER 37

I spotted him standing beside my Jeep the moment I walked out the door.

Damien Spain was planted foursquare in the dirt lot, arms crossed over his ample chest. He locked eyes on me. Didn't matter that he was wearing sunglasses. I felt his high beams on me from all the way across the lot.

No choice but to approach him.

"Word is you're going to surrender yourself to Santiago," he said.

"Stop following me," I said. I unlocked the Jeep door, put my hand on the opener, and pulled it open.

He reached out, pressed his hand against the door, and closed it back up.

I turned to him. "What do you want from me?"

"Two minutes of your time," he said. "I knew that if I called, you wouldn't answer."

"You and your pals find anything interesting inside my project trailer?"

His face turned visibly red.

I stole a glance at my wristwatch. "One minute, fifty seconds," I said.

"I told you I'm under the employ of Albany County to look into Farrell's business practices. I was called to that meeting this morning at the project trailer by Santiago himself. Now that Farrell is officially registered with missing persons, I've been instructed to shift the focus of my investigation on behalf of the county. They want me to see if I can find out what the hell happened to him."

"You and me both…One minute, forty."

"Ms. Harrison, do you have any idea why I haven't been able to nail Farrell with anything substantial since my investigation switched from Tina Farrell to Albany County a few weeks ago?"

"You're pacing yourself?"

"Not exactly," he said. "It's because I can't get anyone who's ever worked for him or with him to talk with me, much less come forward as an expert witness."

"You ever seen an asbestos removal in progress, Spain?"

He shook his head.

"It's not brain surgery. Mostly just some taping and prepping. Two or three people can handle the removals. Farrell hired only temporary help—transients, probably uncertified, probably didn't know the first thing about proper removal procedures. Maybe he paid them in cash, then fixed the books. It's a no-brainer, even for a genius like Farrell."

"Transients would give him control of the situation, keep people moving in and out of the revolving door before they had a chance to snitch on his act."

"Especially if the act involved cheating in exchange for a little under-the-table cash."

He was quiet for a beat. Then, "Still, temporary or not, employees have eyes and ears. You would think one of them might poke their heads out from the dirt pile."

"Listen, Spain," I said. "If it turns out Farrell really did use unskilled labor instead of certified asbestos-removal technicians, they would have been ten-dollar-an-hour unskilled labor. They won't want any trouble. They go where the work is. There's no work, they take off. Or there's trouble sticking to the work, they don't hang around very long. Now, if you'll excuse me, I—"

"Wait, please, Ms. Harrison."

One more glance at my watch. "Fifty-three seconds," I said.

He cleared his throat. "You're about to be indicted by Santiago for asbestos-removal negligence and conspiracy to falsify asbestos removal and testing procedures, both of which carry hefty state penalties, including possible prison time."

"Let me guess," I said. "If I decide to work with you in every way possible, you'll spare me the burden of a drawn-out state investigation. But, of course, I'll have to pay a severe penalty. Am I getting warm, Spain?"

He shook his head. "That's what Santiago will offer," he said. "What I can give you is better."

A last look at my watch. "Twenty-five ticks. How much better?"

"I need a person who's worked with Farrell. A person who knows the ins and outs of the construction trade. On the other hand, you need someone with an in at the DA's office. Someone with solid investigative skills, someone with friends on the inside and solid resources on the outside."

"So what is it you're offering me, Spain? In exchange for my cooperation, you'll help me find Farrell, bring him back to Albany? Santiago know about all this?"

"Yes and no."

"Which is it?"

"Santiago will approve my plan, but not in public."

"What do I get if I say yes?"

"Full immunity, no arrest, no fines. If we locate Farrell and uncover the people he's been working with, you'll be free of the heat—a clean slate."

"What about Santiago? You trust him? What about the indictments? His pristine political future? His support of that PS 20 kid with mesothelioma?"

He smiled for the first time. "Santiago is a political peacock showing off his tail feathers. He saw opportunity for TV time and jumped at it."

"Why?"

"Because now a woman construction project manager is involved and a woman is good press. A woman shows he's an equal-opportunity prosecutor."

"What about those Albany County indictment wheels already set in motion?"

"My investigation will take precedence. Santiago will have to drop his indictment or else face obstruction of his own county-investigated case. Farrell has performed removals in over ten different New York State towns and cities. He's worked on public buildings, schools, libraries, restaurants, you name it. Who knows how many people could be infected with mesothelioma or asbestosis because of him?"

"Time's up," I said.

He uncrossed his arms, placed a hand on the Jeep door. "Ms. Harrison," he said, "in the end, you may very well be the only associate of Farrell's I can persuade to come forward and testify. And in the end, you'll need someone who can prove on your behalf that you didn't knowingly assist Farrell in contaminating that school."

I rolled the car keys around in my hands. "Have you presented this scenario to my lawyer?" I asked.

"I'm not that sneaky. I wanted to talk with you about it first."

"That why you been following me?"

"Maybe it's none of my business," he said. "But far as I'm concerned, I would have fired Joel Clark, Esquire, first chance I got after I found out about his cooperation with Santiago behind your back."

I felt myself trying to bury my anger, but not succeeding.

He added, "Did you know Clark allowed Santiago to confiscate your bid files without a warrant? And that he claimed to be acting on his client's behalf?" Shaking his head, disgusted, "Give me fucking break, if you'll pardon my lingo, Ms. Harrison. But if I hadn't convinced Santiago to give you a shot at working with me, you might be busted right now."

I looked into his narrow face. I'm not sure what came over me, but I was beginning to like Spain. Rough spots and all. He seemed like a straight shooter. Something you don't always come across in the construction industry.

I opened the Jeep door, slipped behind the wheel. "Give me a chance to think this all over," I said.

"You always this stubborn?"

"I'd tell you to ask my dad, but he's six feet under."

"You don't have much time," he said. "You need me, and I need you. You're about to face a summons to appear in court before a grand jury. But I can spare you all of that if you agree to work with me."

I fired up the Jeep. "I'll call you in one hour," I said, pulling the door closed.

He backed away.

I burned some rubber.

CHAPTER 38

Spain had one very good point.

I should have fired Joel for acting without consulting me first.

But what Spain didn't know was that, like Tommy, Joel had known me ever since I was a young pup, back when he was a green lawyer just having passed the bar and newly employed at the firm for which he would one day become a partner.

Joel was used to acting on my behalf without my knowledge. I kept him on retainer, just like my father had for years and years. Over the lifetime I'd known him, Joel hadn't just gotten the Harrison Construction business out of a few scrapes. He'd also handled the occasional traffic violation, including a DUI I got nailed with back when I was still in college. When Joel managed to have the charges reduced to a speeding ticket, my father and I were elated. Since that time, I'd always looked up to him as a legal friend who would always be there if I needed him. So to fire him now was not exactly an easy decision for me.

There was also something else to consider.

I had three major lawsuits pending for the job site accidents that had occurred months ago, and that didn't include the civil lawsuits that would surely arise out of the PS 20 asbestos contamination situation. Nor did it include the work that went into bonding the liens made against my bank accounts.

Who knew how many phone calls Joel had made or decisions he'd had acted upon on my behalf without my being the least bit aware of it?

Driving, I retrieved my new messages from my mobile.

Speak of the devil.

Joel, telling me what I already knew—that I could expect a summons to arrive via processor sometime late that afternoon.

However, the sooner I turned myself in after receiving the summons, the more I would be perceived by Santiago as acting on good faith. Santiago would have no choice but to take my cooperation into consideration when it came time to dig up a deal.

But I wasn't about to dig up a plea deal with Santiago. Without having to think about it anymore, I knew I was going to accept Spain's offer to cooperate with his investigation. I was going to have to step out of my protective, hardheaded shell and trust him. At this point, what the hell did I have to lose other than Santiago's indictments? The way I looked at it, so long as I was working for the good guys, I could keep on searching for Farrell and my money.

Problem was, who the hell were the good guys?

CHAPTER 39

Back home, I found a young man standing by the front entrance to my apartment building. Just an average-looking college kid in jeans, sneakers, and button-down, the tails hanging out. He was wearing those slim, wraparound sunglasses you see a lot of construction workers wearing under their hardhats.

As I approached, he locked onto me with those alien sunglass-covered eyes. "Ms. Ava Harrison," he posed.

"Gee, that a multiple-choice question?"

He held out folded sheet of paper.

I took it in hand.

"You've been served," he said.

He quickly pulled away from the door and jogged across the green to the visitors' parking lot.

I slipped the key into the lock, let myself in through the front door, then down the short flight of stairs to my basement-level unit. I opened the door, stepped inside. Closing the door behind me, I tossed the summons onto the living room desk—hard enough that it shot off the other side, crash landing on the wood floor. I pulled the BlackBerry out, speed-dialed Joel's office.

"Joel Clark," I said when the receptionist answered.

He came on the line.

"I've been served," I said.

"Standard operating procedure," he said. "Meet me at my office in one hour. Santiago's office is in the old county building slated for demotion later this year. It's down a ways from mine on Pearl Street. We'll head there together on foot."

"I've changed my mind," I said.

Dead air filled the connection.

Until Joel said, "I don't understand."

That's when I told him about my meeting with Spain.

When I was through, Joel exhaled. "I don't know the guy."

"You were with him this afternoon when they sequestered my files."

"The hooligan in the black leather jacket?"

"That would be him."

"I still don't know him and I don't know about any investigation on behalf of the county into Farrell's business, secret or not. But I do know this: Even if Spain's polishing Santiago's helmet head on a daily basis, it doesn't mean he can protect you. It also doesn't mean that Santiago still won't come after you when all is said and done."

"Spain gave me his word that the DA's office would take a back seat to the county investigation," I said, not sure I believed it myself.

"But it's no guarantee they won't prosecute you down the road. Especially if they feel certain you and Farrell were working together to cheat the system."

"That's not going to happen," I said.

"Spike, listen to me—"

"No, you listen to me, Joel. Since I'm getting nowhere trying to find Farrell on my own, Spain is going to help me find him, arrest him, put him in prison. Get it?"

"So you're using Spain?"

"Damn straight. And Spain is using me. It was either that or go to the police with my side of the story and my evidence."

"You were going to surrender the evidence to me, Spike."

"Not anymore," I said. "If anyone gets it, it'll be Spain.

"Spike, you don't know him."

"No, I don't. But I do know we both need to find Farrell. And after the golden boy is busted, I'm going straight to the *Times Union* and Channel Thirteen to expose precisely how I've been set up to take the full blame for something I did not do all by myself."

"I need to find out more about this Private Detective Spain character and if he's really been meeting with Santiago and why I'm the last to know about it."

My heart was pounding, palms sweaty, breathing labored. It was the first time in my life I'd ever defied Joel's counsel. It felt a little like disobeying my dad.

"Have you been drinking, Spike?" Joel added after a beat.

"Jesus, Joel—"

"OK, I'm sorry, but I had to ask." Pausing, he added, "There's no changing that pigheaded brain of yours?"

"What do you think?"

"At least give me time to check out Spain's bona fides."

"My mind's made up, Joel. Has been since you agreed for them to take my bid files without a fight. After all we've been through together…after all these years…"

He cleared his throat. Not out of necessity, but because I called him out on something.

He said, "I'll call the DA's office right away. You don't hear back from me in an hour, you can assume the summons you were just served is powerless. Which means no convening of the grand jury and that the county investigation is in fact taking a back seat to some highly questionable but secret county investigation."

"Thank you," I said, but I'm not sure I really meant it.

When I hung up, I pulled Spain's card from my jeans pocket, dialed his cell.

"Spain," he said.

"I'm in," I said.

"You're doing the right thing," he said. "'Bout time."

"My lawyer says I could still be indicted by Santiago down the road."

"Your lawyer is a construction lawyer. He's probably never been inside a criminal court in his life. You won't be indicted. I'll make sure of it."

"How?"

"You didn't do anything wrong other than trusting Farrell to do the job he was paid to do."

"Thanks for that. If only it were that simple, I might never have to worry about guilt. But truth is, he was—*is*—my responsibility."

"Fair enough. If we can find him, we'll make him fess up to his portion of that responsibility."

"My lawyer is making a check on you. See if you are who you say you are. He called you a *hooligan*."

"He won't find a thing," he said. "That's the way hooligans work. You and he are just going to have to place your faith in me."

"Faith," I said. "What's that?"

"It's believing in something you can't see, hear, or feel."

"Like Farrell," I said.

"Like microscopic asbestos fibers," Spain said. "Sit tight and lay low. I'll be back in touch with you very soon."

"Reassuring," I said.

"Have faith," he said.

I hung up.

CHAPTER 40

What's a stubborn girl like me in way over her head to do?

I went into the bathroom, stood over the sink, turned on the cold water. Leaning over the basin, I cupped my hand under the flow, splashed the cold water onto my face. Repeated the process a second time.

Was I doing the right thing by agreeing to work with Spain to track down a missing man? Maybe a dead missing man? If it was the right thing to do, then why did I feel like I just made a deal with the devil?

Maybe I was digging a deep hole in the sand that would only keep collapsing the more I shoveled.

Spain said that Farrell had operated in several towns and cities across the state. This was going to be a long and lengthy investigation. I knew it could take weeks, maybe months, to resolve. But at least I wouldn't be indicted by Santiago.

Or would I?

I turned off the water and dried my face with a towel. I hung the towel back up behind the door, looked at myself in the mirror. I gazed at the pale face, the dark hair that draped it, at the crow's feet that accented my eyes. Running my hands through my hair, I began to realize exhaustion like I've never felt before. Just walking the short distance from the bathroom back into the living room seemed to take a terrific effort. Maybe I shouldn't have stayed up drinking the night before.

I laid myself down on the couch, face-first, left arm and leg dangling off the side.

I fell immediately to sleep.

I'm standing bedside inside a brightly lit ICU.

There are no rooms here, only Plexiglas partitions and sea-green curtains.

Jordan is laid out on his back on the bed, a white, blood-spotted sheet tucked up tight under his chin. Both his braced arms are extended out by his sides. There's an intravenous line needled into his forearm. The IV drips from a clear plastic bag that hangs from a portable metal post on wheels. An assortment of wires and pads have been attached to his chest. The wires are connected to a vital functions monitor. On the monitor, I can see Jordan's heartbeat in the form of a green line that moves across an electronic readout in a constantly interrupted, arrhythmic, up-and-down motion. I can also hear the heartbeat coming from the monitor. The pulse is rapid and uneven, as are his rattling breaths.

An alarm sounds.

The jagged, up-and-down green line goes flat.

A nurse comes running in, pulls me out of the way. But that's when Jordan does something unbelievable: he sits up, blood oozing out his eyes and ears. I back away from him. I see him holding his arms out for me. He wants me to come to him, wants me to listen to him. He's trying to tell me something. But he can't speak and I am leaving him…

CHAPTER 41

The BlackBerry woke me.

I opened my eyes, saw that the late-afternoon sun was settling in over the lush green lawn located directly behind my apartment terrace.

How long had I been asleep?

I sat up, placed booted feet on the wood floor, rubbed the life back into my face with open hands. Standing, I waited to regain my sense of balance before I took a step toward the desk and my phone.

The ringing had stopped by then. But whoever called had left a message.

I checked the caller ID.

Joel.

I punched in the numeric code to retrieve the message.

Joel's voice.

"You got your wish, Spike. Santiago has agreed to postpone the indictments of you and Farrell. Pending whatever your boy Spain has up his sleeve. *Postpone* being the key word here. In any event, our illustrious county DA seems to know Spain pretty well. That's one up on me. Listen, let's hope Santiago doesn't use the extra time putting his ADAs to work digging up even more dirt on you and the asbestos fuckup at PS 20."

That was it.

End of message. No good-bye. No thanks for doing business with Joel Clark, Esquire. Standing there in my quiet half-lit apartment, I wondered if Joel would have hung up on my dad without saying good-bye.

I set the phone down, made my way over to the terrace door, and set the deadbolt.

I was now secure. But I did not feel secure.

Back in the kitchen, I found Diana's cigarettes—or what was left of them—inside the crumpled-up pack. I pulled one out. It was bent in the center but still OK. Thank God. I lit it up with Jordan's old lighter, saw his face in the bright orange-and-yellow flame.

The nerve of Diana hanging onto one of my late husband's mementos. I was the grieving wife. She was the wannabe.

I checked my watch. A little past five o'clock. I found a beer in the fridge, uncapped it, took a sip. I'd dodged the indictment bullets. But only for now.

Leaning back against the kitchen counter, I tried to figure out my next move.

I was on my second beer when the doorbell rang.

I set the beer down on the counter, finger-combed my hair, and slapped some color into my cheeks. I couldn't imagine who would knock on my door uninvited. But the way my week was going, I should have been expecting anything.

In the living room, I stood by the intercom and pressed the speak button. "Yes?" I said, the hint of trembling in my voice taking me by surprise.

"It's Spain." Behind the tinny voice I could make out the sound of crickets chirping and a truck rushing by on the main road. "Can I come in?"

I hit the second button below the speaker—the one that unlocked the front door.

"Watch your step," I said.

There was a loud buzz, the opening of the door. He was in.

I heard the building's main door close behind him, the sound of heavy-soled boots descending the stairs, then a gentle knock. I opened the door to a face that was neither smiling nor frowning.

"Don't mind the mess," I said, heading back into the kitchen with my heart beating fast. I took another cold beer from the fridge, uncapped it, and brought it back into the living room. I gave it to him without asking permission.

He took a generous swallow. "Seven years of marriage and not once did my wife ever hand me a cold beer when I came through the door at night."

It struck me as odd that Spain might actually have a personal life. Past or present.

"She married you, didn't she?"

"She also divorced me two and a half years ago."

"I'm sorry."

"Don't be. It'd been coming for a long, long time. We were one of those couples who were great together unmarried. But married, a disaster."

"Your work," I surmised.

He nodded, pursed his lips, his narrow cheeks caving in on themselves. "I'm not always able to be exactly forthright with those closest to me. Sometimes I'm required to…" He threw up his hands.

"Fib a little," I finished for him.

Another nod, chock-full of guilt.

"Kids?"

He turned his eyes to the wood floor. "A little boy," he said. "Well, not so little anymore."

"What's his name?"

"Jack," he grinned. "Like jack-o'-lantern…Born on Halloween morning."

"Get to see him much?"

Spain's grin dissolved into a sudden sadness. An emotion I sensed he wrestled with often. "They both moved out to California a couple of years ago so that my ex could pursue her music." Looking back up at me, "She's really very good. A soprano with the Los Angeles Opera."

"Impressive," I said. "But you also have rights as a father."

He shrugged his shoulders sadly. "What about you? You must have a skeleton or two. A bad past marriage. Or maybe something you're afraid of."

"My marriage was a good one. Maybe too good. My husband fell from a scaffolding tower and was killed. As for fears, I'm not afraid of anybody or anything. Except…"

"Except?"

"When I was seven years old, I visited a job site with my dad. I fell into a footing trench. The trench caved in. My dad pulled me out before I suffocated."

"I can see how that would stick with you for a while."

"The doctors said another minute trapped under the earth and I would have been brain dead. Or just plain dead. It's something I'll never forget."

"Not the greatest fear to have for a construction pro," Spain said, trying to work up a smile.

"We all carry our crosses. I deal with it."

"I'd love to continue chatting with you, Spike," he said, "but we have business to get down to. When you decided to play detective yesterday morning up at Lake Desolation, did you find anything from the public fishing access site that shouldn't be there? Anything from Farrell's BMW?" Spain wasted no time getting to the nitty-gritty.

"You didn't give the car the once-over yourself?"

He nodded. "All I found was a couple of buckets in the trunk. They were filled with a dark, bad-smelling liquid. Had little insects or clams floating on top. Weird."

"Yep. Saw those myself." I set my beer down, went into my bedroom, opened the desk drawer, retrieved everything I'd found—the stuff that Joel wanted. Then I went back into the living room, set it all down onto my late mother's antique dinner table.

One spent 9mm shell casing.

One still-full chewing tobacco tin.

One Thatcher Street Pub business card, the name *Natalie* scrawled on the back over lipstick red lips.

One sheet of paper, sketch side up.

Spain's face took on a glow. He rested his drink on the table. For a time, he just stared at the objects, not touching them, as if he might contaminate them with his prints. I told him where I'd found each item: the Skoal tin and shell casing by the stream bank, the business card inside the glove box of Farrell's black BMW, the misspelled "Closed Untill Further Notice" note with the odd sketch on the back outside the locked A-1 Environmental Solutions doors.

He gazed up at me. "Why didn't you tell me about any of this stuff yesterday?"

"You and me gonna work together, Spain," I said, "we gotta get one thing straight. This is my show, my ass on the line. My hard head on the chopping block. I decide not to show you something, don't take it personal. I had my reasons, the primary one being I didn't know who the hell you were or if you could be trusted. Still don't know, in fact."

He pursed his lips, bobbed his head. "Let me put it another way," he said. "I'd appreciate you letting me in on what you discover as soon as you see fit to let me in on it."

He smiled.

So did I.

He said, "You have any large plastic freezer bags?"

I retrieved one from the storage cabinet above the refrigerator, handed it to him. He pulled a white hanky from his back pocket, placed everything inside the bag, then sealed it closed.

"What about prints?" I said.

"The lab will know enough to separate our prints from Farrell's—that is, if his prints are on any of this stuff at all."

His comment took me by surprise. "Who else could it belong to?"

He shrugged. "You just don't assume anything in this business."

"Mine, either," I said. "I've learned that lesson the hard way."

He left one object out of the bag: the sketch scrawled on the back of the "Closed Untill Further Notice" note. He picked it up with both hands, examined the parallel lines and the letters "S" and "C" under them.

"S," he said. "C. What can they stand for?" His eyes flicked to mine. "You have a map of North America hanging around?"

I shook my head. "We can go online," I said.

We went into my bedroom, looked up North America on MapQuest.

"Go north," Spain said. "To Canada."

I did it. When the border between Canada and New York State appeared, he pressed the sketch up against the screen.

"The parallel lines don't match exactly," he said. "But what if they represent the Canada–New York border? What if that box attached to the far left is really the Great Lakes region?"

"S," I said. "Southern?"

"C," he said. "Canada?"

"Southern Canada?" Seemed a little sketchy to me. "Who ever talks about 'Southern' Canada—or would mark it on a map that way? Wouldn't you just put 'Canada' on it? It's not like it needs to be labeled. Everybody knows it's up there. Even Jimmy isn't that dense."

Spain nodded, shrugged. For a split second, I thought I made out a hint of a smile on his face.

"Still, we are talking about Jimmy Farrell here," I went on. "Maybe he went north to Lake Desolation to meet up with someone on the sly, then he caught the Northway, made the straight, vertical run to Canada."

"Seems reasonable," he said.

"Maybe," I agreed. "Though, Jimmy had a pretty nice life down here." The two of us stared at the map for another quiet minute before I said, "That nine-millimeter slug tells me that if he went to Canada, he might have very well crossed the border in a pine box."

I folded the sketch and put it back in my desk drawer.

"We can keep on mulling it over until we can be sure what it means," I said. "If it means anything at all."

I remembered the MPEG. Leaning over him, I set my hands on the keyboard, triggered the keys that brought it back up.

"Next item," I said. "Check this out."

I played the MPEG.

"Correct me if I'm wrong," he said. "But now we know for certain that Natalie wants to help us out. We also know she and Jimmy had a pretty friendly relationship and that Marino was aware of it, and even willing to put it on film."

He closed the MPEG for me.

"You sure that's all the evidence you got collected thus far?"

I thought about the lighter. It was Jordan's and I wasn't about to surrender it. Not yet. But the Desolation Kill also came to mind, and the lake of the same name that it fed. I recalled the trash that littered the stream bank—the empty beer can, the used cigarette butts, the used condom. For all I knew an entire slew of evidence pointing to Farrell's disappearance still occupied the site—evidence that I might miss but that a professional detective might spot right away.

I stole a glance at my twenty-five-dollar Target wristwatch. "Six ten," I said. "Still two hours of daylight left." Walking out of the bedroom, I asked, "Wanna take a ride, Spain?"

"Where to?"

"Lake Desolation," I said, picking up my beer, downing what was left of it. "Now that my new partner is a real honest-to-goodness licensed private detective, I'm thinking it might be a good idea to retrace some footsteps."

CHAPTER 42

It took just under a half hour to make it from my North Albany apartment to Greenfield in my Jeep. As we came upon the metal bridge that spanned the stream, I slowed down, pulling into the gravel-covered public fishing access area parking lot.

I got out.

Spain followed.

"Private place when the fish aren't biting," he said, hands stuffed in his jacket pockets. "Peaceful. Good spot to set up an out-of-the-way meeting."

He crouched, studied the lot's gravel surface, focusing his eyes on the many tire tracks that crisscrossed it, the many foot and boot prints that tattooed it, then stood. "Mind showing me where you found the shell casing?"

I did it.

He gazed down at the spot as if it had something more to reveal other than rock and dirt. I moved on toward the path and the stream. Spain took my lead, following me down the path until we came to the edge of the rushing water. I took another look around—under the bridge and beyond it. I stared into the fast-moving water, at the deep green pool. I looked for trout holding steady in the water, just like I used to do when I was a little girl. But I saw nothing but stream and rock.

Strange. Usually there'd at least be fingerlings out there.

Turning back to Spain, I saw him pick up a small stick, saw him pick at the empty beer can and a cigarette butt. He picked and poked at the used condom, the gray, semi-translucent rubbery material flopping over grotesquely with each thrust of the stick. He pulled out a hanky from his back pocket, put the used condom into it, along with its baby-blue wrapper. Out of the corner of my eye, I saw him grab the beer can and a couple of the hand-rolled cigarette butts, setting it all inside the handkerchief as well.

Then, pocketing the evidence in his leather jacket, he pulled out his mobile.

"You mind?"

"Be my guest."

"I've got friends who can help us with this stuff."

"You think that's Farrell's cum inside that condom?"

Spain's face went red. "Yeah, I think it could very well be his DNA in there."

"Won't know for sure unless we have it tested, right?"

He nodded. Called his friends.

"I have a job that needs attention," he said into the phone a beat later. He mumbled a few other directives that didn't make a whole lot of sense to me. When he hung up and pocketed the phone, he looked into my face.

"APD Forensics?" I said. "They your friends?"

"Sort of," he said.

"You don't think the condom and beer can belong to a couple of local kids doing a little partying and…well…whatever?"

"What do you think?" he said. "There's a reason you brought me out here, and I think this is it."

"You're right, Spain. What if that condom and those cig butts belonged to a particular couple of people long past adolescence?"

He looked all around—at the running stream, then beyond it to the still lake, the setting sun reflecting off of its glass-like surface. "Jesus, it's pretty here. But if you're an adult, why not just get a room somewhere? I mean, why meet here, of all places, on the same Saturday you're trying to split town for good?"

I shook my head. Suddenly, the taping compound buckets stored in the back of Farrell's car came to mind as if my gut were trying to alert me. Trying to alert me to a connection. But I couldn't figure out anything to do with the image. With any of this. "Doesn't make a whole lot of sense, does it?"

But I did know this: I did believe Farrell came to this place, and there had to be a reason for it. There had to be a reason he met someone at this very spot. And there had to be a reason for that spent 9mm casing.

I started walking back up the bank. "Let's get back in the Jeep, Spain."

"Where to now?"

"Back to Dott's Garage," I said. "I want to take another look at those stinky buckets, together."

CHAPTER 43

I stopped about a hundred yards up from the main entrance to Dott's garage. I pulled the Jeep off the rural road, parked it inside a thick patch of pine trees and briars across from the yard. It was almost full night, but we waited for total darkness to fall outside the tall perimeter privacy fence before approaching the gate on foot.

It was chained and padlocked, but that was good news. It meant Dott had gone home for the night.

"Got a plan, Spike?" Spain said.

"Underneath the Jeep driver's seat you'll find a framing hammer," I said. "Go grab it for me."

He took off. When he came back with the equalizer, I took it from him, told him to take a step back.

"I've got a sidearm," he said. "I can blow a hole in it."

"Or I can use my quieter equalizer, avoid attracting unwanted attention."

I raised the hammer, brought it down onto the padlock. It shattered on the first swing.

Spain smiled. "You're pretty handy with that thing," he said.

"It's in the blood," I said.

We slipped in through the gate, using the light of the moon and the few pole-mounted spotlights to guide us through the darkness. Far as I could see, old man Dott didn't believe in surveillance security cameras. But that didn't mean they weren't there somewhere, filming our every step. It was a chance we had to take.

We found Farrell's BMW where we had left it.

"I suppose you have the keys," Spain said.

"You didn't keep them yesterday when I handed them over to you?"

"I set them on the hood of the car and split before Dott caught sight of me."

I held up the equalizer.

"That should work," he said. "But I don't think Farrell would like it."

I inverted the hammer, claw end down, jamming the claws into the narrow space between the trunk and the lock that secured it. I yanked back with both hands. The lock released and the trunk rose slowly.

The buckets weren't there.

Spain stared into the trunk along with me. It was as if we expected the buckets to somehow reappear out of the thin night air.

I turned, faced the dark yard. "I think that whatever was in those buckets was important enough for somebody to come back here and take them away."

"Ya think?" Spain grinned.

"OK, wiseass," I said, "whoever wanted the buckets just wanted the buckets. They didn't want anything to do with Farrell's impounded ride. Which tells me they snuck in here and somehow opened the trunk without jimmying it open."

"Who'd have a key other than Dott?"

"Tina," I said. "Maybe her father."

Just outside the front gate, a truck pulled up. It was Dott's old tow truck.

"Run away," I said.

Together, we ran for the perimeter fence. Ducking down, we watched as the grease-pit-overall-wearing Dott examined the broken padlock. We watched him peer over one shoulder and then the other, like he got the feeling he was being watched. After a time, he got back inside his tow truck and drove in through the gate.

Spain and I held our ground, tucked out of sight.

Dott wasn't about to take any chances. Once through the gate, he stopped the tow truck, got out. He had a pistol gripped in his right hand. He walked the few feet back to the gate, looked over his left shoulder, then his right. After a nervous beat, he made his way back to the truck's passenger side. He opened the door, and even though we couldn't see him from our angle, I knew he was reaching for something inside his glove box. He came back out with a flashlight.

Making his way around the front of the truck, he scanned the immediate perimeter with the white beam of light. Once satisfied that nobody was out there waiting to jump him in the dark, he made his way to the office door, where he pulled on the doorknob. It was still locked. Much to his relief, I was sure. Still, he pointed the beam of flashlight into the office through the door glass, just to be sure. When he found the office to be empty, he killed the flashlight, made his way back around to the passenger side of the truck. He pulled out two white five-gallon taping compound buckets identical to the ones that were now missing from Farrell's ride. He carried them to his office, where he set them down to unlock the door. Opening the door, he carried the buckets inside, then came back out and retrieved two more, then one more after that.

Spain turned to me. "Looks like Dott's been keeping busy."

"Working for Farrell and Marino," I said. "Let's go."

We ran for the open gate and snuck our way back out onto the main road. Under the cover of the night, we sprinted the hundred yards of open road to the Jeep.

Funny how the course of events can change in an instant.

CHAPTER 44

I called Tommy, asked him to look up as much dirt on Dott as he could find. Where he lived or stayed; if he had partners, silent or otherwise. In my head, I saw Tommy seated at Lanie's, perpetual bottle of Budweiser set before him on the bar. I knew his laptop would be stored inside his pickup. I pictured him sliding off the stool, heading out of the bar to use it.

By the time he called me back, we were ten minutes out from Albany.

"Dott's first name is Victor," he said. "Owns the garage outright. Bought it off his partner back in seventy-nine—one Robert Becher, mean old bastard who shot himself in the head when one of his daughters married a Catholic behind his back."

"Where's Victor live these days?"

"This is where it gets a little interesting. Victor Dott owns most of the north side property that abuts Lake Desolation. You know, right where the Desolation Kill feeds the lake at the Malden Bridge. The state owns the right-of-way to the public fishing access area, but Dott owns the rest of it. About two hundred fifty acres."

I felt my pulse pick up a little. "Quite the little land baron," I said, the warm phone pressed against my ear as I drove. "Who owns the rest of the lakefront property?"

"Assorted farmers, most of them living just above poverty level, or out of business entirely. Word is they're looking to sell out—excuse me, fucking *desperate* to sell out. But here's the catch. They want to sell, but only for a premium, like they can have their cake and swallow it too. My uncle was a farmer. You know how fuckin' stubborn those old-timers can be?"

Interesting, I thought. *The entire lake is for sale by a bunch of broke but hardheaded farmers. The few hundred acres that surrounds the Desolation Kill is owned by a guy who's probably connected to Farrell and Marino.*

"Anything else?"

"That's about it," Tommy said.

"Keep your phone close," I said.

I told Spain what Tommy told me.

"The reason for the Desolation Kill becoming a popular destination for Farrell is suddenly taking shape," he said.

"Be nice to know what kind of shape," I said. "But what we do know is that the stream, the lake, the property, old man Dott, and those five-gallon buckets of stinky little clams have a whole lot to do with it."

"So does a nine-millimeter shell casing, maybe." Spain grinned. "And maybe a used Trojan."

"Sex marks the spot, maybe," I said. "Which is precisely why we're going back to the Thatcher Street tittie bar."

CHAPTER 45

The usual collection of pickups and Harleys were parked outside Thatcher Street.

Before we got out of the Jeep, I told Spain to hang on a minute. Told him I had a plan. When I finished relaying it to him, we both got out. But before I made my way to the front door of the pub, I reached under the driver's seat, felt for the equalizer, and made certain the handle was positioned perfectly, just in case I needed it in a hurry.

I nodded toward the bar's front door. "You go first," I said. "Just like I told you."

"You sure about this?" he said. "Could be a tough crowd in there."

"I'm a construction project manager, Spain. I'm used to tough crowds. 'Sides…"

"Besides what, Spike?"

"Things get rough, I'll protect you."

"Thanks," he said. "Anything else you might wanna say to complete my castration?"

I grinned.

He frowned and led the way through the door of the Thatcher Street Pub.

Exactly as I'd planned.

The place was dark and subdued. It smelled like a cross between old beer and twenty-four-hours-without-a-shower armpits.

To our immediate left, a couple of bikers dressed in black leathers were shooting pool. To our right, about half the barstools were occupied with solitary drinkers hunched over bottled beer and whiskey chasers. I knew that, once Albany Development had its way, this hole-in-the-wall would be torn down to its foundations to make way for a high-end casino. The bikers and barflies would have to find another topless juke joint to pickle their livers.

We approached the bar at the far end closest to the door and sat down on two free stools. When a young woman came out of the kitchen at the bar's opposite end, it was immediately apparent she was not Natalie. This woman was a small but well-built Asian, long, smooth black hair draping her chiseled face. She wasn't topless, but wore a skimpy baby-blue string bikini, the material of which would have fit inside my right fist. She took notice of her new customers and approached us. But the closer she came, the more she looked like a teenager, not a young woman. Maybe a high school senior, if that.

"What can I getcha?"

When she smiled, I couldn't be sure if it was out of politeness or how out of place we looked. I guessed the latter.

Spain went to work playing cop, pulling out a false cop badge he kept in his wallet, flashing it. "I'm inquiring about an employee," he said. "A bartender named Natalie. Maybe you know her."

I took a glance around the bar and its leather- and denim-clad patrons. I didn't recognize anyone from the previous evening. Not even Gray Beard was there. Maybe he didn't show up unless Natalie showed. I guess it didn't matter. Everyone was keeping to themselves. You might think a couple of strangers like us would be the object of their fascination. Maybe even ridicule. But rather than expose their faces to a cop, the sparse crowd laid low. One guy went so far as to bury his face in his arms, feigning booze-induced sleep.

"Yes, of course I know Natalie," the bartender said. "I'm filling in for her tonight."

"And your name is?" Spain asked.

"Leesa," she smirked. "No I, two E's."

"Natalie couldn't make it tonight?" I barged in.

Leesa without an "I" looked at me. "Who the hell are you?" she said.

"I'm the bad cop, missy," I said. "By the way, you old enough to be working in a place where you show tits and ass? Maybe I should be asking for some real ID rather than that fake shit you been showing the owner."

The place went dead-zone quiet.

The attitude on Leesa's face melted away. "Natalie never showed up this afternoon for her shift," she said.

"That common for Natalie?" I pressed.

She shrugged narrow shoulders, pursing her lips. "Not common. But not uncommon. If you know what I mean."

"No, Leesa," Spain said, "we don't know what you mean."

"Well, sometimes people party too much the night before. Can't make it in the next day." She laughed a little, cocked her head like, *Shit happens.*

"Natalie a big drinker?" I asked.

"Come to think of it, not really."

"You know if she's on the pill?"

Leesa blinked. "What?"

"She use rubbers, she take the pill, use a diaphragm, an IUD, or all of the above?"

"How would I know? And what's it to you?"

"It means something, trust me. You guys work together. You like her, I can tell. You're close. So I figure birth control might have come up in conversation one way or another."

Another shoulder shrug. "Condoms, I think," she said. "She smokes. The pill was gonna give her a heart attack sooner or later or some shit like that."

I shot a glance at Spain. I knew we were thinking the same thing: another crumb of evidence pointing to the used condom now tucked away in his jacket pocket, along with some spent cigarette butts.

"You know what brand cigarettes she smokes?" I said.

She cocked her head. "Rolls her own. Too much cancer-causing nastiness in commercial cigs, she said."

It took all of my willpower not take hold of Spain's arm and scream, *Bingo.*

"Any idea when she'll be working again?" I pressed.

"She's on the schedule for tomorrow, two to eight." Another grin. "I'm kind of hoping she doesn't show again. I could use the extra hours."

"Good tips?" Spain said.

"Ching…It's what it's all about," Leesa said.

I got up off the stool, fished inside my jeans pocket for a business card, set it down on the bar. Stealing a stubby pencil from the lotto quick-draw display, I wrote on the back of the card, *We need to talk.* Then I dug a twenty I couldn't really spare out of my pocket, folded the card in it.

"Can you make sure Natalie gets my card?" I said, replacing the pencil to the quick draw. "She can call me day or night."

Leesa dug the cash and the card off the bar with black-painted stiletto fingernails that made the teeth on a backhoe bucket look small. She tucked away the bill in her bra and stole a glancing look at my card. "Thought you were a cop?" she said.

"I am," I said. "That's my cover."

She squinted at me, not sure if she should believe me. "Natalie in some kind of trouble?"

"Not at all," I lied. "Just need to ask her a few questions about one of her regular customers."

I got up, tossing Leesa a nod. No smile.

Before we turned to leave, Spain took a good look around the room again, at the men hiding their faces. "You boys can go back to your livers," he barked. "And let's not forget the child support payments."

Half the guys in the place winced, but no one said a word.

The PI knew how to play a role.

He opened the door for me. I stepped out into the night. I hadn't opened the Jeep driver's side door all the way when a hand reached out and grabbed my arm.

I was thrown against the Jeep's rear side panel.

Out of the corner of my eye, I saw someone grab Spain. Then the Jeep separated us, my back to the driver's side.

The man facing me was tall, weight-lifter stacked, biceps bursting through a black T-shirt that had the sleeves cut off. Printed on the black T-shirt was *Black Cat Elliot.* I recognized the name. It belonged to a local punk rock band famous for its loud, fast, violent electric noise. The man's head was shaved. He sported a black goatee and mustache. His tight Levi's were stained with gray ready mix spatter. So were his work boots.

"Pouring a little concrete today?" I said. "Or were you just playing in it like a good little slammer?"

He glared at me, showing me his brown teeth. I could smell the booze on his breath and the concrete lime on his clothes. "You know what happens to butch bitches can't mind their own fuckin' business?" he said.

"No, what happens, Slammer?"

Slammer reached into his back pocket, pulled out a sheetrock knife, thumbed open the razor blade, held it up in front of my face.

My right hand moving slowly, I felt inside the already open driver's side door. Bending at the knees, I quickly reached under the seat, grabbed the equalizer, and yanked it out. Gripping it tight, I raised the hammer like I was about to shatter his skull with it.

"Tell me, Slammer," I said. "What happens to butch bitches who don't mind their business?"

I felt my mouth go dry, my heart pounding against my ribs. Behind me, I heard Spain issue a heartfelt "Fuck you" to the goon trying to take him on. "Go ahead," Spain added, calm and cool, like he was used to this kind of thing. "Try me. Take a swipe with that little bitty knife."

"He got a sheetrock knife on you, Spain?" I said.

"Black and Decker," he said, following with a laugh. The PI was acting tough, but we both knew the damage a sheetrock knife could do once it pierced the skin on your face.

Slammer pressed his lips together. He ground his teeth.

Coming from behind, I heard the scuffle of boots on gravel and a deep thud, like a hammerhead slammed into a pumpkin. That was immediately followed by a body hitting the ground. What followed were the noises a full-grown man makes when he's heaving his guts. Spain must have nailed the goon in the gut with an uppercut.

"One down," Spain said.

"Get in the Jeep," I said.

He did it. I heard the door shut.

Slammer kept shifting his focus from me to his fallen comrade and back to me again. He'd lost his advantage and now he was afraid. His Adam's apple bouncing up and down in his throat proved it.

I reached into my jacket pocket with my free hand, pulled out the keys, and tossed them into the open-topped Jeep.

"Start it up," I said.

Spain did that too.

The equalizer still poised in my right hand, I backed up and slipped in behind the wheel. Shifting the hammer to my left hand, I put the Jeep in reverse and backed out of the lot, my eyes never leaving Slammer.

We didn't say a word for what seemed a while.

Then Spain said, "Let me guess...Marino's men."

"Sent to instill the fear of God in us," I said. "Those guys are used to hard labor twenty-four-seven. Then, for fun, they lift weights, get drunk, and go to death metal punk rock shows. They wanted to fuck us up, they would've fucked us up."

Spain turned to me while I came to a stop at the stop sign.

"You scared?" he said.

"No," I said. "I'm just really, really pissed off."

He was quiet for a beat. Until he said, "You know what happens if Natalie is a no-show again tomorrow?"

"Allow me to speculate," I said. "We'll have no choice but to look for two people."

"Question is," Spain said, "are the two people going to be alive when we find them?"

CHAPTER 46

I hit the directional for hooking a right turn onto the Concrete Pearl.

"Go the other way," Spain said.

"I live that way," I said, cocking my head over my shoulder.

"I'm shaking," he said, running both hands over his cropped scalp. "Happens every time I get into a fight. A drink is the only thing that helps."

I stared out onto a desolate Pearl Street. I knew that if I went home, I would be up for hours thinking about Natalie—about the spent shell casing, about the used condom, about the five-gallon buckets, about my ten grand, about that sick little boy, about Marino's thugs—about *all* the evidence that pointed to the fact that Farrell was into something a lot deeper than cheating on his asbestos removals. And that meant I was in deep too. Buried alive.

"What the hell," I said, switching the directional for a left hook.

I pulled out onto Pearl and drove.

When I passed the now abandoned KeyBank building where Jordan took his final fall, I looked away and swallowed my heart.

At Spain's suggestion, we headed uptown to a watering hole called the Lark Tavern. One of the oldest bars in the city, the Lark was a long, dimly lit place with the interior walls finished off in a glossy red-and-black paint. Almost every bit of wall space was covered with old memorabilia, old photos, and old posters from World War II all the way up through Nixon's '70s to the '80s punk scene. A plaster Elsie the Cow's head was mounted to the wall directly above the jukebox. No doubt it had been ripped off the exterior wall of the old abandoned downtown Sealtest factory.

As soon as we'd stepped through the front wooden door, we were greeted by Tess, Lark Tavern's longtime proprietor and owner. Rather, Spain was greeted by her. Tess hadn't changed a bit since I last saw her, back when I was still in my early twenties. She still had long auburn hair, deep-green pools for eyes, and milk-white breasts that looked like they were about to spill out of her long black velvet dress.

Spain kissed her on the mouth.

"Hello, stranger," Tess said, her voice deep, raspy.

He made a hand gesture at me. "Tess, this is Spike."

Her green eyes lighting up, Tess did something totally unexpected. She opened up her long arms, wrapped them around me, and hugged me tightly. She was all firm flesh and she smelled of roses. "How is the goddamned foot these days, Spike Harrison?"

She had an elephant's memory. Beauty *and* brains.

"God, Tess, you are good," I said.

"Honey," she laughed, "in my business, you start forgetting faces, you might as well count the till for the last time."

The long front bar was crowded just like I remembered it, with a mixture of young, middle-aged, and even gray-haired uptown clientele. Coming from the back dining room was loud rock music. Tess must have noticed me noticing the band.

She said, "Those are my boys, the Blisterz, with a 'Z.' They've got a perpetual Tuesday-night spot on the back stage. You can tell they earn it, huh?" The crowd was thick and thrashing.

Taking me by the hand, she escorted us through the bar to a table in back positioned up against the far wall. It was the only empty table left. Probably reserved for VIPs. We sat down and Tess personally took the drink order for us.

Spain locked his eyes on mine while the Blisterz kicked off into some fast punk melody reminiscent of the Ramones or the Clash. Bands I dug way back in high school and college. Bands I'd still dig if only I had the time to go out to the bars at night like I used to. The bass, drums, and electric guitar were loud and pounding. But the force of their melodic sound was a good thing. And the singer/guitarist's raspy voice came through roaring and clear and haunting.

Raising his right hand, Spain tossed a wave at the lead singer—a tall, salt-and-pepper-haired guy who wore tan surfer-dude capris that fell just below his knees, a cut-off T-shirt, and Vans sneakers. His picking hand left his guitar just long enough to return Spain's gesture.

Spain shot me a sly grin. It gave me the distinct impression that he'd planned all this, that his wanting to go out for an off-the-clock drink hadn't been so spontaneous or prompted by Marino's thugs and our little scuffle with them.

Tess brought our drinks, along with a couple of menus. She didn't bother to talk above the rock and roll. She simply puckered up and blew us a kiss before walking back into the bar.

We sat and listened to the Blisterz finish their set. When it was over and the quiet settled back in, I turned to Spain. "Something tells me you're more than just one of Tess's regulars."

"That obvious, huh?"

He cocked his head, pursed his lips, and took a quick drink of his beer. "Tess has connections," he explained, his gray eyes now peering out onto an empty stage. "On occasion, she's been known to help me out with certain bits of information I might not otherwise be privy to."

"By legal means?" I questioned.

But he shrugged that off to talk about the guys in the house band, the Blisterz with a "Z." "They've been known to run some errands for Tess to make ends meet," he admitted. "And for me."

"They the guys you were talking to on the cell phone up at Lake Desolation?"

Spain nodded, took another drink.

"OK," I said. "Nothing wrong with teaming up, if you're sure about the team."

"I am."

"Good enough for me. So what kind of help are we after from the team tonight?"

He took a quick drink, set his beer back down. He was about to say something when a waitress approached the table, pad and pencil in hand. But before we said a word, she grew a wide smile.

"Uncle Damien!" she said, reaching in, giving the black-clad PI a smack on the cheek. Her voice had an odd quality to it. She couldn't exactly pronounce her words correctly. Then I noticed the smallish hearing aids in both her ears.

He held the small, attractive, dark-haired young lady tightly. "Hello, my beautiful girl," he said. Then, nodding at me, "This is my friend, Spike. We're working on something together." When he spoke, he looked directly in her face so she could see his lips.

She looked at me, gave me an up-and-down glare, obviously sizing me up.

"How do you do?" I said, my eyes locked on hers.

Spain ordered for us both. Two strip steaks medium rare, baked potatoes on the side, oil and vinegar on the house salads. With a nod and a bright smile, his niece turned and took off with our orders.

I filled the silence that followed by asking him if the waitress was really his niece. "In spirit only," he told me. Then I asked him what was on his mind that we needed a nice quiet table in order to discuss it.

He sat back in the booth, the fingers on his right hand tap-tapping his beer bottle.

"I can be certain Farrell's been cheating on asbestos removal for a number of years, which means he's good at it," he said. "So why get caught now?"

"Why not now?" I said.

"My investigation tells me that the PS 20 scenario has likely been played out a dozen times before in a dozen different towns across the state. But for some reason, this time it not only blows up into a major scandal; Farrell, the man ultimately responsible, goes missing. And we got two gorillas threatening to kick our respective asses if we keep snooping around."

I drank down the rest of my beer.

Spain drank the rest of his.

"Where's this going?" I said.

"I've been wondering about Diana Stewart," he said.

"She used to work for me," I said. "For my dad, really."

"Don't you think she's found reason to come down on Farrell in the past for faulty asbestos-removal practices? Correct me if I'm wrong, but as far as I can tell, this is the first time she's actually ordered the red-flagging of a Farrell job site. At the same time, she's making a spectacle of it, calling PS 20 contaminated with asbestos, a cancer factory, unsuitable for human habitation."

"She didn't exactly say all that."

"OK, but she did use the words 'asbestos contamination,' and don't forget about that poor kid Nicolas Boni." He looked away. "Christ, she's making it sound like there's no possible way PS 20 will ever be rid of the asbestos." Raising his hands, he added, "Another Pearl Street building slated for the wrecking ball."

"You smelling a conspiracy in the works, Spain?"

Spain gave a noncommittal shrug. "Maybe. I guess what I'm asking is this: Why has Stewart chosen now to make a big deal over an asbestos scam that looks to me likes it's been going on for years?"

He was asking the right questions, but I wasn't sure if any of them could be answered. And I told him so. Then I said, "Take a step back, Spain. Under normal circumstances, you want to cheat on asbestos removal, you gotta learn to hit and run."

He scrunched his brow, sat back in the booth. "What's that mean?"

"It means, Spain, that you can get away with a lot of under-the-radar shit in this business so long as you don't hang around too long."

"Example."

"OK, I once heard about a general contractor who would cheat on the small stuff in order to increase his profits."

"Small stuff."

"Stuff no one would notice. Not even the engineers and architects when they made their inspections. Maybe he would buy a less expensive brand of aluminum ties for the brickwork—a reinforcing tie that was cheaper and less sturdy than what the project specifications called for. The specified tie might cost two bucks apiece, but by substituting it with a fifty-cent job, you're able to make up some good pocket money, especially if a project calls for ten or twenty thousand of them.

"Or maybe the GC would use a few hundred yards less backfill when paving over a parking lot. Or maybe he'd go with a cheaper concrete design mix on the concrete footing and foundation work."

"Sounds dangerous," he said. "Reckless."

"Not at all. Every contractor knows that engineers over-engineer to protect their licenses and their ever-expanding asses. Listen, two-thousand-PSI concrete will hold up a ten-story building for all eternity just as well as four-thousand-pound PSI and it costs a hell of a lot less."

"Less enough to risk cheating? They test for concrete strength, don't they?"

I nodded. "Yeah, they do. But you wanna know how much a testing tech makes per year?"

He looked at me.

"'Bout thirty and change," I said. "Mason laborers without a high school degree do better than that. A lot better."

"So what are you saying?"

"I'm telling you that bullshit walks."

"All you gotta do is grease somebody, is that it?"

"You gotta grease the right palm, do it all under the radar, and maintain the practice of hit-and-run. Just like Jimmy Farrell, who, by all appearances, has most definitely hit and run away. Dead or alive."

The PI grabbed his surrogate niece's attention with a quick above-the-head wave. Holding up two fingers, he mouthed the words "Two more."

While she retrieved the drinks, I began giving him my personal Diana Stewart history lesson. I continued through all of the second drink, through all of a third, and through much of our steaks. I finished over coffee.

"Personal vengeance," he said, having taken in my whole story. "You both loved the same man. You won."

"But lost when he died," I said.

"So did she. Maybe more so because not only did Jordan choose to love you, he died on your watch."

I felt my dinner go south. But Spain detected the pain on my face plain enough.

"I apologize," he said. "Definitely wrong choice of words."

"You really think so, Spain?"

"Seriously, sorry. But I understand where the motive could come from now," he said. "Stewart has always harbored jealousy of you. Maybe hatred. Now that you're implicated in Farrell's asbestos scam, she blasts you with both barrels—"

"The Tiger Lady has been blasting me with both barrels for more than year." My voice was raised enough for the couple at the next table to turn and stare. I lowered my head. "I'm sorry," I said. "It's been a while now since I lost Jordan, but—"

"But it's never enough time. I know from personal experience."

"You still love your wife?"

"I love my son more."

We drank our coffees. I patted the pockets on my leather jacket for the cigarettes. I guess the habit had already sunk back in. Digging into my jacket pocket, I felt not my cigs, but something else. I pulled it out.

"Last night, when the Tiger Lady came to see me," I said, "she left this behind along with her pack of Marlboro Lights."

I set the lighter onto the table. I was ready to reveal it to him.

Spain picked it up, stared at it. "New York Giants," he said. "My team."

"Jordan's too," I said. "In fact, that was Jordan's lighter."

His eyes went wide. "You sure about that?" he asked. "How would she have it?"

"Look," I said, "she and Jordan worked a lot together. And he was forever leaving his cigarette lighters lying around—"

"How many years since he…"

"Died. You can say it. It's OK."

"Well…"

"Five."

"Then how do you know this particular lighter is his?"

"I just know. I was his wife."

He nodded.

"But there could be nothing to her having the lighter, other than the fact that she's had it for as long as she has."

"And that it still has fuel," he said. "Like she's been saving it, rationing the fuel." As if to lose the flame would be to lose Jordan again. He went to store it in his jacket pocket. "You mind if I hang onto it for a while?"

I shook my head, though the truth of the matter was that I did mind. But we were working together now. "What are you going to do with it?"

"Add it to the physical evidence," he said, pocketing the lighter. "Don't worry," he added. "I won't lose something this precious."

Over my left shoulder, I caught sight of all three Blisterz approaching the table from out of the bar. Two of them just nodded at Spain as they passed, but the tall one—the singer—handed him a manila envelope and kept on walking.

"Thank you, Davey," Spain said to the musician's back and set the envelope down onto the table.

"You gonna show me what's in the envelope, Spain?"

He opened the clasps, pulled out three or four glossy pics—eight-by-ten full-color jobs, probably printed off an ink-jet printer onto some glossy stock. The first pic showed Stewart engaged in various OSHA duties. One shot was taken from a distance with what had to be a high-powered lens. The Tiger Lady was dressed in pressed jeans, work boots, a blue cotton work shirt, and a white hard hat with *OSHA* printed on both sides in bright-red letters. In the photo, she was surrounded by some of her OSHA support staff. They were standing by an exterior brick wall that had collapsed. There was an EMT van parked in the near distance beside a project sign that read, *Renovations to the Historic Albany Public Library.*

"I know that job," I said. "I worked up a bid on it late last year. It was too high. Marino was awarded the contract instead. But after the wall collapsed this past winter, OSHA and its on-staff civil engineers declared the building unsafe for habitation, never mind its historic significance. No amount of temporary shoring or foundation work could save the place. So what had been a pricey historic renovation turned into a demo job for Marino. Today the site's just another empty lot along the lower Concrete Pearl."

"A lot no doubt slated for the future new-and-improved Pearl Street," Spain said. Then, "Next photo."

Stewart in action again. This time standing atop a fifth-floor balcony of another commercial project I recognized—the conversion of a century-and-a-half-old Hudson Riverside textile mill, a turn-of-the-century sweatshop being renovated into luxury condominiums and apartments.

I told Spain as much. I also told him that those new upscale condos were located in South Albany, adjacent to the port, behind Pearl Street. So close to the port, in fact, you could see the docked ships in the near distance. Soon enough those docks would be replaced with a brand-new state-of-the-art aquarium, the port itself relocated south to Hudson. Albany Development Limited would be the financiers. Marino Construction would be the project manager for the job.

I sat back in the booth. "Now that I think of it," I added, "Marino had been the construction manager for the riverside condo complex."

"Did you toss a bid in too?"

"Project principals wouldn't let me, not with my crumbling health-and-safety record."

"Why do you think Stewart got involved?"

"The job contained considerable asbestos removal. It's a good bet A-1 Environmental Solutions was awarded the subcontract for the job. I can't be sure, Spain. But seeing as his father-in-law acted as the construction manager, there's a fair shot that he was."

Spain pointed at the photo with an extended index finger. "What's she holding there?"

In the photo, Stewart was holding a meter of some kind in both her hands—a meter not unlike the one the OSHA team had used for testing the interior air quality at PS 20 on Monday. The only difference was this meter wasn't used for detecting asbestos fibers. It was used to sniff out radon. Or so I relayed it to a very interested Spain.

"The media hounds jumped and humped all over the story," I said. "When the carcinogen radon was found to exist on-site in excessive amounts, the Tiger Lady declared the project uninhabitable. So what had been a high-profile rehab for Marino now morphs into another big-ass demo project and a site eventually slated for the new convention center."

"Looks like we got us a pattern here," Spain said.

Third photo.

This one proved different from all the rest in one respect: it didn't show Stewart and OSHA in the act of inspecting a downtown job site. Instead, it showed her emerging from a downtown steakhouse—677 Prime on Broadway, maybe a block up from central Pearl. The most expensive joint in town. Shocker of shockers, the OSHA chief was walking side by side with Peter Marino. The photo had been shot on a clear, starry evening, million-dollar smiles painting both their faces. Marino in one of his well-cut double-breasted suits, Stewart in a navy-blue miniskirt and matching jacket, red hair bobbing freely at her shoulders.

One more person occupied the background—a man, just coming out of the doors. Tall, lanky, and instead of being dressed in a suit, he had on white trousers and loafers without socks. He also wore what looked to be a double-breasted blue blazer. A golden boy born right out of the *Preppy Handbook*. If I didn't know any better, I would have pegged the man's ID as Farrell in the flesh.

"This ain't all about Farrell and Marino," I said. "It's about Stewart too."

"Is it unusual for Stewart to declare buildings unsafe for human habitation?"

"Not at all. Condemning one site after the other is a big part of her job."

"Especially when it's convenient."

"What the hell is going on in Albany, Spain?"

"The Concrete Pearl is being bought up, that's what's going on. And your school is in the way." Looking me in the eyes, he said, "Let me ask you something. Did Marino put a bid in on the PS 20 project?"

"Sure. But he was high by about thirty grand."

"What was the job's total cost?"

"Little shy of three million."

"What's your profit percentage on that?"

"One or two percent, if I'm lucky."

"How much profit did you actually tack on to the PS 20 final cost?"

"Nothing. I needed work desperately. I took the job at cost, just so I could get it."

His eyes grew wide. "By cutting out your profit," he said, "you stole PS 20 right out from under Marino."

"And now that his son-in-law conveniently contaminated the place," I said, "he's about to get the job back."

A magic lightbulb turned on bright over my head. "Or maybe Farrell didn't have to contaminate the place at all, so long as the test results were rigged."

Spain sat back hard, nodded in agreement.

My BlackBerry vibrated while I shoved the photos back inside the envelope.

CHAPTER 47

I didn't recognize the phone number. I excused myself, got up out of the booth, and made my way quickly out a side door that accessed the Lark Tavern parking lot. I answered the phone on the final ring before the answering service took over.

"Spike!" the caller barked.

Tommy.

"You're shouting," I said.

"From in jail," he said. "Pearl Street precinct."

I felt my heartbeat pick up. "What happened?"

"I went to the PS 20 job site, checked around. I saw that somebody fucked with the top-floor window, broke in through the asbestos protection."

"Christ, Tommy, that was me…last night."

He didn't say anything.

"I'm coming down to get you," I said. "Sit tight."

"Least you can do, Chief," he said.

I hung up, went back inside the tavern, and retrieved Spain.

CHAPTER 48

I drove downtown, parked out front of the police station. The overweight uniformed cop manning the desk asked me my business.

I told him my name, showed him my driver's license. "You arrested one of my men tonight for doing his job. I'm here to bail him out."

The gray-haired cop studied my license then slid it back across the desk for me. "What about the private dick?" he said, referring to Spain, a slight grin forming out the corner of his mouth.

"He's with me."

The cop looked at me. "You're an attractive woman," he said. "Take my advice. Find a new boyfriend."

"Maybe a fat cop like yourself," Spain spat.

The cop glowered at Spain but hit the button that electronically unlocked the door to the precinct. There was a loud buzz and the solid metal door opened by itself.

"Wait here," I said to Spain.

"With him?" he said, cocking his head at the cop.

"Everybody get along," I said, making my way to the door.

Tommy wasn't behind bars. He was sitting at one of the metal desks. A uniformed cop was sitting there with him. They were both sharing a bag of Dunkin' Donuts. They were both laughing.

I felt a ray of sunshine in my stomach. "You want I should come back later?" I said.

Tommy looked up at me, his mouth full of strawberry jelly donut.

The cop stood. He was thin, about Tommy's age. "Tommy and I went to Waterford High School together," he said. "Class of 'sixty-eight. Shipped us both off to 'Nam, same rotation. Just in time for Tet."

"Why the hell you bust him?" I said.

"Take it easy, Spike. Kevin's just doing his job."

"Why'd you bust him for checking out the site like a good contractor, Kevin?" I said.

"Site's been red-flagged," he said. "Unauthorized personnel are considered trespassers."

"How you know Tommy's unauthorized?"

Kevin wiped his mouth with a white napkin. "I didn't, actually. We got tipped off by an anonymous caller. Called himself a 'concerned citizen.'"

Tommy and I looked at one another. "Spies," I said. Marino's henchmen came to mind.

"The establishment is coming down hard on us, Spike old girl."

"I ain't old yet, Tommy. But this keeps up…"

"I personally checked the situation out," Kevin said. "That's when I saw him up on the scaffolding and that, by the looks of it, the fourth floor had been broken into."

Tommy looked at me again. He was keeping his mouth shut, powder-covered lips and all.

"You really bust Tommy, or is he just a detainee?"

"There's no bail to speak of. No hearing. Just a warning." He sat back down, pushing away the bag of donuts. "I do, however, require your signature for him on the complaint."

He handed me a clipboard. I studied it. It had been written in near-illegible handwriting. Cop handwriting. Although it hadn't been signed by anyone at OSHA, the complaint had been officially lodged by them. Interesting. While Marino had his thugs tailing me, OSHA had her spies glued to me, and Tommy also. I signed it and handed the clipboard back to Kevin the cop. He tore off the pink copy and handed it to me.

I folded it, stuffing it into my jacket pocket. "Let's go, Tommy," I said.

He got up and shook hands with his old friend. "Next time, doughnuts are on me, pal," he said.

CHAPTER 49

We dropped Tommy off at his apartment after stopping at a convenience store so he could pick up "a quick six-pack." Then we drove back to my place.

By then it was past eleven. I was dead tired.

Spain followed me to the door. "Good night," he said. But gut instinct told me he wanted to come in. I could read the want in one eye, the loneliness in the other. For a moment, I thought about inviting him in. It had been a long time since I enjoyed some alone time with an attractive man. But then every time I was tempted to take the step, I pictured Jordan's face. The beautiful face I married and the shattered face that stared up at me from down on the ground beside the scaffolding tower.

"Lock your doors when you get home," I said.

"That's supposed to be my line," he said.

As he turned for his refurbished Charger, I let myself into my apartment. The place was dark, like it always is when I come in during the night. But something was different this time. Something didn't feel right.

There was an odd odor in the air. Like cheap cologne. Old Spice, maybe. Same thing my dad soaked himself in whenever he shaved. All cologne smells the same to me. But not Old Spice. That one I knew like I knew my own face.

I flipped on the light, took a look around. Nothing out of place. All books stacked in order on the bookshelves, Mom's antique table set in place up against the wall, television turned off, photos hung level and undisturbed.

For a brief second, I thought about going back outside, grabbing my equalizer. But then I found myself stepping into the kitchen.

Again, nothing out of place.

Inside my bedroom, however, the smell of Old Spice got stronger. I gave the room a quick scan. Nothing had been messed with. Not the dresser of drawers, not my bed. I went to my desk, looked down at the desktop. The laptop was turned off and OK. But when I opened the desk drawer, I got a terrible chill. The chill lodged itself in my sternum. While nothing was missing, my intuition told me someone's hands besides my own had been rummaging around inside the little space. Someone like one of Marino's thugs in search of the evidence I collected up at Lake Desolation?

I pulled out the "Closed Untill Further Notice" note. If one of Marino's men had been in the place, he certainly hadn't known enough to take it.

I took a step back. It had been another long day and I'd had a couple of drinks too many at the Lark Tavern. I might have been imagining things—even the smell of Old Spice.

I tossed the note back inside the drawer, closed it back up, and tried to forget about the whole thing. Back inside the living room, I set the deadbolt and the chain on both doors. In my bedroom, I never bothered to get undressed before I collapsed onto my bed and fell fast asleep.

CHAPTER 50

The BlackBerry vibrating against the nightstand woke me with a start.

I picked it up.

"You awake?" Tommy said.

"You wanna call it that."

He told me to turn on Channel 13. "Now!" he snapped.

I grabbed the clicker off the nightstand, thumbed the power button. The channel was already set to 13 from the previous morning. A commercial was being broadcast—an ad for choosing Time Warner cable over satellite.

"Wow, Tommy, riveting."

"Shut up, Chief. Wait. I caught a little preview."

When the ad was over and the news anchor reappeared, she started in on the headlines for the top of the seven o'clock hour. "The brutal murder of a local Albany bartender tops the news," Chris Collins said into the camera, dark eyes focused on my own through the TV.

She got my attention. I sat up.

The video feed came on. It showed a half dozen APD surrounding the parking lot of PS 20. There was an EMT van parked in the middle of the lot directly beside the construction trailer, the words *Harrison Construction* emblazoned on its side in huge red block letters. Portable sodium lamps illuminated the lot like daylight. Laid out beside the EMT van was what looked like a body with a rubber sheet pulled over it.

A still photograph appeared. It was superimposed over the video feed.

Natalie Barnes, the caption beneath it read, *29-year-old West Albany native.*

Something inside me caved in.

"This the girl Natalie you told me about?" he said. "The topless one from Thatcher Street?"

"Yeah," I said. "That's her."

I told him I'd have to call him back. I hung up.

Collins spewed on about a brutal attack in the parking lot of PS 20, about the local bartender being repeatedly hit over the head with a "common carpenter's framing hammer."

I shot up and out of bed, stood on the bare floor, still dressed in my clothes from the night before. A still shot of a framing hammer appeared on the screen. The hammer was as familiar to me as my own face. A big twenty-two-ounce job with a rounded highbrow head, blue-injected nylon grip, a three-eighths-inch steel band that ran three inches down the handle's backside, and sharply curved raptor claws. A hammer manufactured a whole lot of years ago by a now long-gone company called Dead On. The tool had blood stains on it and little bits of hair.

"Oh Christ," I whispered.

My vision blurred. There was a strange electric hum or buzz coming from inside my head. I grabbed my keys from the counter inside the kitchen, ran back out into the living room, and threw open the back door. I ran around the building to the Jeep. No need to unlock the door, it was already unlocked.

I opened the driver's side door and felt under the seat.

The equalizer was gone.

My heart pushed itself up into my throat.

I ran back inside the apartment and called Spain. He told me to drop everything and run down to the bottom of the Wards Lane hill to the Burger King. He'd pick me up there.

I hung up the phone, threw on my jacket, and stuffed the BlackBerry in the pocket. Keys in hand, I slipped back out of the apartment through the back terrace door.

I ran like hell.

CHAPTER 51

I took a small table set up against the wall by the ladies and men's rooms in the back of the Burger King. There was no one eating in the place that early except for an aged black woman seated at a table a couple up from me, hovering over a breakfast of deep-fried French toast shaped like ladyfingers. She wore a long wool coat even in June and a wool hat that covered her ears.

I pulled the phone out of my jacket pocket and speed-dialed Joel.

He answered after the second ring. He'd heard about the murder and he'd already been on the phone with the DA's office.

The news he had for me was not good.

"Our deal to put a hold on the indictments pending Mr. Spain's independent investigation is off," he said. "Santiago wants to go ahead and prosecute for the PS 20 asbestos-removal negligence case. The APD is in complete agreement with the DA, which means Santiago will also proceed with the indictment for Natalie Barnes's murder. If he's able to fill in the blank spaces between the asbestos scam and Barnes's murder, it could lead to a case of homicide for which you, as an obvious suspect, face probable arrest. Make no mistake about it, this is the real shit, Spike."

I felt numb as I watched the old woman eat her French toast. The voice inside my head kept whispering, *This isn't happening.* But I knew that it was.

"What the hell am I supposed to do, Joel?" I said. "You see me capable of murder?"

"I think if you make an effort to work with Santiago," he said, "maybe work up some sort of plea bargain, things can work in your favor."

"Why would I kill Natalie Barnes? Why isn't somebody finding out who got into my Jeep and stole my equalizer?"

"APD found no prints on the hammer other than your own," he said. "And something else too. The hammer claws have got paint on them. Small amount of black paint they think came off of a car. In this case, Farrell's impounded BMW. It was reported broken into yesterday after the trunk was pried open with a claw hammer. That's *after* somebody smashed open the lock on Dott's front gate, after somebody smashed the taillight on an impounded Hummer, after somebody tried to smash through the window of Farrell's office building."

"I'm trying to find him, Joel—"

"Don't tell me any more. I don't want to know. But I don't have to be a criminal attorney to know that if Farrell winds up dead, those little hammer stunts could very well tie you to his murder after the fact."

I exhaled a breath. "What's the APD cooking up as my motivation?"

"Goes something like this: You've been implicated in an asbestos scam, along with a suspected offender. You've been working with him all along. Colluding with him. And now that he's bolted the scene, you're left alone to take the blame."

"So where does Natalie fit in with this theory?"

"You're lonely, desperate, your construction business failing, your husband dead. Like Natalie, you've fallen in love with Farrell. Maybe you've carried a torch since high school. Now that he ditched you, you want your revenge. Therefore, you killed Natalie."

"A claw hammer to the head," I said. "That poor kid."

"Listen, Spike. The district attorney's office has it all figured out. Nice, neat, and simple."

"So what now, Joel?"

"It pains me greatly to have to do this, Spike," he said while issuing one of his famous big sighs, "but at this point, I'll have to terminate our relationship—"

"Joel—"

"I'm not a criminal lawyer, Spike. I'm a third-generation construction attorney. I know building and construction codes, ASCME specification law, general construction contracts, how to abide by them or how to get out of them in a pinch. But I cannot defend against an accusation of murder."

I hung up just as the old woman stood up, tossing her empty Styrofoam plate into the trash receptacle.

CHAPTER 52

Spain pulled up in his Dodge Charger.

I exited the Burger King out the side door.

Slipped into the passenger side.

He pulled out, hooked a right onto Broadway in the direction of the city.

I stared out the window onto a mirage of concrete and glass.

The world was no longer real for me.

We drove in painful silence.

CHAPTER 53

When we arrived at the Lark Tavern, it was still closed.

The downtown city street outside its black-painted front door was abandoned and littered with empty beer bottles, spent cigarette butts, and discarded pages of newspaper blowing in the wind like tumbleweeds.

Spain drove through the narrow alley to the old building's back lot.

Davey was there to greet us. The tall, black-leather-jacketed rocker was standing inside an open overhead door that led to a garage that housed a red Toyota pickup truck.

"In here," he said, waving us in.

Davey led Spain and me through the garage, down into a basement wine cellar. Tess was waiting for us, along with the other two Blisterz—Drew Blood and Vinnie. Emotionless faces stared at me, their hands buried in their jeans pockets. Like their leader, Davey, they were wearing black leather jackets over black T-shirts. They looked like the second coming of the Ramones.

Tess wore a long red velvet dress, a strand of real pearls dangling from her neck. She looked beautiful, even in the morning after what no doubt had been a long night watching over her bar and its drunken customers.

The cellar was dimly lit and smelled faintly of must and garlic. It wasn't an unpleasant smell. On the opposite side of the room stood a floor-to-ceiling wood-slat wine rack. The Lark Tavern wine cellar was to be my temporary refuge. My safe house.

"How you feeling?" Tess asked.

All I could manage was to shake my head.

Spain asked if he could have a moment alone with me.

Tess turned. "Come on, boys. Let's get the lunch on the fire before we have to open the doors."

Leading the band of aging punk rockers, Tess left the wine cellar, closing the door behind her.

"You don't believe I killed Natalie Barnes," I said after a beat. "So you put your own ass on the line. Tess, Davey, all the rest of them…putting their asses on the line."

Spain bit his bottom lip; his eyes peered down at the tops of his black boots. "Sometimes something comes along you're not equal to. You have no way of beating this alone."

"Like being buried alive."

"I knew on Monday morning you were being set up to take the fall for this shit storm. You knew it too. Otherwise, you wouldn't have abandoned the job site and gone looking for Farrell on your own like that."

"So what about Marino and Farrell?"

"Let's start at the start with what we both know," Spain said. "They've been colluding on specific jobs of their choosing that required asbestos removal, and have been doing so for years now. A general contractor like Marino can slip a subcontractor like Farrell information about the project bids that would guarantee your golden boy getting the project. Let's face it, if Farrell knows the competition's prices, all he has to do is undercut them by a few bucks, and bang-zoom, he's got himself a job.

From there, Farrell removes the asbestos while making it look like he's following standard operating procedure. But in all reality, he's cheating, cutting expensive but specified corners. Not using the right filters or maybe reusing old ones, maybe tossing the asbestos material in some secret landfill that doesn't cost a red cent. Who knows? In turn, his cohorts at Analytical Labs falsify the indoor air quality reports as required."

"So it's really a double scam," I said. "Jimmy and Marino collude on projects that are severely contaminated, and Jimmy cuts corners to save cash. Then there are projects located down on the Concrete Pearl like PS 20 that aren't all that contaminated but that they want for the convention center project. So they get Analytical Labs to pen up some phony reports."

"Bunch of greedy backroom bullshit," Spain commented.

"Collusion and cheating aren't all that different from murder," I said. "Once you get away with the first one, the next one gets a little easier. Especially when your profits start shooting through the roof."

"And then suddenly Jimmy cops an attitude. Dude actually thinks he's contributing to the profits. He thinks he's emerging as this genius businessman. So what if people think he's dumb. He's always known better. He's a late bloomer is all."

"So he gets in his father-in-law's face."

"Exactly. He demands a larger take of the meat pie, or he's closing down the shop, taking his show on the road."

"But Marino won't let him have it. He tells Jimmy to shut up and sit his ass down. Don't bite the hand that's been feeding you."

"Tina employed me to look into her husband's affairs," Spain said. "Although she never said anything about it, I suspect she's known all along about the collusion between her father and husband. How the hell could she not know about it? She must have at least overheard them talking. It would make her complicit in their less-than-legal arrangement."

"Natalie?"

"That's where things get personal between father and son-in-law. We already know Farrell has his blue eyes glued to her. But I now suspect it's possible someone else was falling for her too."

"Marino," I said.

"Marino's wife passed on from stomach cancer fifteen years ago. Lonely man."

"So Natalie maybe wasn't just some video piece of young ass to Marino," I said. "Farrell and his father-in-law could have been fighting over the same woman."

Another one of Spain's half smiles, half smirks. "That would explain the out-of-the-way rendezvous at Lake Desolation. It's possible Marino wanted Farrell dead for two reasons." Spain held up two fingers. "First, he needed Jimmy to die because he'd become a security liability in both the asbestos scam and in the Pearl Street Convention Center." He dropped a finger. "Second, he needed Jimmy gone so that he'd get Natalie all to himself."

"Marino's receptionist made it sound like Peter and Jimmy were fighting over a woman named Natalie this past Saturday morning. But she couldn't be entirely sure what they were fighting about."

"If that's true, Jimmy knew he had no choice but to get the hell out of town. No way he could wage war against his father-in-law and win. So what's he do? He closes down his offices, strips them bare, and fills the Beemer with a tank of gas. He dumps a bunch of hot files at Peter Marino, doodles out a vague map of where he's heading—South Canada. And then—and only a dumbass like Farrell can pull this one off—he absentmindedly uses the same paper to write 'Closed Untill Further Notice' on the other side and Scotch-tapes it to the outside of his office door. From inside his Beemer, he calls Natalie, arranges to meet her at some out-of-the-way destination north of Albany.

"It's a painful, tearful good-bye, but they have one more streamside romp for the road. Jimmy would love nothing more than to stay with her. But Jimmy's in trouble. It's only a matter of time until his father-in-law makes him dead. Jimmy's got to move on, leave the country. Time's wasting. He's got to get back into his Beemer, head north on Highway Eighty Seven, which just happens to be located conveniently right around the corner between Greenfield and Saratoga. From there, it's a straight three-hour shot to the Canadian border. But what Farrell doesn't expect is that his father-in-law has followed him out to the secret rendezvous."

"There's a showdown," I broke in. "Marino pulls a gun, shoots Farrell…Natalie becomes the witness to a murder. Marino thinks she'll stay quiet…But then she sends me that video file. And I blab about it to him." I pressed my fingertips to my eyelids. "Jesus, Spain, did I get the kid killed?"

It was terrible, but it seemed logical enough. But then, I was used to the black-and-whiteness of life. Blue CAD printing on white paper, linear image maps of steel frames, concrete footings, and foundation walls. I was the spoiler the conspiracy theorists hated to have sitting on the next stool when the question came up about why the Twin Towers dropped so fast after those jetliners crashed into them. The answer was simple: steel burns; steel melts.

Spain was burning too. But until his theories could be proven, they were still just theories. If Jimmy wanted to escape so fast, why take the precious time to argue with his father-in-law? Why make the stop at the Desolation Kill public fishing area? Why not gather up all your chips, make your silent escape, and leave it at that?

But then, the answers to those questions weren't as important as proving first that Marino did something bad to Jimmy, and because of it, he had no choice but to do something bad to Natalie, then set me up to take the blame.

"That used condom," Spain said. "We prove the DNA inside that latex balloon belonged to Farrell on the inside, Natalie Barnes on the outside, we got proof positive of their presence and their intimate relationship. Then we try and find a gun that matches that empty shell casing you found in the lot outside the stream and try and find Marino's prints on it. We get all that, we get all three of them at the scene. We get Peter pulling the trigger. Which would also make him the logical suspect in Natalie's murder."

"You still need a body," I said.

"Yes, we need Farrell's body," Spain said.

"Could be that if the golden boy is dead, he didn't make it far from Lake Desolation."

"There's thick state forest land surrounding the lake and the stream," Spain pointed out.

"We gotta take one last look," I said. "This time we need to look *inside* those woods."

"You're the primary suspect in a murder," he pointed out. "The cops and staties will be combing the place for you—for us."

"If Marino killed Jimmy, and Natalie Barnes witnessed it, then it only makes sense that he killed her too. And since the cops already have Natalie's body, we're going to have to try and bring them Jimmy's."

CHAPTER 54

Before we ventured out, Tess came back down into the wine cellar, pulled my dark hair back, and folded it into a tight bun, which she held in place with a series of pins and barrettes. Then she fitted me with a wig of lush auburn hair that matched hers exactly. I had to wonder if the hair that made up the wig had belonged to her once. I didn't ask.

By the time she finished with me I looked like a brand-new woman.

She handed me a set of keys. "My Toyota pickup," she said. "The windows are tinted. Should give you enough cover. For now."

Spain pulled his sidearm and released the clip. He eyeballed the stacked rounds, slapped the clip back home, thumbed the safety on, re-holstered the weapon, and tossed Tess a nod in the direction of his weapon. "Got something for Spike?"

Without a word, the bar owner left the basement room and came back a beat later with a cell phone and something else—a gun identical to Spain's.

She handed it to me. I slipped the pistol into the waist of my Levi's. Easy access. It wasn't the same as having my equalizer on me, but it would have to do. I shoved the cell phone into my back pocket, handing her my BlackBerry in exchange. Tess dropped it to the floor and crushed it with her boot heel.

She must have noticed the shock on my face.

"Cops use those things like LoJacks," she said.

I exhaled a sad breath at the thought of losing my mobile smart phone. Cutting off my right hand might've been preferable.

"Spain," she said, "you're next."

He handed her his. She crushed that one too.

As a last precaution, Tess handed me a pair of white-framed "Jackie O" sunglasses. I slid them on while Spain put on his Ray-Ban aviators.

"Ready?" I said.

I went for the door.

The pro dick followed.

CHAPTER 55

Behind the wheel of Tess's pickup, driving north up Highway 87, I kept my sunglass-masked eyes peeled on the road ahead.

Spain reached into an interior pocket on his leather jacket and pulled out some papers. The pages were folded in half down the center. He unfolded them for me to glance at while I drove. It didn't take me long to realize that I was looking at a photocopy of a mapped-out Pearl Street—the lower Concrete Pearl, in particular.

"On a hunch, I asked Davey to pay a visit to the Albany County Tax Assessor's office. Take a look at the parcels that are crossed off in red Sharpie."

I looked. "They're all crossed off," I said.

"Not all of them," he said. "Look again."

I did it. "PS 20," I said.

"The crossed-off properties are either scheduled for the wrecking ball or have already been leveled, including the entire port and that radon-infested condo project that Marino had been working on right to the south of it."

"Why not the school?"

"The school board refuses to sell out."

"They're in the process of investing millions of tax dollars on a multiphase renovation. I wouldn't want to sell, either."

"Nor would you want to displace three hundred–plus kids to different school facilities—that is, if you possess any kind of conscience."

He slipped the pages back into his jacket.

"'Course, now they got an asbestos contamination," I pointed out. "Stewart has red-flagged the project, shut the sucker down."

"Convenient," Spain said. "Nobody wants to work or learn inside a poisoned building."

"A cancer factory," I added. "Just take a look at Nicolas Boni."

"The convention center's poster child," he said. "And one thing has become obvious: Marino wants that school and he's willing to put your head on the chopping block to get it." Then he said, "Need to ask you a personal question."

I threw him a look.

"Did Diana ever sleep with Jordan?"

Something inside me dropped like a caged elevator. I knew he was searching for something. A motivation. But Jordan's death had been an accident.

"I…don't…know," I said. "But let's leave it."

"Answer enough," he said.

I held back some tears while I drove.

CHAPTER 56

Fifteen minutes later, we came up on the Malden Bridge, which spanned the narrow Desolation Kill, the freshwater source for Lake Desolation. I pulled into the gravel access area parking lot under the protection of the tall pines and got out. We weren't alone. There was a boy coming up the bank from under the bridge. He was wearing shorts and no shoes. He bore a sad expression on his smooth face. He looked up at us, not with surprise, but with dark eyes glassed over in disappointment.

"Don't even freakin' bother," he said as he passed.

"Excuse me?" I said.

He stopped, turned. "There's no fish in that stream and even more no fish in that lake. There never is."

I remembered fishing here as a little girl. I remembered all the trout my grandfather would take out of both bodies of water. "Maybe you're not using the right lure," I said.

The kid rolled his eyes and held up a Styrofoam takeout container of bait. "Ahhhh, *worms*, lady? Worms have always killed 'em here. Believe me, if you can't catch fish with worms, there's no fish to catch, period."

"My bad," I said.

The kid turned, kept walking across the street and into the field. After about a minute, he disappeared into the tall grass.

Like we'd done before (when we weren't in search of a dead body), we made our way down the narrow path to the stream bank. I gave the underside of the bridge and the gravel bank one more sweep of my eyes.

"In the little scenario we've cooked up thus far, this is where Farrell had sex one final time with Natalie," I said. "After that, she smoked, he chewed tobacco. They shared a beer." About-facing,

I started back up the path toward the parking lot where I'd first found the shell casing on Monday. "And this is where Marino confronted his son-in-law."

I moved in a circle around the small lot, raised my right hand, and made a pistol with index finger and thumb. I pointed the imaginary pistol at Farrell's imaginary face, brought the thumb down.

"I think Marino shot his daughter's husband. Right on this spot. Then he turned the gun on Natalie, told her that if she told a soul, she would die. He knew she had to die. But he couldn't get himself to kill the woman he loved, even if she was sleeping with Jimmy. So he grabs her, stuffs her inside his vehicle, maybe ties her up. Puts the fear of God in her as best he can, hopes that'll be enough. Or what the hell, maybe he doesn't call in the goons at all. Maybe he just simply tells her to drive the hell home but leaves Jimmy's ride behind on purpose so that it gets towed."

"Then Marino dumps the piece," Spain said, "and dumps Farrell's body of evidence. Question is, where?"

As if answering his question, I turned away from Spain, walked into the woods.

Spain and I walked the thick woods from the edge of the stream to the opposite side of the public access parking lot. We walked inside the trees one way and then the other, the branches slapping at my face and making my eyes tear, the briars stabbing the skin on my arms, the sweat building up under the red wig and dripping down my forehead into my eyes.

We felt under our feet for any soft spots in the pine-covered soil. Nothing there. We walked the woods for a half hour and then walked them again. Spain knocked off, but hardheaded me kept at it for a while longer. I was about to leave the woods, disappointed, when I felt something out of place underneath the leather sole of my right boot. I knelt down, felt under the thin layer of damp leaves and pine needles, and uncovered something that made my heart skip a beat.

It was a pistol.

I walked out of the woods with the pistol. "Jimmy's body isn't there," I said. "But this was."

I was breathing heavily, my head feeling very hot under the auburn wig.

Spain pulled a white hanky from his pants pocket and took hold of the pistol with it.

"Nine-millimeter," he said. He released the clip, let it slide down into the palm of his uncovered hand. "One spent round."

"But still no trace of Farrell to be found," I said. "No burial mound, no blood trail, no torn or ripped clothing, no hair. Jimmy's a big, wiry guy. Marino's out of shape. No way he's dragging him through those thick woods more than ten or fifteen feet. Not without having a coronary, anyway. No way Marino left the body out there."

"So where is Jimmy Farrell?"

"Only other explanation is that Marino shot him and transported the body out of here."

"So what now?"

"You tell me. You're the private dick."

Spain smiled. "I love the way you say that." He gripped the automatic, stared out onto the empty country road, thought a minute. He then said, "We finally have a weapon that may very well match the nine-millimeter casing you picked up the other day. Plus, we're already working on having the condom, the beer can, and the spent cigarette tested for Jimmy and Natalie's DNA. But we also have to secure matching DNA sequences that come directly from Farrell and Barnes's respective bodies."

"Why bother?"

"The stuff left on the stream bank was contaminated, left out in the open for two days. If Jimmy and Natalie's DNA is found on them, which I believe it will be, it could very well be contaminated—even the condom. And that's something the defense would be sure to pounce on in a court of law.

"But—and this is a big *but*—if we provide pure cross-reference samples that match the contaminated ones, at least according to initial tests, then there will be no doubt about the identity of the individuals we're dealing with here."

"What do you mean by 'pure samples'?"

"Samples of DNA that haven't been contaminated, samples that come from the actual bodies. If they match the DNA on the evidence, even if that DNA is slightly messed up after having been left out in the elements, there will be no question in anyone's mind about who it belongs to."

"OK, so how are we going to accomplish scraping up more DNA samples right off their bodies with one of them definitely dead, the other almost definitely dead and missing?"

"Natalie is still in cold storage in the AMC morgue. She'll be easy. If we can't get at Jimmy's body, we do the next best thing."

"What next best thing, Spain?"

He stuffed the 9mm into his jacket pocket. "We go back to his house in East Hills, steal a pair of his dirty BVDs."

CHAPTER 57

Back in the city. A sunbaked concrete and blacktop jungle.

I glanced at my wristwatch while I drove. "Two minutes 'til four," I said, turning the radio on, the volume down low. "I want to hear the news."

"You think it's possible Tina could be home?" Spain said. "Maybe Peter?"

"Chance we gotta take."

I pulled onto Madison Avenue in the direction of the suburbs. At the top of the four o'clock hour I turned up the volume on talk radio station WGY-13. Sister station to Channel 13 twenty-four-hour news. First came a station identification, then a media voice I recognized:

"...The search continues for a local Albany businesswoman wanted in connection with the brutal slaying of a local bartender. Early this morning, construction company owner Ava 'Spike' Harrison became the prime suspect in the murder of Natalie Barnes, a twenty-nine-year-old bartender and graduate student who worked part-time as a topless bartender at the Thatcher Street Pub located in Albany's Pearl Street district.

"Harrison, along with James 'Jimmy' Farrell of A-1 Environmental Solutions asbestos-removal company, had come under heavy scrutiny by both OSHA and Albany law enforcement officials, including District Attorney Derrick Santiago, for negligence in the gross asbestos contamination of Albany Public School 20. Facing imminent indictment by Santiago, Harrison agreed to cooperate fully with his investigation.

"Late last night, however, the badly mutilated body of Barnes was discovered lying in a pool of blood outside the PS 20 Harrison Construction trailer. The weapon utilized in the crime? A construction framing hammer reputedly belonging to Harrison. Sources close to both the assailant and victim attest that Harrison killed Barnes after discovering the bartender and Farrell had been frequent lovers. It is also being speculated that Barnes was about to cooperate fully with Santiago, possibly revealing fully the extent to which Farrell and Harrison had been illegally collaborating. While a warrant for Harrison's arrest has yet to be issued by Albany County, one is expected shortly. This is Chris Collins reporting…"

I killed the radio, continued driving out of the city. Grabbing Tess's cell, I punched in Tommy's number. As if knowing it was me despite my new cell, he answered after the first ring.

"Tommy, it's me," I said.

"Make it quick," he said. I heard a commotion in the background. Voices.

"Tommy, where are you?" I said.

"You've gotta speak up," he said. "Having trouble understanding you with all these policemen."

Tommy, surrounded by cops.

"You're at my apartment, aren't you, Tommy? You went looking for me."

"That's right, Ma," he said. "I'll be over as soon as I can. Soon as the police are finished going through Spike's apartment and towing away her Jeep. Shouldn't be much longer, Ma. You hang in there. The Albany cops are very thorough, but quick."

"I'll call you back," I said.

"Sounds good, Ma."

I hung up, turned to Spain. Told him the cops and Santiago must have acquired the warrant they needed to go through my place and take my Jeep.

"Whad' you expect?" he said.

I shook my head, eyes peeled on the hilly suburban road bordered by manicured lawns and cookie-cutter houses. Somehow the thought of the police invading my personal space made this all the more real in my hard head.

The pit in my stomach shifted just as I made the hard left turn onto East Hills Drive.

Tina's white Land Rover Discovery was parked in the circular drive.

Correction: half the Discovery was parked on the drive, the other half on the lawn, the driver's side wheels sunk deep in a newly planted flower bed.

"So much for searching the house," Spain said.

"We stick to the plan," I said. "Fuck it."

I pulled off the road directly in front of Farrell's two-story palace, made it across the manicured lawn, past the Discovery, up the marble steps to the front door.

Spain followed close behind.

I rang the doorbell. Tina came to the door dressed in a short tennis skirt and a tight tank top, slim sunglasses masking her eyes, blonde hair tied back in a perfect ponytail, Nike tennis sneaks and peds.

She seemed to be having trouble keeping her balance.

"I'm calling…the police," she slurred, the air sucked out of her lungs. The alcohol on her breath hit me like a tennis racket to the face. I'd forgotten about my disguise. She saw through it anyway, regardless of the booze.

I slid the automatic from my waist, held the barrel on her. "No police," I said. Then, "Spain, go do what we came here for."

Spain bounded up the center hall staircase to check the upstairs for something with Jimmy's DNA on it.

Tina turned, stumbled, looked up. "Whas…happening? Whaddya you doing…inside my home, Mr. Spain?"

We stood inside the vestibule. I held the pistol on her until Spain came back down the stairs a few beats later. A translucent plastic sandwich baggy was gripped in his right hand. Some rich, black, soil-like material inside it, along with what looked to be a clear drinking glass. Spain had found what we needed—Farrell's DNA-rich chewed and used tobacco.

I kept the pistol poised on Tina.

She exhaled a sour booze breath that nearly sent me careening against the door. "Damien," the trophy wife said. "We…have…a con…a contract."

He looked at her, then at me again. "Mrs. Farrell," he said, slow, controlled. "Your husband has gotten himself into a lot of trouble."

Tina's blue eyes filled. Her long legs began to shake, knees about to buckle. "It's true...isn't it, Damien?" she said. "What they're...saying...saying on the news?"

He exhaled. "Your husband's lover was murdered, Mrs. Farrell," he said. "I believe your husband was also murdered."

Tina dropped to the marble floor, a pretty, silver spoon–fed bag of rags and bones.

CHAPTER 58

We shifted her deceptively heavy body into a cherry-wood-paneled library located off the kitchen. We laid her out on the couch, placed a warm washcloth on her forehead. You get used to people passing out in my business. Overexertion, heat exhaustion, slamming your head against a door frame. After a while, you know what to do. Pressing two fingers against her jugular, I counted out her heartbeats for a full minute. Satisfied that she would live to see another Pilates session, I then took a step back, took a quick glance at all the books Farrell never read, but displayed for show anyway.

"Let the poor kid sleep it off," I said.

Spain took the used chewing tobacco into the kitchen, found a plastic baggy in a drawer, stuffed the entire drinking glass inside it. Coming back out into the living room, he said, "Let me show you something."

I followed him out of the living room, back into the inlaid marble vestibule, up the stairs to the home's second floor. When we came to the first bedroom on the left, he stepped inside. I walked in right behind him and felt a silent shudder in my heart.

This wasn't a bedroom, but a nursery.

The room was painted a boy's baby blue. A sky of soft white clouds had been hand-painted against a sky-blue ceiling. A white-railed crib took up the far corner near the long double-hung Pella windows. Below the windows were white cubby-style bookcases full of books: *Dr. Seuss, Thomas the Tank Engine, Grimm's Fairy Tales, Monster Trucks, The Giving Tree…*

In the corner opposite the crib was a mound of large stuffed animals: a giraffe taller than me, a brown bear wider than me, a half dozen fluffy white bunnies, a small pack of black, brown, and white dogs.

This might have been a room designed to welcome a new child into the world. But a palpable sadness oozed from the sheetrock. I couldn't help but imagine what my own child's nursery would have looked like if I'd ever gotten pregnant with Jordan. If he had lived, I would have wanted our baby to have spent her first years growing up in just such a room.

"When Tina first hired me," Spain said, "I didn't just stumble upon Farrell's asbestos-removal scam. I also discovered this room…the things inside it. Turns out they were all meant for a boy named Greg. Tina carried him until close to her second trimester when miscarriage ended the pregnancy. The baby— the fetus—had to be delivered stillborn inside a hospital. Tina insisted on remaining conscious for the entire procedure so she could see his face. That's what she told me."

Immediately, I was transported back in time. Two days had passed since I first visited the East Hill's house in search of her husband. I saw her standing inside the marble vestibule, her open hand placed over an exposed tummy, as though there was a baby growing inside her womb. Now I pictured her going through all the pain and agony of delivering a stillborn child just to see his face, just to know for a moment what her son looked like, his eyes, nose, and mouth.

"Does she somehow blame Jimmy for the child dying in utero?"

Spain cocked his head. "He put her through a lot. Not only with his affairs, but with the ever-strained relationship he had with her father. Farrell was running an illegal operation. Marino was a part of it. There must have been bitter fights in this house. It was a lot for Tina to swallow."

I didn't want to hear any more.

I stood silent on the carpeted floor.

Silent and numb.

How does a childless widow with a stubborn streak avoid being buried by sadness?

She makes a beeline out the nursery door. "Screw this place," I said. "We need to get to the morgue, grab a sample of Natalie's DNA. By the time we get that, Marino Construction will have closed up for the day."

"Marino will be closed. What difference does it make? I don't understand," Spain said, the plastic tobacco-filled baggy still gripped in his hand.

"Here's where I become *your* invaluable partner," I said. "We're going to break in, dig through Peter and Jimmy's stored records, and find a way to link up the asbestos scam with the two murders."

CHAPTER 59

We blew out the front door and shot across the lawn to the sidewalk.

From behind the wheel of the pickup, I called Tommy back and asked him if he was still at my apartment.

He wasn't.

I told him my planned moves—the first being the AMC morgue, the second being the Marino Construction offices off Wolf Road. I told him we may be in need of his assistance at some point.

"All this ends tonight," I said. "One way or another."

I hung up and set the cell down beside Jimmy's DNA.

"Can Tommy be trusted?" Spain said as I hooked a left onto New Scotland and the boulevard that would take us directly to the hospital.

"When my father died," I said, "Tommy took his place."

CHAPTER 60

Spain knew his way around the AMC campus. Instead of driving into the main lot, he told me to turn left into the service delivery entrance. I followed the road around the back side of the main hospital. At the guard shack, he leaned forward to make himself more visible to the attending security guard. He then made as though tipping the brim of an invisible fedora. The guard returned the gesture with an identical one of his own. Spain was taking a chance. The guard would have heard the news about me, and maybe about Spain being with me. Maybe not. No point it thinking about stuff. Just do.

I pulled up to a pair of sliding service entrance doors, stopped the truck.

We got out and approached the doors. The electronic door opener had to be slapped manually before the glass sliders would open. Spain did it.

We went inside.

Although I'd overseen the occasional interior fit-up inside the Albany Medical Center, I'd never before been exposed to its bowels. It was a dark, creepy place. The floor was constructed of rock-hard terrazzo, the walls protected with a wainscoting of ceramic tile that was chipped in places. I knew the chips had been caused by the metal caskets that were wheeled in and out of there on a daily basis. Above us, the ceiling was an exposed maze of heating and ventilating ductwork and lightbulbs protected inside little metal cages. A prison cell block came to mind. A prison in hell.

That silence was broken by the distinct hum of an electric saw, the not-unfamiliar sound of a diamond-studded blade cutting through rigid material. Spain stopped in front of a set of double doors with the word *Pathology* stenciled onto the frosted glass in black letters.

He opened the door and stepped inside.

I followed.

"Don't come any closer," he said as the door closed behind me.

The place smelled like worms. Natalie was laid out on a steel table set in the center of the room. She'd been placed on her back, the back of her head propped up on a kind of half-moon-shaped metal block. She was naked, except for a medical green sheet that covered her sex. Her skin was stark white and blanched like newly cut Italian marble. Part of the skin that covered her forehead had been pulled down over her eyes. A portion of the exposed skull had been sawed according to a precise line. Like passing by a bad car wreck, I didn't want to look. But I couldn't help it.

A doctor stood over her. He was dressed in surgical scrubs. A long translucent shield masked his face. A green skullcap covered the top of his head. Green latex gloves protected his hands. His left hand supported an electric saw with a circular, diamond-studded blade. He wore an electronic headset with an attached microphone. He'd been speaking something into it when we entered the room unannounced.

The doctor eyed Spain. His Adam's apple bobbed up and down in his neck like a turkey the day before Thanksgiving.

"It's favor time, Doc," the PI said. Then, turning to me, he said, "Step outside for just a moment, won't you please, Spike?"

I did it, gladly enough.

Alone in the dark corridor.

I was reminded of Jordan…of the day his heart stopped. The doctors and nurses called his death a gift from God. Although he had been going in and out of a coma in the twenty-four hours since he'd fallen from the scaffolding, one medical expert had assured me that he would never walk again, never lift a finger. If he were to survive, Jordan would spend the remainder of his days a severe quadriplegic—a basket case.

The door opened, startling me. In Spain's hand was a small white bag marked *LAB* in blue letters.

Natalie's DNA.

I said, "That was quick."

We started walking back toward the double exit doors.

"The doc's got a nasty habit of playing the field. Even though he's got a beautiful wife, three kids. He's even got a million-dollar home in guess where?"

"Picture-perfect East Hills."

"Plus a condo in Jupiter, Florida."

I was beginning to see the picture. "You blackmailed him a little," I said.

"I've worked for his wife, just like I worked for Tina. Totally confidential, of course. Up until now, that is. I showed the wife what I had, and—this happens—she just nodded and that was it. Didn't confront him, didn't leave him. Just wanted to know, I guess."

"People are funny."

"Not always happy-go-lucky funny, though. At least he wasn't laughing in there when I showed him what I had for him."

"Photographs," I guessed.

"Imagine the ensuing scandal if I were to distribute the pictures of him and a sixteen-year-old Craigslist Casual Encounter girl laid out in the backseat of his Lexus?"

"Pretty picture," I said. "And pretty fucking sad."

CHAPTER 61

Back in the pickup, Spain placed the "LAB" bag in his briefcase, along with the chewing tobacco. I pulled out of the lot, drove the service road back to New Scotland, hung a right toward West Albany and the Marino Construction offices.

We got off 90, made the turn onto Wolf Road, began slowly cruising the former site of pristine apple orchards for as far as the eye could see. Now that the farmers had been forced out by the developers, the place was filled on both sides with chain restaurants and strip malls. Red Lobster heaven; Dunkin' Donuts' glass facade covered with big glossy posters of Rachael Ray swallowing a chocolate long john.

"Something I've been meaning to ask you," I said, feeling my temples begin to pound under Tess's red wig. "If you're only a PI, how did you get Santiago to hold off on his original indictments?"

"Santiago wasn't always a DA," he said. "I wasn't always a PI. We both started with the APD. Partners assigned to Pearl Street. In those days, anything could and would happen on the Concrete Pearl. It was a regular old-fashioned Times Square. Dope pushers, prostitutes, porn, pretty much anything. Everything was bought and sold on Pearl…Everything had its price."

"I'm only about ten years younger than you," I said. "Pearl Street was one place my dad always warned me about—Lower Pearl, anyway. Down by the port…the real Concrete Pearl."

"For good reason. The little stretch of riverside roadway was a microcosm of everything that could go wrong with a lost-in-time city like Albany. Santiago and me, we did our best to clean some of it up, return some shine back to the Pearl."

"I'm sensing a 'but' here," I said, eyes on the double-lane boulevard before me.

"But," Spain said, "two men trying to shore up the sides of a sand pit ain't no damn good. Those were the days when most of the drugs that entered into Manhattan were dropped in Albany first, cut up, and then shipped south. Only way we could stem the flow was to buy information. And who better to buy from but a young Pearl Street brothel madam by the name of Tess. Beautiful long auburn hair, the greenest eyes you ever saw...Tess swept Derrick Santiago off his feet."

"Tess," I said, both hands pressing against my wig. "As in *our* Tess?"

"The very one."

"She and Santiago?"

"Surprise you?"

"Not at all," I lied.

"Leverage can be a real bitch," he smiled. "Especially when it's being weighed against a DA with hefty political aspirations."

I turned into Aviation Industrial Park. In the near distance, on the left side of the deserted single-lane road were the offices and warehouse of Marino Construction. Directly to the north of it were the empty offices of A-1 Environmental Solutions.

"Memory Lane ends here," I said. "What happens now is the future."

CHAPTER 62

It might have been late in the evening, but it was June. Summertime. We didn't have the advantage of pulling off what amounted to a B&E under the cover of darkness. It was just approaching dusk when I pulled off to the side of the road, close enough to give us a clear eyeball view of the offices, but far enough away not to raise suspicions.

We gave it a quiet fifteen minutes before we slid out of the truck.

We didn't go to the front door and risk getting caught out in the great wide open. Together, we went around back to the warehouse entrance. Spain pulled from his pocket a device that allowed him to jimmy the padlock on the gate. When the pit bull came sprinting at us, wet fangs poised for the kill, he slammed the gate closed.

Sonny crashed face-first into the chain-link.

The little black-and-white monster barked and yelped— loud, short bursts of pure anger and vengeance. Spain pulled his weapon, aimed it at the dog. The 9mm trembled in his hand.

"Jesus," he said. "I can't do it."

I pulled my piece, held it in two hands, took aim, and squeezed. I grazed one off the dog's ass end. It didn't kill him, but it was enough to send the beast barking and howling blindly in the direction of the newly dug-out pole barn trenches. When Sonny reached the trench's edge, he didn't even attempt to stop. He just jumped into the hole.

"Nice shot," Spain said.

"You hesitated," I said.

"I love dogs."

"That monster is more killer than dog."

He opened the gate and we stepped on through. The gravel yard was filled with timbers and construction material for the new pole barn. There was a Komatsu backhoe, a John Deere bulldozer, and two Ford one-ton pickup trucks similar to the four Chevys I once owned for my business. There was a mound of sandy soil that would serve as backfill once the pole barn piers were poured, plus stacks of concrete frames and angles.

As we made our way past the open trenches to the back door beside the warehouse overhead door, I felt that familiar but uncomfortable tight feeling in my chest. The sensation transported me back to seven years old when I fell into a trench and was buried alive. It was a sensation I've been fighting all my life.

"Go to it, Spain," I said.

He used the pick device to unlock the solid metal door. When he pulled it open, there came the immediate *beep-beep-beep* of the triggered alarm system about to explode in a cacophony of sirens and flashing lights. Spain quickly punched in a four-number sequence. The alarm disengaged.

I asked him how he'd become privy to the code.

"Tina can be quite the font of information when sufficiently lubricated," he said.

I ran my hand along the exterior wall, found the overhead light switch. When I flipped it on, the big room lit up under the four ceiling-mounted halogens. The interior wasn't like any construction warehouse I'd ever seen. Nothing like the one I'd left behind at the old Harrison Construction offices, anyway. This one housed very few tools and only a couple of pieces of light construction equipment—a table saw and a gas-powered generator.

The space had been emptied out to make room instead for what had to be a couple dozen banker's storage boxes. I might have ignored them entirely, had Marino not bothered to lock them inside a metal storage cage that could have doubled for a holding pen inside a county jail.

I pressed myself up against the cage, took a closer look. Every box seemed to be marked "A1" in black Sharpie.

"A1." *A-1 Environmental Solutions.*

But that was about all I could make out.

"Spain, can you open this lock with that device?"

He approached me and went to work picking the lock, which was embedded into the steel door. He labored hard enough to begin working up a beaded sweat along his brow, until the metal pick broke off in the lock.

He took a step back. "That answers that," he said, pulling out his cell phone.

I took a quick survey of the room. "We need to get into the office," I said, "find the keys for that lock, or at the very least, the machinery outside."

"You do that while I get a few pictures with my cell phone of the A1 boxes inside Marino's warehouse."

To our left was a door that would lead us into the main office.

I went to it, turned the knob.

Open.

I walked right into the general offices of Marino Construction like I owned the joint.

To my left was the kitchen. I kept moving, past a project manager's office on the left and a blueprint room beside it. At the end of the hall was another, more spacious office. I knew this one belonged to Marino because I'd seen him stick his head out of it on Monday morning.

The dark room was lit with the setting sun that leaked in through the wide windows. A placard from the Associated General Contractors hung on the wall. It named Marino Construction as the year's number one Capital District General Contractor. There were six or seven identical plaques hanging on the wall beside it. My dad had also earned a few of the same trophies back in his day.

I had earned none.

On the opposite side of the office was a large drafting table. A big wood job like the old-time architects used before CAD took all the artwork out of drafting. There were several blueprints laid out on the drafting table. I made my way over to it, took a look at the masthead in big bold letters on the drawings:

THE PEARL STREET CONVENTION CENTER AND NORTH ALBANY REDEVELOPMENT PROJECT

The drawings had been stamped with a warning by the project architects (Marino's own architects, it turns out): *Drawings not for Construction. For Value Engineering and Review Only!* In other words, for Marino's eyes only. Marino Design—a company within a company I had no idea existed.

I rolled up the documents, stuffed them under my arm. Then I crossed back over to Marino's desk and opened the top drawer. There were several sets of keys stored inside, all of them marked with individual ID tags.

One set had *Backhoe* written on the attached tag. Another said *Dump No. 1*, yet another, *Dozer*, and so forth. No keys that went to the padlocked cage. No doubt Marino himself was carrying them on his personal key ring. I took the keys for the bulldozer and one of the one-ton dumps.

"Spike, how's it going in there?" Spain was clearly getting nervous while he photographed Farrell's caged boxes.

I couldn't help myself. I started flinging open drawers. In the lower right-hand drawer, I discovered a couple of blank CDs or maybe DVDs enclosed in cheap plastic cases. I grabbed them. Then I opened up the other two drawers, found some personal files. One of them said *Farrell* on the top tab; another said *The Concrete Pearl.*

I pulled the files from the desk.

"Spike, for Christ's sake!"

Cradling the mother lode, I ran back down the hall to an awaiting Spain.

"Do a little shopping?" he said, his cell phone no longer in hand.

I set everything down on a stack of copy machine paper stock. "Pilfered evidence," I said.

"What about the boxes?" Spain said. "You find a key to the cage?"

"No, but what I got will give you a hard-on."

Turning away from a red-faced Spain, I went to the overhead door and hit the green button that triggered the opener. The door exploded to life, raising itself up in a racket of metal against metal. I made my way outside, across the gravel lot to the bulldozer. Careful to keep my eye out for Sonny, I climbed aboard the bulldozer, put the key into the ignition, and turned it clockwise. The bulldozer roared to life.

I pulled back the lever that raised the blade, then pushed the throttle forward. The machine bucked, its heavy treads squealing and squeaking. Spain stood in the doorway, a big smile planted on his face while he waved me toward him. I knew then he was getting a big kick out of all this action. What boy doesn't like tractors?

I pushed the stick all the way forward and the dozer tracked its way across the lot to the open garage. I didn't stop there. I drove all the way inside, aiming the lower right corner of the big blade for one corner of the cage. When the two connected, the cage exploded and collapsed.

That was my idea of fun.

The boxes immediately before me were marked March of this year. I approached one such box atop a stack of four on the far left end of the cage. I unwound the thin black shoelace-like string that secured the box. Inside, I found dozens of manila folders containing documentation of some sort neatly stacked on their sides.

I reached into the box, slipped dirty fingers into the first folder, pulled out a document.

A spec sheet for a project in Buffalo.

The sheet was stapled to a test result that came from the George Washington High School removal. The numbers printed in pencil on the sheet meant nothing to me. I flipped the page back over, took another glance at the spec sheet. What I noticed was that the specification numbers matched the numbers (or levels) of the end specification result, as they were supposed to in a testing situation. Who knew if the numbers had been fabricated, though?

Behind me, Spain once more had his open cell phone raised before his face. He was snapping a few more pictures of the boxes, careful to get the "A1" identification in each of the frames.

"Jackpot," he said.

"We need to load up and go," I said.

"Even the Toyota can't hold all this."

"Outside," I said, "the one-ton pickup truck...We've got the keys."

"It's got Marino's logo on both doors."

I took a quick look around. On the far wall was a shelf rack. There were cans of blaze-orange spray paint stored on it. The same kind of paint contractors use to mark areas on existing walls, floors, or roads that need to be chopped or cut out. I went to the rack, pulled down two cans, then took them with me outside. Aiming the first spray can at the side of the blue truck, I sprayed the big-lettered name *Marino* with the orange paint.

No more Marino.

I sprayed until the door was covered in orange and the can was empty, only the little steel ball bearing rattling inside the hollowed tin.

Then, using up the second can, I repeated the process on the other side.

Hopping in the driver's seat, I turned the truck over, threw the gearshift in reverse, and backed it up to the open garage door. Spain started loading up the dump truck's back bed with the A-1 Environmental boxes. I pulled the brake on the dump truck; went back inside the warehouse; grabbed the Pearl Street prints, computer disks, and personal files I'd snatched from Marino's office; and tossed it all into the front seat. Then I tossed Spain the keys to Tess's pickup.

"It'll be dark in a few minutes," I said. "Meet me back at Tess's."

"You want me to follow you?"

"Don't worry about staying close. Too dangerous. Just get there as fast as you can."

CHAPTER 63

We pulled into the Lark Tavern's back lot within thirty seconds of each other.

I watched from behind the wheel of the idling one-ton dump as Spain engaged the parking brake on the Toyota. He got out, opened the overhead garage door. Slipping back behind the wheel, he undid the brake and slowly pulled into the garage.

As usual, Davey Blister was our greeting party. He took the keys from Spain, asked him if he'd retrieved the "materials."

The PI nodded and moved around the pickup to the passenger side. He opened the door. That's when I got out of the one-ton. He set his briefcase onto the hood of the Toyota, opened it. Spain retrieved the 9mm, the bag of chewed tobacco, and the white "LAB" bag. He handed it all over to Davey. It was now the punk rocker's turn to get behind the wheel of Tess's pickup.

He fired it back up. When he backed out, Spain waved me in.

Slowly, I maneuvered the dump into the garage. It was a tight fit, but I took it extra slow and got it all in without doing damage to the garage walls.

Spain closed the garage door and locked it from the inside, then pulled the first A-1 Environmental box off the truck.

"Wine cellar," he directed.

CHAPTER 64

Tess was standing at the cellar door. She stepped up behind me, gently removed my wig, and unclasped the barrette, allowing my own sweat-saturated hair to fall against my shoulders.

I asked her if I could use her computer.

Her laptop was stored upstairs in her office. She'd bring it downstairs for me.

Spain, along with the ever-silent Vinny and Drew Blood Blister, emptied out the Marino dump truck, setting everything down inside the wine cellar. By the time they were done, there was barely room to move.

I went to work opening box after box, rummaging around like a kid in a video game store. There were records of asbestos-removal jobs from all over the state. No surprise there. But what did take me by surprise was the third box I opened. A banker's box that didn't contain A-1 Environmental solutions records at all, but records from another company altogether: Analytical Labs, the independent testing firm employed by PS 20 to keep track of Farrell's interior air test samples. Four entire boxes were filled with Analytical Lab documents. The box was full of testing folders from various projects all over New York State.

"I'll be damned," I said, holding up a file. "Guess who owns Analytical Labs?"

Spain bit his lip. "Our boys Farrell and Marino," he said, stating the obvious.

In my mind, I saw the empty storage space that served as the "office" of Analytical Labs.

"It's illegal for owners of environmental cleanup companies to own testing outfits," I added. "No wonder they passed all those tests for as long as they did."

"Until they *purposely* didn't pass," Spain pointed out.

I couldn't help but smile. "Right on," I said. "Until they got the chance to prove that PS 20 was so contaminated no one would want to inhabit it any longer. The results had been rigged all along."

Spain leaned into me, gave me a kiss on the cheek. For the first time in days, I felt a wave of relief wash over me. It was my responsibility to monitor the asbestos removal and to sign off on those daily worksheets. But the quality of the work inevitably depended upon those interior air quality test reports. But now that we knew they'd been rigged all along, I didn't feel quite so guilty for having put all those kids at risk. "We go no further," he said. "There's enough here to prove to my ex-APD partner that Marino was in collusion with Farrell. Enough evidence to prove that a construction conspiracy existed. Enough to take the heat off of you for collusion and murder."

The little light flashed on inside my head. "Not so fast," I said. I grabbed the blueprints I'd stolen off Marino's drafting table, set them on top of the banker's boxes, and unrolled them.

Spain looked over my shoulder as I flipped over the title page, skipped over the architectural and mechanical drawings, went right to the heart of the matter—the site plan. The sheet was covered in blue CAD-produced lines, two of which created the outline of lower Pearl Street. Nearly every building represented on the plan from the Port of Albany to the south, to one very special site to the north, was slated for demolition.

Spain shook his head. "Translation," he said.

I pressed my index finger against the "special site" to the north. "You see that right there, Spain?"

He looked down at the rectangular blue-lined architectural representation of PS 20.

"That's my asbestos-contaminated school," I said. "It says, 'Condemned School to be Demolished.'"

Spain looked at me quizzically. "Condemned? The asbestos thing didn't hit until this past Monday."

"Now take a look at when these progress drawings were created," I said, straightening up.

Spain looked closer. "April third," he said. "That's more than two months ago."

I smiled.

He smiled.

"How long will it take Davey to have that stuff processed for DNA?" I asked.

"Couple hours or so for initial results," he said. "Maybe a week for conclusive results."

"We don't have a week, much less those two hours," I said. "But we'll go with what we've got. Until then, we'll chill out here. When Davey comes back, we'll wake up Santiago, arrange an emergency meeting."

"We might just have enough evidence here to shift the burden of suspicion away from you, Spike. Even without the DNA evidence."

"Let's hope so," I said. "I'm not taking any chances when it comes to getting me off the hook for murder."

A beat later, the young woman who'd waited on us the other night stepped back into the half-lit, four-walled room. She was carrying a small tray. Atop the tray were two plates of food covered with tin warmers. She set the tray down on the table. Before she left, she walked up to Spain, gave him a kiss on his cheek. He reached into his pocket, pulled out a twenty, set it in her hand.

She tried to give it back. But when he tossed her a look that meant business, she kissed him again, pulled the tins off the dishes, revealing plain spaghetti and sauce, then made her way out of the room, back up the stairs to the main restaurant.

That's when Tess came back in with her laptop already opened and booted up. I grabbed one of the CDs, set it into the computer tray and waited for the media player to engage.

"Eat something," Tess said.

"Bless you, Tess," I said, knowing I wouldn't able to stomach a single bite.

"Don't bless me," she said. "I'm getting paid." Cocking her head in Spain's direction, she added, "Bless Spencer-for-Hire."

When the media player emerged on the screen, it became immediately apparent that the inserted CD wasn't a CD at all, but a DVD.

On the computer, a familiar but disturbing image appeared.

CHAPTER 65

What can you say about a home movie shot from a remote-controlled camera set up on a tripod inside the bedroom of some hotel-no-tell? What do you say about the sight of a tight golden boy going at it doggy style with a twenty-something concrete blonde? What can you say about his very own father-in-law servicing a second peroxide job, same position? What the hell can you say about the mirror set out on the bed, the cut-up coke laid out in neat little lines in the center of it, along with the gold AMEX they used in place of a razor blade and a rolled-up twenty-dollar bill for a straw? What can you say about the cries of passion, the sloppy laughter, and the empty bottles of Dom strewn across the bed?

Maybe what you'd say is this: "Hey, this is the construction business and I'm not the least bit fucking surprised."

There was, however, something to be said of the discovery I made when rolling up the convention center blueprints. A separate site plan slipped out from in between the electrical drawings.

I laid it out on top of the banker's boxes.

Spain looked over my shoulder. "Another site plan," he said.

"Yup," I said.

"More Pearl Street?"

I set an extended index finger on the title bar.

"Lake Desolation Estates," he said. "Marino-Farrell Development."

"That's the Desolation Kill right there," I said, setting my index finger on the lower right corner of the plan. "See how it snakes its way through the center of the site?" My finger traced the path of the winding stream. "And that's where it empties into the lake."

Spain studied the plan. "What's all this stuff, then?" he asked, pointing his own finger to the many squared-off parcels of land set side by side one another.

"That, my PI friend, is what's commonly called a subdivision. Looks to me like Marino and Farrell were planning on developing that beautiful rural area way up north. Making it a hot spot for a bunch of McMansions."

"That's not all," Spain added, pointing with his index finger. "That say 'Casino'?"

He was right. Butting up against the lake was a large parcel with the outline of a big box-shaped building in the center of it. The word *Casino* was printed inside the box.

"You're getting pretty good at reading these prints, Spain. Maybe one day you can come work for me."

"We keep you out of Sing Sing first," he said.

"Priorities," I said.

"Where you think they were gonna get the money for developing all that land?"

"The convention center would be my guess. What better way to launder bad construction money than to invest it in another bad construction project?"

Over the next hour, we viewed the other DVD. It was a lot different from the first one. The plot didn't revolve around a sex party hosted by Farrell and his extended family. This one was all about landscapes. More specifically, it showed Lake Desolation and then moved on to show the Desolation Kill. It also contained panoramic shots of the pine- and oak-tree-covered hillsides that would be leveled to make building lots.

The disk also revealed something else: a video of Farrell dumping something into the lake from out of a five-gallon taping compound bucket. The stuff was dark and watery, with little clumps of something unrecognizable in it. It was the same stuff I'd sniffed in the back of Farrell's ride and nearly threw up over, the same stuff that old man Dott was transporting from his tow truck to his garage offices.

This is exactly what I relayed to Spain.

He got up, moved closer to the computer, pressed He pointed an extended finger at the still shot like a shooter and his pistol. "Marino and Farrell were trying to poison Lake Desolation," he said. "No wonder that little kid couldn't catch any fish. There aren't any."

"But why film your own crime?" I posed.

"Marino was the photographer. He was always the photographer." Turning to me, he continued. "He filmed Jimmy kissing Natalie in the Thatcher Street Pub; he filmed himself and Jimmy getting down with two blonde pros. Now he films your golden boy doing this. Maybe he made the film to prove to some filthy, nameless investors that he was taking care of business."

"Or it could be that he'd been setting Jimmy up all along, and Jimmy was too stupid to realize it—or too drunk and too in lust."

"Jimmy probably trusted Marino implicitly. At least initially, Spike. The old man probably tossed him a line every time he broke out the camera. You know, 'Hey, Jimmy, smile, you're on *Candid Camera*.' Or, 'Hey, Jimmy, I'm just shooting the beautiful landscape for our future development investors.' I mean, how many crime videos you seen on cable television? People being filmed in the act?"

He had a point. Put people in front of a camera—even criminals—and they suddenly become Brad fucking Pitt.

He turned to me, still pointing to the picture on the laptop. "You see that there?" he said, the tip of his finger on one of the little black clumps of solid that was pouring out of the bucket. "Those tiny little clams...I can bet you dollars to donuts they're parasites."

"You poison the lake, no more fish. No tourists or sportsmen."

"They weren't poisoning the lake so much as they were poisoning the property values," Spain deduced.

I nodded. "They could buy up the land on the cheap from those pigheaded farmers, move in with the bulldozers. And Dott not only owns some of that lakefront property, he was assisting them with the poisoning. He probably swallowed a brick when I showed up to get a look at Farrell's car."

"I'm guessing Dott was willing to take a hit on his portion of the property now," Spain added, "for huge backend dividends."

Davey arrived back from his mission. In his hand, he gripped a plain plastic shopping bag. The bag held two sealed envelopes containing initial DNA matches for both Natalie and Farrell—or more precisely, matches that proved the two had indeed shared the condom found on the stream bank.

Davey turned his attention to Spain. "You know they won't let you use this stuff in court," he mumbled in the same raspy Joe Strummer voice he belted out his punk songs. "You fought the law to get it, and you know that the law's gonna win every time."

"Santiago is my former APD partner," Spain said. "I know more about his past than most wives know about their husbands. All I have to do is supply enough to prove that Marino and Farrell were colluding on asbestos-removal projects, that they'd formed an asbestos-removal racket that included a very affordable and agreeable independent testing outfit, that things went bad for them both when they starting sleeping with the same woman and when Jimmy started screaming for more of the profits."

"Greed, the great motivator," I said. "Lust, the great equalizer."

"Love stinks," Davey said, a semblance of a smile cracking on his hard face.

"Listen," Spain said, the initial DNA results in hand, "I don't have to prove any of their actual crimes. That's for the police to do later. All we have to prove is that a conspiracy existed to nail Spike with the PS 20 asbestos scam and with Natalie's murder. Maybe even with Farrell's murder when he turns up dead. They both had to die, and they needed someone to pin it on. That alone will shift the burden of guilt from Spike back to Marino." Cocking his head over his shoulder, he said, "All this stuff behind me—the A-1 Environmental records, the Analytical Labs records, the Pearl Street Convention Center site plans calling for PS 20 to be contaminated long before last Monday—all that stuff is the backup in our case against Marino. And as for Spike? You're going to be the state's number one witness."

Spain put his jacket back on, pulled his automatic, released the clip, gave it a quick visual, then slapped it back home, returning the piece to his belt holster.

"You want me to call the DA?" Davey posed. Then he sang like John Lennon, "*He's only sleeping...*"

The call to Santiago—the wake-up call that would get him out of bed, wake him up to the truth.

"Nope," I said. "That one's for me to make."

Spain punched in a seven-digit number on Tess's cell. He handed it to me. I put it to my ear, waited for a connection.

"Santiago," I said when he answered groggily, mouth full of cotton. "This is Spike Harrison. I'm turning myself in to your office—half an hour. No staties, feds, no APD, no ADAs. Just you. I'll be bringing along an old partner of yours. I understand you share quite a history together."

"Spain," he said.

"See you in a half hour."

I slapped the phone closed. "How much do you trust Santiago to be in his office alone?" I asked Spain.

"About as far as I can pick him up and toss him. Alliances have changed for us over the years."

"If we're bringing him evidence that will not be admissible in court, but that proves my innocence in all this beyond the shadow of a doubt, I want it all caught on video tape. And not just any video. I want the media to know about it."

"Collins," Spain said. "News Channel Thirteen. You promised her the exclusive."

"I'll make this call from the Charger," I said.

CHAPTER 66

How does a headstrong girl like me go about saving my ass from prison?

By working up some quality one-on-one face time with the city's top prosecutor.

Spain and I sat inside Santiago's office at a long conference table. The DA sat directly across from us. His dark, wavy hair was disheveled from sleep, his white button-down wrinkled as though he'd just picked it up off his bedroom floor, his expression teeth-clenched tight.

At the opposite end of the room stood Chris Collins and her cameraman. Collins was real put together in her red miniskirt suit, as if she had somehow anticipated the unplanned early morning get-together. She stood off to the side without comment. Not a field reporter so much as a documenting witness to the proceedings.

Without ceremony or comment, Spain handed over the evidence, piece by piece.

A single box that contained A1-Environmental and Analytical Labs files and that represented just a part of all the boxed files that had been stored inside the Marino Construction warehouse. A box that also included the 9mm I discovered tossed in the woods with Marino's prints on it, the empty Skoal tobacco container found on the stream bank, the used condom, the spent shell casing, the initial DNA results taken from Farrell's chewed tobacco and from Natalie's corpse matching the DNA samples lifted off the used condom—all of it proof that the three players had been present at the public fishing access area on the Desolation Kill and proof that a murder could very well have taken place there.

We also handed over the in-progress contract documents for the convention center along with the site plan for the proposed Lake Desolation Estates and Casino. Finally, we presented two DVDs, the first showing Jimmy and his father-in-law sexing it up together, and the second, the poisoning of Lake Desolation by parasitic clams, better known to environmentalists and scientists as Pohnpei clams. Or so the very thorough Davey Blister informed us.

"And one more thing," Spain said, turning toward the camera, looking into it as if addressing his maker, "I want to go on public record that Ava 'Spike' Harrison and I spent the entire night of Tuesday, June sixteenth together. She never left my side for any reason. There's no possible way she left her North Albany apartment, got in her Jeep, drove to PS 20, and killed Natalie Barnes. And for that, I am willing to submit myself to a lie-detector test." He turned his eyes back on Santiago. "I believe Peter Marino, in a further attempt to hide his complicity in both the A-1 Environmental Solutions asbestos scam and the murder of his son-in-law Jimmy Farrell, stole Ava Harrison's framing hammer from her parked Jeep, then used it to kill Ms. Barnes. In doing so, he would make it appear that Ms. Harrison was the murderer."

Santiago maintained a stone face throughout the proceedings. It was a great risk Spain was taking. Not only in accusing Marino of the murders, but also in publicly and openly fibbing about spending the entire night with me. If in the end our plan was to backfire and I was still accused of murder, he could now be charged with conspiracy.

Santiago sat back, staring at us both.

He then looked at the camera as opposed to looking into it. I knew if he could have, he would've insisted that Collins kill the tape. But no way in hell could he do that without raising some kind of suspicion about himself. He was a public figure, voted into office. Already, he was eyeing the attorney general's seat. Or was it the mayor's office?

In his low, steady voice, he said, "You both realize that much of this so-called evidence won't be admissible in a court of law.

Nor would your polygraph be admissible, no matter the outcome, Mr. Spain."

"We understand that," I said. "But what's right is right, Mr. Santiago. And I, for one, felt the need to go after the truth."

"Mr. Santiago," Spain went on, "I have the good fortune of knowing an extraordinary young woman about to enter law school. Her name is Stella, and she's a waitress at Tess's Lark Tavern. Stella has been legally deaf from birth. She's a bright, attractive young woman who plans to spend her life in the defense of children who are abused and neglected and have nowhere to turn. Now, how in the world could I face a brave young woman like that if I didn't seek out the truth when someone like Spike Harrison has been wrongly accused?"

Quiet filled the office for a long moment. Santiago stared into me, eyes wide, unblinking. From across the table, I watched his Adam's apple tremble inside the loose skin on his neck. Until he sat up straight, bit down hard on his bottom lip, nodding. I believe then he'd begun to see the light.

"From this point forward," he addressed the rolling tape, "this office will redirect the focus of its investigation into both the murder of Barnes and the asbestos negligence case at PS 20." Shifting his brown eyes to me, he added, "Ms. Harrison, this office no longer considers you a suspect in a homicide. You are hereby free to go."

For a split second, I thought about asking for a public apology.

Instead, I stood.

Spain stood.

Together, we turned and bolted from the DA's office, free at last.

CHAPTER 67

It was dawn on Thursday by the time we got back into Spain's Charger. The sun was rising red over the Berkshire Mountains to the east, its reflection glistening off the Hudson River as we pulled away from the curb and began driving the Concrete Pearl in the direction of my apartment.

Just up ahead was the Miss Albany Diner.

"Let's grab some breakfast," I said. "For the first time in days, I'm hungry."

Without hesitating, Spain pulled into the parking lot. It was empty except for a pickup truck that pulled in right on our tail, parked beside me. Just another construction worker grabbing an early breakfast before the workday began, I thought.

"Maybe Tommy would like to join us," I said.

"He up at this hour?" Spain asked, pulling the key from the starter.

"Trust me, he's been up for an hour." I opened Tess's cell phone, dialed the old mason laborer's number.

He answered right away.

I said, "How does bacon and eggs and a free-as-a-bird Spike sound for breakfast this morning?"

"You buyin', Chief?" he said.

The window shattered.

Blood spatter strafed my face.

Spain slumped over into my lap.

A black barrel stared me down.

The phone fell onto the floor at my feet.

Glancing to my right, I caught the logo printed on the side panel of the parked pickup.

MARINO CONSTRUCTION

A gloved hand reached for me through the window.
"Tommy," I screamed, "Marino…Marino Construction!"

CHAPTER 68

Duct tape wrapped around our mouths.

Wrists and ankles bound behind our backs.

Tossed hog-tied into the bed of the pickup.

Only when the bastards got back inside the cab and started to drive—the same two beefy bastards who threatened us outside Thatcher Street—could I see that Spain was still alive. He was awake now, wide-eyed, the star-shaped hole in his cheek caked with thick black blood. It dribbled down his chin and neck. The bullet he took to the face had entered and exited his cheek. It must have just missed me and the asshole with the gun on my side of the Charger.

They drove for maybe fifteen minutes, but it seemed like forever as I bounced around in the back of that truck on the hard bed liner, trying to breathe through my nostrils, knowing that what I faced was the same thing Natalie faced, that Farrell had no doubt faced.

When we came to a stop, Slammer and his buddy got out and opened the tailgate.

First, they pulled Spain out by his feet, letting him fall to the ground like a bag of mason's sand. They did the same to me, yanking me feetfirst, my body falling hard to the ground. Slammer kicked me in the stomach, knocking the wind out of me.

When I got my breath and my bearing back, I could see that the two Marino laborers were not alone. I heard voices, but I could not see faces.

I looked up from the hard-packed ground, recognized the back side of the Marino Construction Company building. Shifting my eyes over my left shoulder, I made out the incomplete construction of the pole barn. When Slammer began dragging me by my feet, I made out a long swath of open, excavated trench that was surrounded by yellow ribbon that bore the words *Warning: No Entry.* Coming to a stop at the edge of the trench, I looked down. A partial naked footing had already been poured, bulk-headed off by a dyke framed out of two-by-fours and two-by-tens.

I saw something else too.

At first, I didn't recognize the ball-shaped object partially buried in the hardened concrete. It didn't immediately register that the object was not a round rock or a pumpkin or a big rubber ball that had gotten stuck in the pour. It didn't make sense that what I was looking at might in fact be human—but then it did. The object was a head that belonged to a body buried in the naked footing. A head, much of the lower jaw portion also buried in the now rock-hard concrete, leaving only half a gaping mouth and two wide-open eye sockets, the once blue eyes they'd housed now eaten away by the crows. A head with wavy blond hair. The head belonged to a man who had been alive when his body was buried in ready mix. The head belonged to a man who tried to avoid suffocation by lifting up his head from out of the soft concrete, but not far enough to avoid the mix filling his mouth, hardening in place inside him and all around him.

I'd finally found Jimmy Farrell.

In my racing mind, I saw the note that he had left on the front door of his asbestos-removal business: *Closed Untill Further Notice.* I knew then that the document hadn't come from Farrell at all. It had come from Marino. The note still sat in my desk drawer at home. It had a diagram of parallel lines on the back, the letters "S" and "C" beneath them, along with a question mark.

Quite suddenly, I knew the meaning of that sketch. It must have been passed along to Marino by somebody at the Albany Building Department. By law, Marino had to seek city approval for the construction of the new pole barn. When he received his building permit, the building department must have insisted that he pour a long "naked footing" instead of the less sturdy concrete piers. The soil around the Wolf Road industrial park was pure crap—red clay mixed with unclean fill. You couldn't trust the structural integrity of the piers in that kind of precarious, foul-smelling soil. Clay shifted; trash settled. You'd have to build something that would provide stability, stop the earth from shifting under your feet. Something long, hard, and thick. Something that would last forever.

The letters "S" and "C" didn't stand for South Canada any more than they stood for Santa Claus. The letters stood for "Soil Conditions." The building department had questioned the soil conditions behind Marino Construction. In turn, they'd required Peter to pour a naked footing to properly underpin the piers.

That naked footing had become the burial plot for James Atkins Farrell. It would become a hard-curing ready-mix grave for me, and for Spain. Easy-peasy burial. No one would find our bodies. We would go forever missing. No body, no proof of murder.

I looked away, felt my body turn cold. I tried to focus on the clear morning sky. I knew now that I'd been preparing for this moment for most of my life—since I was seven years old, when I was buried alive. Only, this time, my dad would not be here to save me.

I felt Slammer's boot heel dig into my side. "You're gonna love burning in hell, butch," he said.

His words made me laugh.

The boot heel sent me down into the ditch, flat onto my back. Dazed, I looked up to see Spain being flung into the ditch not far behind me. I struggled against the duct tape to free myself. But the struggle was useless. I couldn't begin to move. My ribs were on fire. I had no idea how to save myself.

I heard voices. And a dog barking. I recognized the voices. They came from the people who stood at the very edge of the trench. I could see them. Marino dressed in a seersucker suit, crisp white shirt, white-and-black rep tie, a barking Sonny by his side. Marino looked sharp, wore tortoise-shell sunglasses with round lenses. Looked like he was on his way to a power breakfast with Albany Development Limited. In his hand, he held the leash that reined in the pit bull. The dog's hindquarters were covered in a bandage that resembled a diaper. The bullet grazing I'd given it didn't seem to make an ounce of difference. The dog was baring white fangs at me.

Diana Stewart wore black jeans and a pressed blue-jeaned work shirt. Her earrings glistened in the warm morning sun, red hair parted just above her right eye. I couldn't make out the words she and Marino spoke to one another. But I knew that the subject of their discussion was important, that it had to do with murder.

The rumble and noise of something else caught my attention.

A ready-mix truck had arrived on the scene. A heavy-duty cement truck, its never-still, heavy weight making the naked earth tremble beneath my body. When it came to a sudden and abrupt stop, air brakes hissed and spit. Then came the unmistakable *beep-beep-beep*—the standard, OSHA-mandated warning that accompanies all heavy mobile equipment engaged in reverse mode.

From my paralyzed position down inside the trench, I listened to the truck backing up. For a quick second, I thought it was going to drop into the trench. But then the heavy machine stopped so close to the trench's edge that the rear wheels sent stinging shards of stone and dirt raining down onto my face. I heard the driver's door open, the sound of two boot soles slapping the bare earth.

"Who's the super?" the operator belted. "Who the fuck orders a half load at six-thirty in the morning?"

A sudden gunshot shattered the plateglass atmosphere. A body collapsed deadweight to the ground.

"Toss him in with shit-for-brains," Marino ordered.

The body tumbled into the trench, coming to a rest up against Spain.

There was a slight commotion—people moving one way and then the other. Then the concrete truck engine revved up, along with the cement mixer. I sensed my fate the way people near death see a white light at the end of a tunnel. There came the clanking and banging of heavy aluminum concrete chutes being pulled off the truck and connected together.

When I heard Marino shout, "OK, let her rip!" I knew exactly what was coming. I'd been in the construction business all my life. First was another RPM injection and the whine of the concrete mixer spinning rapidly counterclockwise, its corkscrewed interior sending the wet concrete mixture up through the opening. I could hear the wet, muddy, gravelly mix sliding down the chutes.

And then I felt the heavy *plop-plop-plop* of warm mud, stone, and slag cement mix.

I felt the pain of its collision against my legs and bruised ribs. I smelled its raw, earthy smell.

It took only a few short seconds for the concrete to build up and bury my feet. The lime burned through my boots and jeans. The weight of the concrete pressed against skin, flesh, and bone. The spatter slapped my face, stung my eyes; the acrid taste of dirt, mud, and lime befouled my lips and tongue. In my head, I saw flashes of Jordan's face. First, an incomplete picture: the eyes, the slightly crooked nose, the flat forehead, the black brows. But then I saw the whole face looking at me, calling me to him.

The cement poured from the chutes and into the trench. It had covered my legs, had begun creeping up my torso. It buried my belly and most of my chest. Its weight pulled me down, dragged me under, suffocating and entombing me.

I struggled, screamed against the duct tape. But the weight and the heat of the cement was too much. I struggled until I stopped struggling. Until I died in mind before my heart followed.

Then a gunshot. And another.

And then the cement stopped pouring.

CHAPTER 69

Someone jumped down into the trench.

Footsteps followed.

Heavy, rapid footsteps slogging through the wet cement. I could barely see through the tears. But I recognized Tommy.

He had a shovel in his hand. With no words spoken, he started digging me out. He shoveled fast until he freed most of my upper body. Like my father had done all those years ago, he bent down at the knees, dug his arms under my shoulders, and slid me out of the naked footing like a doctor delivering a baby. He pulled out a pocket knife and cut the duct tape that bound my ankles and wrists. He then moved on to Spain, cut him free of the tape.

As if back in Vietnam, Tommy had the sense to make a bandage out of the kerchief he stored in the back pocket of his jeans. He pressed the kerchief against Spain's bullet-damaged face, held it in place with a slice of the cutaway duct tape. It was already too late for the concrete truck diver.

The rescue took less than a minute. But time had lost all meaning for me.

I stood up, shin-deep in hardening ready mix, ripped the tape from my mouth, never feeling the sting. My cold body was trembling, shivering.

Tommy, stocky body in a T-shirt and baggy jeans now covered with ready mix, pressed an extended index finger to his lips. He pointed the finger up toward the sky as if to indicate that something bad was going down outside the naked footing trench.

"Tina," he whispered.

It took some effort, but we climbed out. That's when we saw Tina Farrell. She must have followed her father out to this place. She must have known his intentions. She must have also known that he insisted upon his business partners being present for the festivities. All for one and one for all even when it came to murder—*especially* when it came to murder.

Tina held a pistol in her hand. She'd already shot the laborer who'd been operating the cement truck. He lay facedown on the ground by the back wheels of the truck, his right arm still extended upward toward the sticklike controls.

The second laborer, Slammer, was down on his knees, hands clasped against the top of his shaved head. He didn't seem so threatening now. Not like he'd been when he was waving a sheetrock knife at my face. Now he was crying, tears soaking his mustache and goatee. But the tears weren't about to place even the slightest hairline crack in Tina's stubborn resolve. Slammer was staring up at her with big wet eyes when she shot him in the face, the back of his head and a chunk of brains hitting the ground before the rest of his body slumped forward.

Now she had the barrel aimed dead ahead at her father and Stewart. The two partners stood shoulder to shoulder, hands raised in surrender like prisoners of war.

The expression on Tina's face had shifted from resolve to pure hatred. She struck an almost comic figure in her tennis skirt, white sneakers, ped socks, and cropped white acrylic top. The top exposed a belly that had given life to a baby she had no choice but to deliver dead.

"Put the gun down, baby," Marino said, yanking back on a lunging Sonny. "You don't want to shoot your own father. Come on now, sweet baby doll, put the gun down. Please, baby, please put the gun down…"

But Tina never wavered, never hesitated, thumbed back the hammer, and settled the pad of her manicured index finger on the trigger.

Stewart took a brave, angry step forward. "Tina," she said, "think about what you're doing…about what you'll be giving up if you do this."

Tina shook her head. "I give up nothing I haven't already given up," she said, voice strangely detached.

"You have a life, Tina." Stewart softly smiled while slowly extending her left hand, reaching out with it like a mother trying to console her daughter.

"I had a life," Tina said. "He was inside of me. A little baby boy."

Marino's face went pale, eyes glossy.

Stewart's jaw dropped. She started crying—the Tiger Lady, *crying*.

"Tina, please," she sobbed, the tears falling from her face. Like her Virginia accent, it was one hell of an act.

Farrell's widow took a step forward.

There was a shot.

Peter's face exploded the split second before his body crumpled and dropped. Another shot followed and Sonny was put down for good. Then a third shot made certain Stewart exited this world right behind them.

Tina pulled back the pistol, opened her mouth, and swallowed the barrel.

When the fourth and final shot followed so did all hope for the Marino Construction bloodline to be carried on.

CHAPTER 70

Uniformed APD surrounded the backyard of the Marino Construction Corporation in their vans and cruisers. Outside on the road, two state trooper cruisers, flashers flashing, blocked the entrance to the yard. EMTs washed my shivering body down with the cement truck hose. They took care of Spain's facial wound as best they could. A forensic team photographed and recorded the scene of the murder/suicide, along with Farrell's frozen-in-time, half-exposed face. Soon, they'd have to hook up a ninety-pound jackhammer to a compressor, cut his body out of the footing, ship him off to be autopsied. Maybe they'd find a bullet hole somewhere on his body. A 9mm slug. A slug that didn't take his life, but only wounded him, leaving him alive long enough for Marino to enact a classic construction vengeance on his son-in-law: burying him alive in raw ready mix.

Why he never bothered to finish the job of entombing the golden boy's head, I'll never know. Maybe he left it exposed as a reminder to himself about never trusting a dumb-as-a-box-of-rocks-jock-star like Jimmy. Or maybe he left the head exposed because it made him feel good to look at it once in a while. Maybe that's how much hatred Peter Marino had for his son-in-law, the man who stole both his daughter and Natalie. Or who knows? Maybe the truck simply ran out of ready mix.

Not long after, Spain and I occupied the back of an EMS van. He wasn't able to speak, but his eyes screamed volumes. As we motored our way toward the Albany Medical Center, I got the feeling that he hadn't had any idea of the extent the Farrells' and Marinos' corruption when he first took on the job of spying on an adulterous Jimmy Farrell, and later, a Farrell who cheated on asbestos removal.

As the hospital approached, I knew that the whole truth and nothing but the truth was on its way to being spilled.

But not right away.

CHAPTER 71

I spent a full day in the hospital being treated for bruised ribs and lime burns before I was given the OK to go home.

But I didn't leave for good.

Spain lost a couple of teeth and a whole lot of blood when the .22 caliber round tore through his left cheek. His lower left jaw was broken only in one place. However, his injuries were severe enough to require three nights of forced hospitalization.

I spent considerable time at the hospital keeping him company while Tommy took care of something I did not have the stomach for—the closing of the Harrison Construction doors. That meant settling all debts, collecting all outstanding accounts receivable. The receivables alone neared the mid-six-figure range, most of which we owed to the various subcontractors and material suppliers for PS 20, our lone project on the books. Plus, there were the outstanding OSHA fines and pending civil lawsuits.

But then something happened that changed everything.

Joel Clark received a call from the Albany School Board requesting that our contract to renovate and rehabilitate PS 20 be reinstated in the wake of Marino's death. Not even another civil lawsuit lodged against Harrison Construction and A-1 Environmental Solutions on behalf of Nicolas Boni's family could prevent us from finishing the job we'd started many months ago.

I'd been extended one final reprieve, and I wasn't about to blow it.

First item on the construction agenda?

A complete reevaluation of existing asbestos-removal procedures. We'd also have to look into decontaminating the entire school facility of asbestos fibers—a costly but necessary job.

As the GC in charge of the project and as its health-and-safety manager, I would personally oversee every step of the final contaminate removal process. This time I would watch the job like the most hardheaded hawk you ever did see. Even if it meant sleeping on-site inside the construction trailer.

Three days after Spain was released from the hospital, Joel called me into his Pearl Street office to sign new, revised contract documentation that would guarantee our reinstatement as the PS 20 general contractor. Tommy and I took the elevator up to his penthouse office, met up with the dapper lawyer over coffee and fancy pastry.

"I really should apologize for quitting on you, Spike," Joel said while pouring the coffees and as we took side-by-side seats at the far end of a heavy safety-glass conference table. Outside the floor-to-ceiling glass windows, we had a bird's-eye view of the port and the massive demolition project that Marino Construction had already initiated to make way for the Pearl Street Convention Center. Now that Marino was dead, however, the project had come to a standstill. From what the local rumor mill was churning up, the venture would remain closed down until District Attorney Santiago had thoroughly investigated the records of Marino Construction and his now suspect connections with Albany Development Limited.

I sipped my coffee while Joel neatly laid out the new contracts in triplicate.

"You're a construction lawyer, Joel," I said. "Not a criminal attorney."

I pulled a ballpoint pen from my work shirt pocket and signed the first document. But in my mind, I flashed back to two weeks ago. I recalled Joel standing alongside Marino and Stewart outside the PS 20 construction trailer the day I'd been tossed off the job. I recalled their happy, smiley faces despite a major construction project that had been red-flagged due to asbestos contamination. I recalled my records being confiscated before I had the chance to get at them. I recalled Joel asking me to hand-deliver the physical evidence I'd collected at the Desolation Kill public fishing access parking lot, including a spent 9mm brass cartridge, and I recalled the smell of Old Spice permeating the air of my apartment—especially the bedroom. It was precisely the odor that filled my nose inside Joel's penthouse office.

I sat back in my chair and looked up into the lawyer's face. "You were Marino's lawyer, weren't you, Joel?"

His eyes blinked rapidly beneath round tortoise-shell glasses. Puffy cheeks filled with blood. "Obviously, you're not my only client," he said, his tone defensive. A little too defensive.

I turned, shot Tommy a glare over my left shoulder. The former Vietnam grunt raised his right hand, extended an index finger, ran it across his neck. Sign language for *Mr. Clark is finished with Harrison Construction.*

I executed the final two contracts, dated them. Then I picked up all three copies, handed them over to Tommy.

"I'll need one for my records," Joel said.

I stood up, pushed out my chair. "How much do you have invested in the new-and-improved Concrete Pearl?" I said.

Joel half smiled, shook his head. "I'm not sure that's any of your—"

"It is my business when you favor one client over another. So how much? Three, four, five million? Ten million?" A laugh. Bitter, but sweet too. "Christ, Joel, maybe you were in bed with Marino all along."

He stood up, that half smile now replaced with a tight-lipped expression best described as false dignity. Joel had favored Marino Construction over my firm. He made sure the numerous lawsuits lodged against me last year were never resolved. What he had done was not only unethical, it was illegal. My lawyer was trying to bury me alive—bury me so deep that another client would remain the number one construction firm in Albany, the very firm chosen to oversee the Construction Management for the Pearl Street Convention Center.

"Please listen to me, Spike," he said, altering his tone. "Here's your shot at the big time. Marino is no more. We need a construction manager with your talent. We need the Harrison touch."

Standing tall, he had the floor. Joel, the big-daddy lawyer. Me, back to being the sixteen-year-old daddy's girl playing construction worker. He really started to pour it on.

"Think of your father," he said. "Think of his memory, your legacy. Think of all those pending lawsuits. With Stewart out of the way, OSHA will be up to its neck trying to find her replacement. They won't be paying attention to your cases. In the meantime, I'll take on the insurance agencies, make them settle for far less than they're asking. Spike, I'll make you my number one client. I'll—"

"Fuck you, Joel," I said.

The eyes beneath the tortoise-shell lenses went wide. He was a lawyer, after all. A proud member of the Albany Bar Association and the Albany Fort Orange Men's Club. He also happened to be a resident of picture-perfect East Hills. Farrell's neighbor, in fact. No one ever said "fuck you" to a lawyer like Joel. Especially a stupid, hardheaded girl like me.

"Excuse me?" he said.

"You heard me. You'll be hearing from my new attorney. *She'll* want all my records and files transferred to her offices immediately. In fact, she'll want to go through all the paperwork you have pertaining to me and the firm's pending lawsuits. She'll want to make certain you've been defending me to the best of your ability while entertaining your relationship with Marino and your investment in the convention center."

I stole another glance at Tommy.

"I have an idea, Tommy," I added. "Maybe we should get Chris Collins on the phone, tell her about how, back in April, Mr. Clark and Mr. Marino were going to strongly recommend that PS 20 be leveled, along with its entire campus, due to gross asbestos contamination. We'll let her in on how they were also going to recommend to the Albany School Board that PS 20 be relocated somewhere else entirely, thereby vacating the very last parcel of badly needed riverfront acreage along the Concrete Pearl. We'll let Collins in on what had been Joel and Marino's little secret: They had controlled Farrell all along. It was Marino who used Farrell as the front man for A-1 Environmental Solutions, made him submit a lowball price for the asbestos removal. He then made Jimmy purposely screw up the job in order to contaminate the school.

"For the first three phases, he made certain that Analytical Labs and Stewart's OSHA gave their *Good Housekeeping* seal of approval on the project. Because after all, Stewart, too, was a vested member of the Pearl Street Convention Center project. Stewart, Marino, Victor Dott, and Joel Clark. That's the *real* Albany Development Limited. A lawyer, the chief safety agent for upstate, a Lake Desolation landowner, and Albany's largest construction firm—all come together in a foolproof development scheme to get rich beyond their most fucked-up, greedy dreams.

"Who'd bother to check up on such valued members of Albany society? Not even the school board or the Albany Common Council would question them, especially after the Tiger Lady finally came down on me for gross asbestos negligence. I became the perfect patsy—the screw-up-her-daddy's-business, too-stubborn-to-quit broad. Not only that, they could say I was jealous that Jimmy had formed a relationship with Natalie Barnes. Not only was I furious with him for leaving me holding the contaminated bag for PS 20, but he was sleeping with Natalie. I wanted him dead. I wanted him dead in the worst way."

Joel's clean-shaven face turned as white as the paper my useless PS 20 contracts were printed on.

Tommy turned, but not before shouting, "The jig is up, Counselor!"

Good old Tommy. I got the feeling he'd been waiting for a moment like this since Tricky Dick Nixon tossed him into the Tet Offensive.

"How close am I to the truth, Joel? You set me up to take the heat away from Marino and the rest of your Albany Development Limited operation. By shifting the blame onto me, you were free to run with the new Pearl Street. Together, you were going to bypass the common council. You weren't going to give the school board a chance to fight it. And why would they? Their PS 20 was contaminated now. A child was dying because of it. It would cost too much to clean it up. Who needs eminent domain when the property is poisoned?

"You people—Albany Development Limited—were going to tear down the Concrete Pearl and build it right back up with businesses that would make you more filthy rich than you already are. You were then going to launder the profits by investing them under a new name in a second development way up at Lake Desolation. But only after poisoning the water so that property values plummeted and you could buy out the entire lake for dirt cheap. But what you didn't count on, Counselor, was Spain and me teaming up to go after the truth."

"Get out," Joel said. His voice sounded like dried-up asbestos insulation being ripped away from some old piping. "Get out of my office before I call the police."

"Not if I do it first," I said.

I smiled at Tommy. Like he did many years ago when I stepped on a sixpenny nail, he held the door open for me while I exited an unhealthy place.

CHAPTER 72

Another forty-eight hours had passed.

I was fixing dinner in my apartment and glancing at the six o'clock news when my new iPhone vibrated a single time against my hip.

See U in 10, the text message read.

It had come from Spain. It was the first time I'd heard from him in a few days. At his urging, I was not to contact him until he contacted me first. He was working something, he told me. Work took his mind off the pain of his healing facial and jaw wounds.

Back to the television news.

"...The drama continues tonight for Albany's troubled Pearl Street Convention Center project," said Chris Collins into her handheld mike from where she stood just outside the soon-to-be-reactivated PS 20 job site. "What began as a simple case of asbestos removal at the old Pearl Street school has ballooned into a complicated plot of deception, greed, and murder. When high levels of asbestos were discovered at the school and the subcontractor responsible for its removal, James Farrell of A-1 Environmental Solutions, was reported missing, Harrison Construction president Ava 'Spike' Harrison took it upon herself to go hunting for the asbestos-removal tycoon.

"What she found instead was an accusation of murder when Farrell's longtime adulterous interest, Natalie Barnes, showed up at the PS 20 job site brutally murdered—the victim of blunt-force trauma to the head via Harrison's own framing hammer. Forensic investigators now tell us that Peter Marino, the late CEO of Marino Construction Corporation and contracted construction manager of the convention center, stole the hammer from out of Harrison's

Jeep. Then, having lured Barnes into a clandestine rendezvous at the construction project trailer, proceeded to assault her with it.

"Why would a longtime respected businessman like Marino carry out such a heinous criminal act? By all appearances, to silence Barnes after she'd been witness to Farrell's shooting and eventual murder. It's also possible she knew all about Farrell's longtime asbestos-removal scam the local contractor ran in partnership with Marino, who also happened to be his father-in-law.

"In silencing Barnes, Marino set the stage not only to make Spike Harrison look like a corrupt general contractor but also a woman capable of murder. With Marino and Upstate New York's OSHA chief, Diana Stewart, having suffered fatal wounds during the June eighteenth murder/suicide enacted by Marino's daughter, Tina, the fate of the grandiose half-billion-dollar Pearl Street project is up in the air.

"The first of two surviving Albany Development Limited partners, the organization in charge of the redevelopment project, is noted construction attorney Joel Clark. Clark is presently being charged by Albany County prosecutor Derrick Santiago with several counts of conspiracy to collude with Marino Construction, as well as three counts of accessory to murder and two counts of accessory to attempted murder.

"The second known individual is Victor Dott, sixty-two, of Wilton, who is being held for questioning by state police.

"This is Chris Collins with a special live report from the Albany Public School 20 construction site."

I shut off the TV, opened the fridge, reached in for a beer, and twisted off the cap. I took a swallow, felt the good, cold beer swimming down my throat.

When Spain came in without knocking, I was already half-finished with the beer. He was wearing Levi's, black motorcycle boots, and a T-shirt that fit tight to his arms and chest. He appeared the epitome of health. Except for his face. The face was bandaged where the .22 caliber bullet had entered and exited the cheek, and his left eye was still colored a combination black, blue, and purple. As for his jaw, it would remain wired shut for six more weeks. He could talk, but without the benefit of lower jaw movement, making it easier for him to bang out text messages from his new cell phone.

"Let's go," he mumbled.

"Let's go where?" I said.

But he didn't answer. It hurt too much to talk.

CHAPTER 73

We got in Spain's Charger. He pulled out of the apartment complex, went left onto the main road, then made a beeline down to the Concrete Pearl.

We drove for a bit until we came to a section of ten or twelve abandoned town houses that had been long ago boarded up with old sunbaked sheets of plywood. Spain pulled up against the curb out front, shut down the Charger. He reached across my lap and opened the glove box. He grabbed a flashlight and opened his door.

Together, we got out.

He walked up to one of the old brownstone entrances, stuffed the handle of the flashlight in his pants. He then reached out with both hands, pulled the plywood off the entrance, popping the nails. We slipped inside and were greeted by a vestibule that was covered in dust, dirt, and spiderwebs. He led me to a room on the left. He opened the old wood-paneled door and shined the flashlight inside, revealing a bare space that housed an old spring mattress positioned atop a metal bed frame. There was an old dresser of drawers in the far corner, a standup lamp set beside it, the shade long gone.

In his muffled, constricted voice, he said, "In this room, Tess gave birth to Derrick Santiago's baby. He refused to send her to a hospital. He was married, a cop on the way up. A detective. Eventually, he'd become a lawyer and a district attorney. He had goals and a vision. The birth of an illegitimate child to a prostitution madam would mean certain shame. He refused a hospital and a doctor. He forced Tess at gunpoint to deliver her baby with some strung-out quack doctor attending to her. When complications arose, the baby would lose her hearing."

I found myself pressing both hands against my belly. I was a woman, after all. Didn't matter that I lived in a man's world.

"Tess," I said. "*Our* Tess."

"They named her Stella. It all had to be kept quiet. Santiago and Tess together, the pregnancy, the birth. He was a top cop. Tess was a well-known madam with a half dozen girls working under her."

"If word were to get out…"

"End of career for Derrick P. Santiago. End of his cop life in Albany—or anywhere in Upstate, for that matter."

"What happened to baby Stella?"

A shrug of the shoulders. "Whatever happens to a kid born under those circumstances? A secret kid. Tess could have terminated the pregnancy at any time. But she wanted a child. She wasn't about to blackmail Santiago, even though she had the power to destroy him if she'd wanted to. But that wasn't Tess's way.

"So, in the end, she had Stella with Santiago's service weapon staring her down. Later on, she would ease her way out of the prostitution racket, move uptown, buy the Lark Tavern with her bankroll, raise Stella while she worked her ass off as a legit businesswoman."

The face flashed before my eyes. Stella. A beautiful young face.

"Sometimes Santiago tried to do the right thing," he said. "He'd go through bouts of taking care of her needs when she was growing up—medical, private grammar school, private high school." Spain shook his head. "But then he drops out and sends nothing. Eventually, it's Tess who pays up for private college. Now it's law school. Stella's going to be a lawyer, work on behalf of neglected children, abused children. Her life's goal is to make deadbeat parents step up to the plate."

"And what about you? How did you help?"

"I took care of the extra stuff—spending money, new clothes when she wanted to go shopping. On occasion, I footed the tuition bill." He pressed tight lips together. For a second, I thought he was going to shed a tear.

I said, "When we met with Santiago on that early morning, with Collins filming our every word, you spoke about Stella. But what you were really doing was sending a message to the DA. Back off and do the right thing, or your life in Albany is over."

With a slow shake of his head, Spain turned and walked out of the bedroom.

CHAPTER 74

We weren't done with Pearl Street yet. Its quiet road and the empty buildings that flanked it held more secrets. From the looks of things, Spain was determined to reveal them to me.

Making a tight U-turn, he slowly drove until he hit lower Pearl Street.

Over one shoulder, you could see Nipper the Dog sitting up atop the old RCA building. The plaster dog looked down at us with big black eyes. Over the other shoulder was abandoned building after abandoned building—old historic town houses and multistory brick-faced office buildings, all of them emptied after being bought out by Albany Development, all of them awaiting a wrecking ball that at this point might never come. One of these buildings included the KeyBank that Harrison Construction had renovated inside and out—the project where Jordan lost his life.

When Spain pulled into the empty parking lot of the old bank, my heart began to speed up. At the same time, my stomach sank.

"What are we doing here?"

But he didn't answer me. I knew it was a profound effort for him to talk.

He drove the Charger around the back of the ten-story structure. The last time I'd been on site, the redbrick facade had been covered entirely with scaffolding and Jordan was lying on his back on the solid ground, his body shattered. We completed the job even after he died, per the signed contract. But I had nothing to do with it.

Spain stopped the Charger. We got out, and I followed close behind while he walked the length of the deserted lot until he came to the empty building's brick wall. About-facing, he eyeballed me.

"How deep is a scaffolding section?" he asked in that pained, mumbled voice.

"About five feet from brace tip to brace tip."

He stepped forward, taking three distinct paces. "That's about five feet," he said to himself. Then he stepped three more paces. "Police and OSHA reports indicate that when Jordan fell from the topmost scaffolding section, he landed right about here." Pointing with both hands at the section of empty lot under his feet. "That's a good ten feet away from the bottommost section."

I had no idea what he was getting at. Or maybe I didn't want to know. I just wanted to get the hell away from that empty building, away from that ghost town.

"You told me that Jordan climbed the scaffolding to the top floor to meet face-to-face with Diana. At that time, she was a Harrison project manager."

I nodded. "He met her up there to inspect the repaired cornice."

Spain tried to purse his lips, like it helped him to think. But I knew with that wired jaw, it wasn't easy to do anything with his mouth. He mumbled, "How could a man with Jordan's athleticism and construction site experience fall off a scaffolding on a beautiful fall day?"

I swallowed something bitter. Then my mouth went dry. "Sometimes even monkeys fall from trees," I said, my eyes filling. In my head, I saw Jordan's beaming face as he refused to take the interior staircase to the bank's top floor, preferring instead to climb the scaffolding. In my brain, I saw him climbing.

"That what you really believe?" Spain said. "Diana loved Jordan. But she could not have him. So what does she do? She meets him at the top of thirteen sections of scaffolding, blocks his path by keeping him on the edge. Before he can say a word, she asks him for a light. He pulls out a New York Giants lighter. And while he goes to light her cigarette like a perfect gentleman, she pretends to have difficulty getting the cigarette to light. Maybe it's the wind, or maybe she just makes it difficult on purpose. Whatever the case, that's when she asks him for the lighter. It will be easier if she lights the smoke herself. He hands her the lighter, and that's when she reaches out with both hands, shoves his chest, sending him over the short safety rail." He glared down at the spot where Jordan landed. "Diana stores the lighter in her pants pocket. A souvenir of the man she loved but could not have."

I saw it all in my head as it happened.

Jordan going over the side.

I saw him falling, saw him dropping from out of the sky on a bright, warm fall day. Saw him hitting the ground. Heard the thud. Saw his crushed face, his shattered body, saw me kneeling over it. I saw him lying in the ICU hospital bed, going in and out of a coma, trying to tell me something, but not able to tell me because he could no longer speak. I saw him the same way I'd been seeing him in my dreams ever since the day he'd died. The dreams that left me feeling like Jordan's story was not complete— that the truth had been kept from me.

"Diana killed Jordan," I said, a single tear running down my cheek. "In the hospital, he tried to tell me she pushed him…But he couldn't get it out."

Spain nodded. "Had he simply slipped and fallen from the scaffolding like the police report stated," he said, forcing his words, "he would have dropped straight down close to it and landed up tight to it. But because he was pushed off, he landed a good ten feet away from the scaffolding. No one in the APD ever questioned it, because why would Diana have done it? Didn't even occur to them, or if it did, they dismissed the idea. She was perceived as an honest, sane woman."

"Diana pushed Jordan," I repeated, making it sink in. A truth I had always suspected, but never accepted. Until now. "Jordan didn't die by accident. He was murdered."

The tears fell hard now—for Jordan, for me, and for all I'd lost at the hands of Diana Stewart. A woman who had to turn to murder in the face of rejection. Maybe someday I'd find it in me to pity her for her fucked-up life. But not today. Today I was glad she was dead and buried. The bloodguilt pouring down heavy and squarely on her soul.

"I need to leave this godforsaken place," I said.

Turning, I walked toward the Concrete Pearl.

CHAPTER 75

The following day, the bodies of Jimmy, Tina, and Peter Marino were laid to rest in an emotional, custom-tailored-for-the-media, triple-casket funeral. The funeral services were conducted at St. Mary's Roman Catholic Church in downtown Albany. Following that, daughter and father were buried on either side of Peter's late wife, Marie, at the Albany Rural Cemetery. Jimmy was buried a few plots down from them in a lonely plot, forever banished at arm's length from the family. But not entirely out of sight, either.

I would have liked to report that no one showed up for the services. Or that the bodies of Farrell and Marino were buried in unmarked graves. But the church was jam-packed with old friends, business associates, almost the entire Schuyler Meadows Country Club roster, most of the East Hills residents, plus business associates past and present.

It was more like a social event than a funeral service, the glamorous housewives decked out in the latest fashions, their husbands standing outside the church in tailored suits, smoking cigarettes, trying to subdue their giggles with fisted hands pressed up against their mouths. If the joke was that Farrell had cheated, the punch line came in his having been caught. After all, Jimmy might have been a golden boy, but he was also as dumb as a box of No. 5 sized gravel.

How the hell did he get so rich so fast? How did the dumb jock become such a huge success?

Well, now they had their answer.

He cheated. Plain and so very simple. He cheated out of pure greed.

And for many of the residents of the East Hills community, bending the rules in the service of greed made perfect sense. Hell, if they raised a flag to fly over their community every day at full mast, greed might have been the motto emblazoned on it.

Fifteen minutes after leaving the funeral services, Spain insisted we head over to the port. When I asked him why, he told me that someone important wanted to meet with us in private.

"Someone *very* important," he stressed.

"Obviously," I said. "And what does Mr. Important want to discuss with us?"

"Not me," he said. "You."

But when I asked Spain if he might find it in his heart to reveal the ID of Mr. Important, he just pursed those sore lips and cocked the scarred side of his face over his shoulder. The silent, you'll-find-out-when-you-find-out treatment—I was getting it whether I liked it or not

Moments later, we stood on the edge of the dock, not far from the warehouses that were no longer being demolished by Marino Construction. Seagulls soared and hovered over the dark river water.

"OK, Spain," I said. "Why are we here?"

"Because I asked him to bring you," came the voice of Derrick P. Santiago. "I knew you wouldn't come alone if I asked you personally."

The DA approached us on the pier, dressed in a dark suit, narrow-framed sunglasses shielding his eyes. He was carrying a brown paper grocery shopping bag.

"And what is it I can do for you, Mr. Prosecutor?"

He looked down at the tops of his polished Florshiems. Then he looked back up at me. "I'd appreciate it if you'd keep everything—*everything*—you've learned about me, about my past, to yourself. Do you understand?"

I felt my blood beginning to simmer. "The past has a name, Santiago," I said. "Stella. And she lives very much in the present."

He nodded.

I looked at him, at his dark eyes protected by the thick brow, the hawk nose, the clean, dark face, his lips pressed together. He knew that I had the power to destroy him and his aspirations.

Knowledge was power, and now I knew more about him than anyone, save Tess, Stella, and Spain.

But then, I needed him.

As much as I hated to admit it, I needed him to help me get rid of that OSHA monkey, to help me get rid of those civil lawsuits. I needed him, but I didn't have to like it. I could destroy him with one phone call to the press, but what good would it do anyone? And besides, maybe in the end, that was a phone call for either Tess or Stella to make.

"Your secret," I said, my heart dropping into my stomach, "your fucking secret is…safe."

He went to hold out his free hand for me to shake, until he remembered the bag he was holding in his other.

"Oh, I almost forgot," he said, opening the bag, digging into it. "Thought you might want this back."

He pulled out my equalizer—the framing hammer that Marino had used to kill Natalie. It had been cleaned of blood, brains, and hair. But that didn't make it any more attractive to me. My stomach dropped to my shins just looking at it.

"No, thank you," I said.

Santiago smiled, as if he didn't understand my apprehension. "You've carried this around for a lot of years," he said. "I just thought—"

"You thought wrong, Derrick," Spain said, pulling the hammer from his hand, tossing it into the drink.

For a beat, we listened to the gulls squeaking and squawking at the splash the hammer made in the river. Until they died down.

That's when Santiago once more tried to hold out his hand for me to shake.

I ignored it.

Tough, hardheaded girls don't go down, I thought. *They survive anyway they can.*

He let the hand fall. "Sure thing," he said. "I get it."

About-facing, he walked the empty pier alone toward a brilliant political future.

CHAPTER 76

Months later, I was back in our old offices, seated behind Dad's big mahogany desk. There was a drafting table set up against the far wall. A cabinet with books about engineering and construction project management methods took up the whole of the opposite wall. There was a leather couch pushed up against the third wall. Scotch-taped to the wallpaper above it were about two dozen Christmas cards I'd received in the last week alone.

I didn't use the couch for lounging.

Like Dad, I used it like a table—an area where I could sort out the separate bids I was presently receiving via fax for a historic cathedral renovation in South Albany. The project called for a boatload of asbestos removal, and thus far, I'd received three quotes—all of them within 10 percent of one another. In the end, only the fair-and-square low bidder would win.

Harrison had been officially hired back to complete the renovation at PS 20. I'd hired a new asbestos-removal outfit to complete the job Farrell started but cheated on. My new lawyer was attempting to secure A-1 Environmental's bid bond in order to pay for the asbestos repair. But at this point, with the three civil lawsuits that had been pending against me all throughout the previous year now settled out of court, I would have gladly paid out of pocket. Small price to pay for getting a second chance to make good in this impossible business, this man's business. And besides, the Harrison bank accounts no longer had liens placed against them. The liens had been successfully bonded. Now it was just a matter of filling them up with pretty green again.

Nicolas Boni, the third-grader who was thought to have developed mesothelioma, did not have the disease at all. He was misdiagnosed. Because of his less-than-stellar living conditions inside the Albany projects, he'd contracted a rare form of tuberculosis, the symptoms of which matched almost identically to those of the fatal form of asbestos cancer, minus the terminal prognosis. Receiving treatment at the children's hospital in Boston, Nick was back in school. Thankfully, his mother dropped her lawsuit. In return, all of us at Harrison Construction chipped in and bought Nick a new coat, snow pants, and a new Wii video game system for Christmas.

For the rest of that summer and through some of the fall, I saw Spain only on occasion. We e-mailed from time to time, sometimes talked on the phone. Judging from our last conversation, he was seriously contemplating pulling up stakes in Albany, packing his bags, and moving west to California to be close to his son. But I suspected that what he also wanted was to try to win his wife's heart back.

I made sure to stop in and see Tess nearly every Tuesday night when the Blisterz rocked out. I'd sit at the bar, have a couple of beers. On occasion, Stella brought me a steak, medium rare, a baked potato, and a garden salad. "On the house," she'd inevitably insist. I had no choice but to accept her generosity. But I did take her clothes shopping before she began her first fall semester at Albany Law School to make up for it.

As for the surviving members of Albany Development Limited, Joel Clark no longer occupied a county jail cell. He'd hired a powerhouse attorney who was fighting his numerous state indictments. But by all appearances, my dad's longtime lawyer was fighting a losing battle.

It also hadn't helped Joel's cause at all when Victor Dott began singing like a bird, agreeing to cooperate fully with both the state and FBI law enforcement officials in exchange for a lenient sentence inside some federal country club prison.

Despite the introduction of parasitic clams to Lake Desolation via the Desolation Kill, New York State EnCon was able to save both bodies of water from irreversible damage. Ironically, however, Marino and Farrell's original idea of turning the area into a high-end casino, hotel, and residential condo development was adopted by the organization that owns and runs the Fox

Woods Casino in Connecticut. By the looks of things, old man Dott would prove the big winner in all of this when he and the development company finally closed on his lakefront property. How's that for the American dream come true? I wondered if he could spend the money from prison.

Marino Construction was still up and running stronger than ever now that Marino's number two had taken over the reins. In fact, Marino would be my direct competition in the cathedral renovation bid, which was scheduled for a public opening at four o'clock that afternoon at the downtown site. In the meantime, I'd keep collecting the subcontractor and material supplier bids just the way my dad taught me, scrutinizing each quotation package item for item, making sure it was complete according to project plans and specifications—apples for apples, oranges for oranges.

It was close to midday.

While a rehired office staff busily decorated the office with garland, colored lights, mistletoe, and a plastic Christmas tree in preparation for the annual Christmas party, I felt my stomach growling. But never fear. Outside the office windows, I saw a big black Ford F-150 pickup pull up to a snowbank. The man driving it was no stranger.

Good old Tommy.

He pounded the horn, waving at me to hurry up. I knew exactly what he wanted. He wanted to grab a quick lunch at the Miss Albany Diner, then get back to finish up the bid so that he could personally drive it out to the cathedral in time for the public bid opening.

As the smooth voice of Nat King Cole sang, "*Chestnuts roasting on an open fire…*" on the radio, I got up from behind the desk and made my way around front. I brushed back my newly trimmed hair. I pulled a cig from the pack set out on the desk and fired it up with Jordan's New York Giants lighter, which Spain had given back to me. I exhaled blue smoke while my eyes shifted to the wall-mounted portrait of my old man—the proud face of John Harrison, construction legend.

"Going to lunch," I said out loud. "And Merry Christmas."

How's a headstrong girl like me succeed at running a general construction outfit?

She listens closely to her old man. In my mind, I heard his exact words: *"Make it quick. You've got a bid to put together."*

Some things never change.

Not even from the grave.

The End

ABOUT THE AUTHOR

Vincent Zandri is the international best-selling author of *Godchild, The Remains, Moonlight Falls, Moonlight Rises, Scream Catcher,* and *Murder by Moonlight.* He is also the author of the best-selling digital shorts *Pathological* and *Moonlight Mafia.* The *New York Post* called his novel *The Innocent* "[s]ensational…masterful…brilliant!" He has worked as a foreign correspondent and freelance photojournalist for *RT, GlobalSpec,* and *IBTimes,* among others. He lives in New York.